W9-DGV-123

IN PRAISE OF
THE WALL

"*The Wall* is a work of surprising emotional power that both haunts and consoles me. Told in a plain, practical style and translated from the German by Shaun Whiteside, it's an uncanny fable about isolation, despair, the beauty and horror of nature, and the agony of a caretaker who can't protect her charges. Haushofer's attentive renderings of animals, plants, weather, and the pleasures of the present enable a steady, sober examination of suffering, existence, death, and the labor of survival." —KATHRYN SCANLAN

"An existentialist masterpiece that can offer profound consolation as well as the ultimate lesson in loss."
—MICHEL FABER, *The Guardian*

"*The Wall* is a novel that contrives to be, by turns, utopian and dystopian, an idyll and a nightmare. In her isolation behind the wall, together with her animals, the woman discovers a new life, in comparison with which her existence before she came to the mountains seems trivial and pointless. The natural world which it describes with such rapt attention is cupped in the larger receptacle of a vivid and sinister dream, a dream we seem to have had many times before and which on each retelling leads to the same scene of horror at its climax."
—NICHOLAS SPICE, *London Review of Books*

"It's a dream in reverse, about a woman who wakes to find herself surrounded by a wall—a reverie that, while it lasts, leaves the reader feeling both anxious and protected." —*The Los Angeles Times*

"The story of a woman who lives in a mountain valley with only animals for company: an anti-*Robinson Crusoe*."
—ANNIE ERNAUX, *Frieze Magazine*

"Subtly surreal, by turns claustrophobic and exhilarating, fixated with almost religious fervor on banal detail, this is a disturbing yet rewarding tale in which survival and femininity are strikingly merged." —*Kirkus Reviews*

The Wall

Marlen Haushofer

THE WALL

translated by Shaun Whiteside

A NEW DIRECTIONS PAPERBOOK

Copyright © 1968 by Ullstein Buchverlage GmbH, Berlin
Translation copyright © 1990 by Shaun Whiteside

All rights reserved.
Except for brief passages quoted in a newspaper, magazine, radio, television,
or website review, no part of this book may be reproduced in any form or
by any means, electronic or mechanical, including photocopying and recording,
or by any information storage and retrieval system, without permission
in writing from the Publisher.

Originally published in German as *Die Wand*
by Claassen Verlag GmbH, Düsseldorf, in 1968

Cover art photos © O. Vaering / Bridgeman Images and
© Odon Wagner Gallery, Toronto, Canada / Bridgeman Images

Manufactured in the United States of America
First published as a New Directions Paperbook (NDP1537) in 2022

Library of Congress Cataloging-in-Publication Data
Names: Haushofer, Marlen, 1920–1970, author. | Whiteside, Shaun, translator.
Title: The wall / by Marlen Haushofer ; translated by Shaun Whiteside.
Other titles: Wand. English
Description: Second edition. | [New York] : [New Directions Publishing], [2022]
Identifiers: LCCN 2022000238 | ISBN 9780811231947 (paperback) |
ISBN 9780811231954 (ebook)
Subjects: LCGFT: Robinsonades. | Novels.
Classification: LCC PT2617.A425 W313 2022 | DDC 833/.914—dc23/eng/20220107
LC record available at https://lccn.loc.gov/2022000238

4 6 8 10 9 7 5

New Directions Books are published for James Laughlin
by New Directions Publishing Corporation
80 Eighth Avenue, New York 10011

for my parents

The Wall

Today, the fifth of November, I shall begin my report. I shall set everything down as precisely as I can. But I don't even know if today really is the fifth of November. Over the course of the past winter I've lost track of a few days. I can't even say what day of the week it is. But I don't think that's very important. All I have to rely on is a few meager jottings; meager, because I never expected to write this report, and I'm afraid that much that I remember will be different from my real experiences.

All reports probably suffer from this shortcoming. I'm not writing for the sheer joy of writing; so many things have happened to me that I must write if I am not to lose my reason. There's no one here to think and care for me. I'm quite alone, and I must try to survive the long, dark winter months. I don't expect these notebooks will ever be found. At the moment I don't even know whether I hope they will be. Perhaps I will know, once I've finished.

I've taken on this task to keep me from staring into the gloom and being frightened. For I am frightened. Fear creeps up on me from all sides, and I don't want to wait until it gets to me and overpowers me. I shall write until darkness falls, and this new, unfamiliar work should make my mind tired, empty and drowsy. I'm not afraid of morning, only of the long, gloomy afternoons.

I don't know what time it is exactly. Probably around

three in the afternoon. I've lost my watch; but it wasn't much use to me before. A tiny, gold watch, really nothing but an expensive toy that never showed the right time. I have a ballpoint pen and three pencils. The ballpoint is almost dry, and I very much dislike writing in pencil. My writing doesn't stand out clearly against the paper. The delicate gray strokes blur into the yellowish background. But I have no choice, after all. I'm writing on the backs of old diaries and yellowed business paper. The writing paper belonged to Hugo Rüttlinger, a great collector and hypochondriac.

This report should really start with Hugo, since had it not been for his mania for collecting and his hypochondria I wouldn't be sitting here; I probably wouldn't be alive at all. Hugo, my cousin Luise's husband and a fairly wealthy man. His money came from a saucepan factory. They were quite special saucepans, produced by nobody but Hugo. Unfortunately, although I had it explained to me often enough, I've forgotten what was unique about those saucepans. And it's irrelevant to the matter at hand. Anyway, Hugo was so wealthy that he needed to do something special. So he organized a hunt. He could just as easily have bought himself racehorses or a yacht. But Hugo was afraid of horses, and felt sick the minute he set foot on a boat.

He only kept up the hunt, too, for appearance's sake. He was a bad shot, and loathed shooting innocent deer. He invited his business partners along, and they, together with Luise and the huntsman, were the ones who bagged the game while Hugo sat in an armchair in front of the hunting lodge, hands folded across his belly, and dozed in the sun. He was so agitated and overtired that he nodded off the minute he sat down in a chair—an enormous, fat man, tormented by dark anxieties, with too many people making too many demands on him.

I was very fond of him, and shared his love of the forest

and a few quiet days in the hunting lodge. It didn't bother him if I stayed somewhere nearby while he slept in his chair. I went for little walks and enjoyed the silence after the hubbub of the city.

Luise was a passionate hunter, a healthy, red-haired character who threw passes at every man who crossed her path. Since she hated housework, it was very pleasant for her that I was there to pay a bit of attention to Hugo, make cocoa and mix his innumerable potions. He was obsessively concerned with his health, something I didn't really understand at the time, because his life was one constant rush and his only pleasure a little nap in the sun. He tended to feel very sorry for himself, and apart from his efficiency in his business (which I had to take for granted), as fearful as a little child. He had a great love of perfection and order, and always traveled with two toothbrushes. Of the things he used every day, he had several of each; this seemed to give him a sense of security. Otherwise, he was thoroughly cultured, tactful and bad at cards.

I can't remember ever holding a conversation of any importance with him. Sometimes he would make little moves in that direction, but would quickly stop himself, perhaps from shyness or simply because it was too much of an effort. In any case, this was very pleasant for me, because we would only have been embarrassed.

At the time everyone was talking about nuclear wars and their consequences, and this led Hugo to keep a little store of food and other important things in his hunting lodge. Luise, who found the whole business ridiculous, got annoyed, and worried that he would tell everybody and encourage burglars. She was probably right, but where these matters were concerned Hugo could develop an obstinacy that brooked no opposition. He got pains in his heart and cramps in his stomach until Luise gave in. But she basically didn't care either way.

On the thirtieth of April the Rüttlingers invited me to drive with them to the hunting lodge. I had been widowed for two years at the time, my two daughters were almost grown up and I could use my time as I saw fit. Not that I made much use of my freedom. I had always been sedentary by nature, and felt happiest at home. But I seldom turned down Luise's invitations. I loved the hunting lodge and the forest, and was happy to take on the three-hour car journey. On that thirtieth of April, too, I accepted the invitation. We were to stay for three days, and no one else was invited.

The hunting lodge is actually a two-story wooden villa, built out of massive branches and still in good condition today. On the ground floor there's a big rustic kitchen with a bedroom next to it and then another little bedroom. On the first floor, ringed by a wooden veranda, are three little bedrooms for the guests. It was in one of these rooms, the smallest one, that I was staying at the time. About fifty yards away, on a slope leading down to the stream, there was a little log cabin for the huntsman, merely a one-room hut, in fact, and beside it, just next to the road, was a wooden garage that Hugo had had built.

So we drove for three hours and stopped in the village to collect Hugo's dog from the huntsman. The dog, a Bavarian bloodhound, was called Lynx, and although he was Hugo's property he had grown up with the huntsman and been trained by him. Curiously, the huntsman had managed to teach Lynx to acknowledge Hugo as his master. Certainly he paid no attention to Luise, he didn't belong to her, and stayed out of her way. He treated me with friendly neutrality, but liked being near me. He was a beautiful creature with a dark, reddish-brown coat, and an excellent hunting dog. We talked to the huntsman a little, and it was agreed that he should go out stalking with Luise the following evening. She intended to shoot a roebuck; the close season finished on the first of May. This conversation dragged on as they will in the country, and even Luise, who could never understand this, checked her impatience, so as not to put the huntsman, who was indispensable to her, in bad humor.

We didn't get to the hunting lodge until about three o'clock. Hugo immediately set about carting new supplies from the boot of his car into the bedroom beside the kitchen. I made coffee on the spirit stove, and after our snack—Hugo was already starting to nod off—Luise suggested that he go back to the village with her. It was pure badness, of course. But she was very clever about it, saying that movement was imperative for Hugo's health. At around five o'clock she'd finally persuaded him, and set off with him triumphantly. I knew they would end up in the village inn. Luise loved to mix with the wood-cutters and farmhands, and it never occurred to her that the sly fellows might be laughing at her behind her back.

I cleared the crockery from the table and hung the clothes in the wardrobes; when I'd finished I sat down in the sun on the bench by the house. It was a fine, warm day, and according to the weather report it was due to stay bright. The sun slanted over the spruce trees, and was close to setting. The hunting lodge is in a little basin at the end of the gorge, beneath steeply ascending mountains.

While I sat there and felt the last warmth on my face, I saw Lynx coming back. He had probably disobeyed Luise, and she had sent him back as a punishment. I could see she'd scolded him. He came up to me, looked at me fretfully and laid his head on my lap. We stayed sitting there like that for a while. I stroked Lynx and spoke comforting words, because I knew Luise treated the dog in quite the wrong way.

When the sun disappeared behind the spruce trees it grew cool, and bluish shadows fell across the glade. I went into the house with Lynx, lit the big stove and started preparing a kind of risotto. I didn't have to, of course, but I was hungry myself, and I knew that Hugo liked a proper hot dinner.

My hosts still hadn't come home by seven o'clock. It seemed hardly likely now that they would be home before half past eight. So I fed the dog, ate my portion of risotto and, by the light of the oil lamp, read the newspapers that Hugo had brought with him. I grew sleepy in the warmth and the silence. Lynx had withdrawn into the stove door, where he panted quietly and contentedly. At nine I decided to go to bed. I locked the door and took the key with me to my room. I was so tired that I went to sleep immediately, despite the cold, damp quilt.

I was awoken by the sun shining on my face, and immediately remembered the previous evening. As we had only one key to the lodge, and the huntsman had the other one, Luise and Hugo would have had to wake me when they came back. I ran down the stairs in my dressing gown and unlocked the front door. Lynx welcomed me, whining impatiently, and dashed past me into the open. I went into the bedroom although I was sure no one would be there, since the window was barred and Hugo couldn't have pushed his way through even an unbarred window. The beds, of course, were untouched.

It was eight o'clock; they must have stayed in the village. I was very surprised. Hugo couldn't stand the short beds in the inn, and he would never have been so inconsiderate as to leave me alone in the hunting lodge overnight. I could find no explanation for what had happened. I went back up to my bedroom and got dressed. It was still very cool, and the dew glistened on Hugo's black Mercedes. I made tea and warmed up a bit, and then set off toward the village with Lynx.

I barely noticed how cool and damp it was in the gorge,

because I was brooding about what might have happened to the Rüttlingers. Hugo might have had a heart attack. As always happens when you're dealing with hypochondriacs, we had stopped taking his condition seriously. I quickened my pace and sent Lynx on ahead. Barking cheerfully, he made off. I hadn't thought to put on my climbing boots, and stumbled clumsily along behind him over the sharp stones.

When I finally reached the end of the gorge I heard Lynx howling with pain and shock. I walked around a pile of logs that had been blocking my view, and there was Lynx, sitting wailing. Red saliva was dripping from his mouth. I bent over him and stroked him. Trembling and whining, he pressed close to me. He must have bitten his tongue or chipped a tooth. When I encouraged him to go on with me, he put his tail between his legs, stood in front of me and pushed me back with his body.

I couldn't see what he was so frightened of. At this point the road emerged from the gorge, and as far as I could see it lay deserted and peaceful in the morning sun. I reluctantly pushed the dog aside and went ahead on my own. Fortunately, thanks to Lynx's obstruction, I had slowed down, for a few paces on I gave my head a violent bump and stumbled backward.

Lynx immediately started whining again, and pressed himself against my legs. Baffled, I stretched out my hand and touched something smooth and cool: a smooth, cool resistance where there could be nothing but air. I tentatively tried again, and once more my hand rested on something like a windowpane. Then I heard a loud knocking sound and glanced around before realizing that it was my own heartbeat thundering in my ears. My heart had been frightened before I knew anything about it.

I sat down on a tree trunk at the side of the road and tried to think. I couldn't. It was as if all my thoughts had abandoned me all at once. Lynx crept closer, and his bloody saliva dripped onto my coat. I stroked him until he calmed down. And then we both looked over to the road, so quiet and glistening in the morning light.

I stood up three more times and convinced myself that here, three yards from me, there really was something invisible, smooth and cool blocking my path. I thought it might be a hallucination, but of course I knew that it was nothing of the kind. I could have coped much more easily with a momentary insanity than with this terrible, invisible thing. But there was Lynx with his bleeding mouth, and there was the bump on my head, which was beginning to ache.

I don't know how long I stayed sitting on the tree trunk, but I remember my thoughts kept hovering around quite trivial matters, as if they wanted to keep away at all costs from this incomprehensible experience.

The sun rose higher and warmed my back. Lynx licked and licked and finally stopped bleeding. He couldn't have hurt himself too badly.

I realized I had to do something, and ordered Lynx to sit. Then I carefully approached the invisible obstruction with outstretched hands and felt my way along it until I bumped into the last rock of the gorge. I couldn't get any further on that side. On the other side of the road I got as far as the stream, and only now did I notice that the stream was slightly dammed and was flooding its banks. Yet it wasn't carrying much water. It had been dry all April and the snow had already thawed. On the other side of the wall—I've grown used to calling the thing the wall, because I had to give it some name or other now that it was there—on the other side, then, the bed of the stream was almost dry, and then the water flowed on in a trickle. It had obviously burrowed its way through the porous limestone. So the wall couldn't extend deep into the earth. A fleeting relief flashed through me. I didn't want to cross the blocked stream. There was no reason to believe that the wall suddenly stopped, because then it would have been easy for Hugo and Luise to get back.

Suddenly I was struck by what might have been unconsciously worrying me the whole time: the fact that the road was entirely deserted. Someone would have raised the alarm ages ago. It would have been natural for the villagers to gather inquisitively by the wall. Even if none of them had discovered the wall, Hugo and Luise would surely have bumped into it. The fact that there was not a single person to be seen struck me as even more puzzling than the wall.

I began to shiver in the bright sunshine. The first little farmhouse, only a cottage, in fact, was just around the next corner. If I crossed the stream and climbed up the mountain pasture a little, I would be able to see it.

I went back to Lynx and gave him a good talking to. He was very sensible, of course, and encouragement would have been much more appropriate. It was suddenly a great source of comfort to me that I had Lynx with me. I took off my shoes and socks and waded through the stream. On the other side the wall ran along the foot of the mountain pasture. At last I could see the cottage. It lay very still in the sunlight; a peaceful, familiar scene. A man stood by the spring, holding his right hand cupped halfway between the flowing water and his face. A clean old man. His braces hung around him like snakes, and he had rolled up his shirtsleeves. But his hand didn't get to his face. He wasn't moving at all.

I closed my eyes and waited, then looked again. The clean old man still stood motionless. I now saw that his knees and his left hand were resting on the edge of the stone trough; perhaps that was what stopped him falling over. Beside the house there was a little garden in which herbs grew along with peonies and bleeding hearts. There was also a thin, tousled lilac bush that had already faded. It had been almost summery that April, even up here in the mountains. In the city even the peonies had faded. No smoke rose from the chimney.

I beat on the wall with my fist. It hurt a little, but nothing happened. And suddenly I no longer felt any desire to break down the wall separating me from the incomprehensible thing that had happened to the old man by the spring. Taking great care, I crossed the stream back to Lynx, who was sniffing at something and seemed to have forgotten his fear. It was a dead nuthatch, its head caved in and its breast flecked with blood. That nuthatch was the first in the long succession of little birds that met their deaths so pitifully one radiant May morning. For some reason I can never forget that nuthatch. While I was contemplating it, I noticed the plaintive cries of the birds. I must have been able to hear them for a long time before I was aware of them.

All of a sudden, all I wanted was to leave that place and get back to the hunting lodge, away from those pitiful cries and the tiny, blood-smeared corpses. Lynx too had grown worried again, and pressed himself whining against me. On the way back through the gorge he stayed close by my side, and I spoke to him reassuringly. I can't remember what I said, it just seemed important to break the silence in the murky, damp gorge, where greenish light seeped through the beech-tree leaves and tiny streams trickled down from the bare rocks on my left.

We were in a bad situation, Lynx and I, and at the time we didn't know how bad it was. But we weren't lost entirely, because there were two of us.

The hunting lodge now stood in bright sunshine. The dew on the Mercedes had dried, and the roof gleamed an almost reddish black; a few butterflies fluttered over the glade, and there was a sweet scent of warm spruce needles. I sat down on the bench, and immediately everything I had seen in the gorge seemed quite unreal. It simply couldn't be true, things like that simply didn't happen, and if they did happen, then it wasn't in a little village in the mountains, not in Austria and not in Europe. I know how ridiculous that thought was, but as it is exactly what I was thinking I won't deny it. I sat quite still in the sun and looked at the butterflies, and I don't think I really thought about anything for a while. Lynx, who had had a drink at the spring, jumped up on the bench next to me and laid his head on my lap. I was pleased by this mark of favor, until it occurred to me that the poor dog didn't have any option.

After an hour I went into the lodge and heated up the rest of the risotto for Lynx and myself, and then made coffee to clear my head and smoked three cigarettes. They were my last cigarettes. Hugo, who was a heavy smoker, had inadvertently taken four packs with him into the village in his coat pocket, and hadn't yet got round to laying in cigarette supplies for the aftermath of the next war. Once I'd smoked the three cigarettes I couldn't bear it in the house any longer, and went back to the gorge with Lynx. The dog followed me unenthusiastically and kept close to my heels. I ran almost the whole way and came to a breathless halt when the woodpile appeared. Then I walked on with my hands outstretched until I touched the cool wall. Although I couldn't have expected anything different, the shock was much more violent this time than the time before.

The stream was still blocked, but the trickle on the other side had grown a little wider. I took off my shoes and set about wading through the water. This time Lynx followed me, hesitantly and reluctant. He wasn't afraid of water, but the stream was ice cold and went up to his belly. It unsettled me that I couldn't see the wall, so I broke off an armful of hazel twigs and started sticking them in the earth along the wall. This activity struck me as the obvious thing to do, and most importantly it kept me busy enough to stop me thinking. So I tidily staked out my twigs. My path now took me uphill a little way, and I got back to the spot from where I could see the little farmhouse.

The old man was still standing by the spring, his cupped hand raised to his face. The little bit of valley that I could see from here was filled with sunlight, and the air trembled, gold and green and clear, at the edges of the forest. Now Lynx could see the man too. He sat down, stretched his head into the air, and let out a drawn-out, terrible howling. He had understood that the thing by the spring was not a living human being.

His howling tugged at me, and something within me tried to force me to howl along with him. It tugged at me as if it wanted to tear me to pieces. I took Lynx by his collar and pulled him away with me. He grew quiet, and followed me, trembling. I slowly felt my way further along the wall, and stuck one piece of wood after the other into the ground.

When I looked back, I was able to follow the new border down to the stream. It looked as if children had been playing there, a cheerful, harmless spring game. The fruit trees on the other side of the wall had already faded, and were now covered with gleaming, light-green leaves. From here on the wall rose gradually uphill to a group of larches in the middle of the mountain pasture. From here I could see two more cottages and part of the valley. I was annoyed that I'd forgotten Hugo's binoculars. In any case I couldn't see a single person, not a living soul. No smoke rose from the houses. The disaster must, by my reckoning, have happened toward evening, and surprised the Rüttlingers when they were still in the village or on their way home.

If the man by the spring was dead, and I could no longer be in any doubt about that, then all the people in the valley must be dead, and not only the people, but everything that had been alive. Only the grass in the meadows lived now, the grass and the trees; the young leaves brilliant in the light.

I stood, both palms pressed against the cool wall, and stared across. And suddenly I didn't want to see anything anymore. I called Lynx, who had started digging under the larches, and went back, keeping to the little toy boundary. After we had crossed the stream I staked out the road as far as the rocks, and then slowly returned to the hunting lodge. After the cool, green gloom of the gorge the sun suddenly overwhelmed us when we walked into the glade. Lynx seemed to have had enough of the whole enterprise, ran into the house and crept into the stove door. As ever, when he was at a loss, he went to sleep straightaway after snuffling and wagging his tail for a bit. I envied him this ability. Now he was asleep I missed the slight disturbance that he always emanated. But it was still better to have a sleeping dog in the house than to be entirely alone.

Hugo, who didn't drink himself, had laid in a little store of cognac, gin and whisky. I poured myself a glass of whisky and sat down at the big oak table. I had no intention of getting drunk; I was in desperate search of a medicine to drive the dazed numbness from my head. It occurred to me that I thought of the whisky as my whisky, so that I no longer believed in the return of its rightful owner. This gave me something of a shock. After the third sip I pushed the glass away disgusted. The drink tasted of straw soaked in lysol. There was nothing in my head that I could make sense of. I had convinced myself that overnight an invisible wall had come down or gone up, and in the state I was in I was quite incapable of finding an explanation for it. I was neither concerned nor desperate, and there would have been no sense in forcing myself into either state. I was old enough to know that it would get me sooner or later. The most important question seemed to me to be whether only the valley or the whole country had been affected by this disaster. I decided to accept the former theory, since then I could still hope that I would be released from my forest prison in a few days. Today it seems to me that I hadn't believed in that possibility even then. But I'm not sure. In any case I was sensible enough not to abandon hope at first. After a while I noticed that my feet hurt. I took off my shoes and socks and saw that I'd got blisters on my heels from walking. The pain seemed to arrive at quite an opportune moment, because it distracted me from fruitless thoughts. After I'd bathed my feet and smeared ointment on my heels and stuck plasters on them, I decided to organize the hunting lodge in the way that seemed most manageable. First of all I moved Luise's bed out of the bedroom into the kitchen and put it by the wall so that I could see the whole room and the door and the window. I spread Luise's sheepskin by the bed, in the secret hope that Lynx would choose to make his bed there. He didn't do this, incidentally, and went on sleeping in the stove door. I took the bedside table out of the bedroom as well. It was only some time later that I moved the wardrobe into the kitchen. I closed the shutters in the bedroom and then locked the door leading out of the kitchen. I locked the upper rooms as well, and hung the keys on a nail beside the stove. I don't know why I did all those things; it must have been instinctive. I had to be able to see everything and protect myself against attack. I hung Hugo's loaded shotgun beside the bed and put the torch on the bedside table. I knew that all the measures I was taking were directed against human beings, and they struck me as ridiculous. But since I had only ever been threatened by human beings before, I couldn't adapt too quickly. The only enemy I had ever encountered in my life so far had been man. I brought up my traveling alarm clock and my watch, and then fetched wood, which lay stacked, cut and chopped up under the veranda, into the kitchen and piled it up beside the stove.

Evening had fallen in the meantime, and the cool air swept down from the mountain into the house. The sunlight still lay upon the glade, but all the colors were slowly growing colder and harsher. A woodpecker was tapping in the wood. I was happy to hear it, and the splashing of the spring that flowed thick as my arm into the wooden trough. I laid my coat over my shoulders and sat on the bench. From there I could see the path into the gorge, the huntsman's hut, the garage and the dark spruce trees behind it. Sometimes I imagined I could hear footsteps in the gorge, but of course I was always mistaken. For a while, quite absently, I contemplated a few enormous wood ants passing by me in a hasty little procession.

The woodpecker abandoned its tapping; the air grew cooler and cooler, and the light bluish and cold. The little patch of sky above my head turned pink. The sun had disappeared behind the spruce trees. The weather report had been right. As I thought this I was reminded of the car radio. The window was half open, and I pressed the little black button. After a moment I heard a gentle, empty hum. The previous day, to my annoyance, Luise had listened to dance music throughout the journey. Now I would have collapsed with pleasure to hear a bit of music. I twisted and turned the buttons: nothing but a distant, gentle hum that might only have come from the mechanism of the little box. I should have realized even then. But I didn't want to. I preferred to convince myself that something in it must have broken during the night. I kept trying, and all that emerged from the box was that humming noise.

I finally gave up and sat down on the bench again. Lynx came out of the house and put his head on my lap. He needed attention. I talked to him, and he listened carefully and pressed himself against me, tail wagging. Finally he licked my hand and tentatively beat on the ground with his tail. We were both afraid, trying to give each other courage. My voice sounded strange and unreal, and I allowed it to drop to a whisper, until I could no longer distinguish it from the splashing of the spring. The spring would often frighten me. From a certain distance its splashing sounded like a conversation between two sleepy human voices. But I didn't know that as yet. Without noticing, I stopped whispering. I shivered under my wrap and watched the sky fade to gray.

Finally I went back to the hunting lodge and made a fire. I later saw that Lynx had gone to the gorge, and stood there motionless, waiting. After a while he turned around and trotted back to the house, head lowered. He did this the following three or four evenings. Then he suddenly seemed to give up. I don't know if he just forgot, or if, in his dog's way, he realized the truth before I did.

I gave him risotto and dog biscuits, and filled his bowl with water. I knew that he was usually fed only in the morning, but I didn't want to eat on my own. Then I brewed myself some tea and sat down at the big table again. It was now warm in the hunting lodge, and the oil lamp cast its yellow glow over the dark wood.

It was only now that I realized how tired I was. Lynx, who had finished eating, jumped up and joined me on the bench and watched me long and attentively. His eyes were reddish-brown and warm, a little darker than his coat. The white around the iris gleamed damp and bluish. Suddenly I was very glad that Luise had sent the dog home.

I put the empty teacups away, poured warm water into the tin bowl and washed myself, and then, since there was nothing else to do, I went to bed.

I had closed the windows and bolted the door. After a little while Lynx jumped down off the bench, came over to me and sniffed at my hand. Then he walked over to the door, from there to the window and back to my bed. I talked to him for a good while and at last, after a sigh that sounded almost human, he sought out his sleeping place in the stove door.

I let the torch burn for a while, and when I finally turned it off the room seemed as dark as it could be. But it wasn't all that dark. The remains of the fire in the stove cast a weak, flickering glow on the floor, and after a while I could make out the outlines of the bench and the table. I wondered whether I should take one of Hugo's sleeping tablets, but couldn't bring myself to do it, afraid that I might miss hearing something. Then it occurred to me that the terrible wall might slowly move closer in the silence and darkness of night. But I was much too tired to be afraid. My feet still hurt, and I was lying stretched out on my back, too tired to turn my head. After everything that had happened I had to prepare myself for a bad night. But once I had come to terms with this thought I went straight to sleep.

I didn't dream, and woke up refreshed around six o'clock, when the birds started singing. I immediately re-membered everything, and closed my eyes in terror, try-ing to sink back to sleep. I couldn't, of course. Although I had barely moved, Lynx knew I was awake, and came to my bed to greet me with a happy wag of his tail. So I got up, opened the windows and let Lynx into the open. It was very cool, the sky was still pale blue and the bushes wet with dew. A bright day was dawning.

Suddenly it seemed quite impossible that I would sur-vive that bright May day. At the same time I knew I had to survive it, and that I had no means of escape. I had to stay quite calm and simply get through it. It wasn't the first day of my life that I had had to survive like this. The less I resisted it, the more bearable it would be. The dazed state of the previous day had entirely vanished from my head; I was able to think clearly, as clearly as I ever had, but when my thoughts approached the wall it was as if they too bumped up against a cool, smooth and quite insuperable barrier. It was better not to think about the wall.

I slipped into my dressing gown and slippers, walked along the wet path to the car and switched the radio on. A gentle, empty hum; it sounded so strange and inhuman that I switched it off straightaway.

I no longer believed that there was something broken in it. In the cold light of morning it was quite impossible for me to believe that.

I no longer remember what I did that morning. I only remember standing motionless beside the car for a while, until I was startled by the damp seeping through my slippers.

Perhaps the hours that followed were so terrible that I've had to forget them; but perhaps I only spent them in a state of numbness. I can't remember. I only know that I came to again around two in the afternoon, when I walked through the gorge with Lynx.

For the first time I didn't find the gorge charmingly romantic, but merely damp and gloomy. It's like that even at the height of summer; the sunlight never touches the ground there. After thunderstorms the fire salamanders creep out of their stone lairs. Later, in summer, I was sometimes able to watch them. There were so many. I often saw ten or fifteen in a single afternoon; glorious creatures mottled black and red, more like certain flowers—tiger lilies or Turk's caps—than their relations, the plain grayish-green lizards. I have never touched a salamander, while I'm happy to touch lizards.

That day, on the second of May, I didn't see them. It hadn't rained, and I still had no idea that they were there. I got out quickly to escape the damp green gloom. This time I was better equipped, with mountain boots, knee-length socks and a warm cap. The coat had been a nuisance the day before; it had dragged along the meadow while I was marking out the boundary. I had taken Hugo's binoculars with me as well, and in my rucksack I had a thermos flask of cocoa, and sandwiches.

Apart from these, as well as my little penknife (for sharpening pencils), I'd taken along Hugo's sharp jackknife. I couldn't use it, because it was too dangerous to cut down branches with; I would only have cut my hand. Although I was reluctant to admit it to myself, I carried the knife for self-protection. It was something that gave me a deceptive sense of security. Later on, I often left it at home. Since Lynx died I have carried it with me wherever I go. At least I now know precisely why, and no longer convince myself that I need it to cut down hazel branches. The wall was, of course, still where I had marked it, and hadn't shifted nearer to the hunting lodge as I had imagined in the evening. It hadn't moved back, either, but I wouldn't have expected that. The stream had returned to its usual mirror surface, so it had clearly found it easy to penetrate the loose rock. I was able to cross it, jumping from stone to stone, and then followed my toy boundary to the vantage point by the larches. There I broke off fresh branches and began marking out the wall again.

It was an arduous task, and my back soon ached from all the bending. But I was almost obsessed with the idea that I had to get the task finished as best I could. It comforted me and brought a bit of order into the huge, terrible disorder that had invaded my life. Something like the wall simply could not exist. In marking it out with green sticks I was making my first attempt—since it was there—to assign to it an appropriate place.

My path led over two mountain pastures, through a young growth of spruces and over an overgrown patch of wild raspberries. The sun was burning, and my hands were bleeding, torn by thorns and splinters. Of course I could only use the little sticks in the pasture, while in the thickets I needed real posts; here and there I marked the trees near the wall with my pocketknife. All this held me up, and I made very slow progress.

From the top of the raspberry patch I could see almost the whole valley below me. Using the binoculars I could see everything very clearly and sharply. In front of the coach maker's cottage a woman sat motionless in the sun. I couldn't see her face, her head was lowered and she seemed to be asleep. I watched for such a long time that tears came to my eyes and the image dissolved into shapes and colors. A sheepdog lay unmoving across the doorstep, its head on its paws.

If this was death, it had come swiftly and softly, almost lovingly. Perhaps it would have been more sensible to have gone to the village with Hugo and Luise.

Finally I tore myself away from the peaceful scene and went on planting my branches. The wall now dipped into a meadow, with a one-story farmhouse in it; only a little smallholding such as one often finds in the mountains, not like the big square farms in the open countryside.

The wall divided the little meadow behind the house, and had cut two branches off an apple tree. They didn't look as if they'd been cut off, incidentally, but rather as if they'd been melted, if you could imagine melted wood.

I didn't touch them. Two cows lay on the other side of the wall in the meadow. I looked at them for a long time. Their flanks weren't rising and falling. They too looked more asleep than dead. Their pink nostrils were no longer damp and smooth, and looked instead like prettily painted fine-grained stone.

Lynx turned his head and looked away into the forest. He didn't break into that terrible howling, but simply didn't look, as if he'd decided not to take in anything on the other side of the wall. My parents had once had a dog that turned from mirrors in a similar way.

While I was still watching the two dead animals I suddenly heard a cow mooing behind me, and Lynx barking excitedly. The noise whipped me round, and then the undergrowth parted, and out of it, followed by the excited dog, stepped a living, mooing cow. She walked straight up to me and bellowed out all her pain to me. The poor creature hadn't been milked for two days, her voice sounded quite hoarse and raw. I immediately tried to relieve her. As a young girl I had learned how to milk for fun, but that had been twenty years ago and I was completely out of practice.

The cow patiently complied, having understood that I wanted to help her. The yellow milk spurted onto the earth, and Lynx set about licking it up. The cow gave a great deal of milk, and the unfamiliar grip made my hands ache. All of a sudden the cow was quite content, and leaned down and brought her big mouth close to Lynx's brown nose. This mutual assessment seemed to be favorable, for both animals were content and calm.

So there I was in a wild and strange meadow in the middle of the forest and suddenly I was the owner of a cow. It was quite plain that I couldn't leave the cow behind. It was only now that I noticed bloodstains on her mouth. She had obviously been desperately running against the wall, which was stopping her getting home to her byre and her people.

There was no sign of those people. They must have stayed in the house when the catastrophe happened. The drawn curtains over the little windows convinced me yet again that all of this had happened in the evening. Not too late, because the old man had just washed himself, and the old woman with the cat had still been sitting on the bench in front of the house. In the early morning, when it's still cool, an old woman doesn't sit on the bench by her house with her cat. Also, if the disaster had occurred in the morning, Hugo and Luise would have been home ages before. I considered all this and immediately told myself that considerations such as these were absolutely no use. So I abandoned them and searched through the copse, calling encouragingly for another cow, but nothing stirred. If there had been a bull somewhere in the vicinity, Lynx would have flushed it out a long time ago.

I had no alternative but to drive the cow back home, over hill and dale. The boundary I had marked out suddenly served a useful purpose. For in the meantime it had grown late; it was about five o'clock in the afternoon, and only narrow shafts of sunlight fell on the glade.

So the three of us walked home. It was a good thing that I had planted the branches and didn't have to slow myself down by feeling my way along the wall. I walked slowly between the wall and the cow, continually anxious that the animal might break a leg. But she seemed used to walking in a mountainous landscape. I didn't have to drive her on ahead of me, but simply made sure that she stayed at a safe distance from the wall. Lynx had already grasped the meaning of my toy boundary, and kept at a safe distance.

All the way home I didn't give the wall so much as a thought, I was so preoccupied with my foundling. Sometimes the cow would suddenly stop and start grazing, and then Lynx would lie down nearby and keep a constant eye on her. If she went on for too long, he pushed her gently and she obediently started moving again. I don't know how right I was, but during the time that followed I sometimes had the impression that Lynx had a very good notion of how cows were to be treated. I think the huntsman must sometimes have used him as a watchdog when he drove his cows to the meadow in the autumn.

The cow seemed completely calm and happy. After two

terrible days she had found a human being, had been freed from her painful burden of milk and hadn't a thought of running away. Somewhere there had to be a byre that this new human would take her to. Snuffling hopefully, she trotted along by my side. When, with some difficulty, we had crossed the stream, she even sped up, and in the end it was all I could do to keep up with her.

In the meantime I had realized that this cow, while certainly a blessing, was also a great burden. There could no longer be any question of long reconnaissance missions.

An animal like this wants to be fed and milked, and needs a settled master. I was the owner and the prisoner of a cow. But even if I hadn't wanted the cow I couldn't have left her behind. She was dependent on me.

When we reached the clearing, and it was almost dark, the cow stopped, looked backward and mooed quietly and happily. I led her to the huntsman's hut. There was nothing inside but two bunk beds, a table, a bench and an oven in the wall. I carried the table into the open, tore the straw sack from one of the beds and led the cow into her new byre. There was plenty of room for a cow. I took a tin pot off the stove, filled it with water and placed it in the empty bed. It was all I could do for my cow that evening. I stroked her, explained the new situation to her and then bolted the door.

I was so tired that I could barely get myself back to the hunting lodge. My feet burned in my heavy shoes and the small of my back ached. I fed Lynx and drank cocoa from the thermos flask. I was too exhausted to eat the sandwiches. That evening I washed with cold water at the spring and then went straight to bed. Lynx also seemed to be tired, for immediately after he had eaten he crept into his stove door.

The following morning wasn't as unbearable as the previous morning had been, because the minute I opened my eyes I thought about the cow. I was immediately wide awake, but still very fatigued by my new efforts. I had also slept rather late; and the sunlight fell in yellow stripes through the slats of the shutters.

I got up and set to work. There were a lot of pots and pans in the hunting lodge, and I chose a bucket as a milking pail and took it into the byre. The cow was standing quietly by the bed, and greeted me by happily licking my face. I milked her; it was harder than the day before because every bone in my body ached. Milking is an extremely strenuous job, and I would have to get used to it again. But I knew the right grip to use, which was the most important thing as far as I was concerned. Since I had no hay, after I had milked the cow I drove her to the forest meadow and let her graze there. I knew without a doubt that she wouldn't run away from me.

Then at last I had my breakfast, warm milk and the stale sandwiches from the day before. The whole day, I remember quite clearly, was dedicated to the cow. I arranged the byre as best I could; I spread out green branches for her, since I had no straw, and with her first dung I laid the foundations of a dung heap beside the hut.

The "byre" was solidly built from tough timbers. Under the roof, in the corner, was a little room that I later stuffed with straw. But back in May there wasn't any straw as yet, and until autumn I had to make do with fresh branches.

I thought about the cow as well, of course. If I was especially lucky she would be expecting a calf. But I couldn't rely on that, I could only hope that my cow would give milk for as long as possible.

I still saw my situation as a transitory condition, at least that's what I tried to do.

I had little notion about cattle-rearing. I had once witnessed the birth of a calf, but I didn't even know the length of a cow's gestation. I've learned that in the meantime from a farmer's diary, but I don't know much more than that to this day, and have no idea how I could find out anything more about it.

I wanted to take out the little oven in the byre, but later found it to be quite practical. If necessary I could heat up water there. I carried the table and a chair into the garage, where there were a lot of tools. Hugo had always made sure that he had good tools, and the huntsman, an honest, tidy man, had made sure that they were always in working order. I don't know why Hugo set such great store by the tools. He never touched them himself, but looked at them with great satisfaction every time he visited the place. If it was a fad of his, then that fad was a blessing. It is thanks to Hugo's mild eccentricities that I am still alive today. Dear old Hugo, God bless him, I'm sure he's still sitting at the table in the inn with a glass of lemonade in front of him, finally unafraid of illness and death. And there is no longer anyone to send him to those business conferences.

While I was busy with the byre, the cow stood grazing in the forest meadow. She was a pretty animal, fine-boned, rounded and grayish-brown. She somehow looked cheerful and young. The way she turned her head in all directions when she tore leaves from the bushes reminded me of a graceful, coquettish young woman looking over her shoulder with moist brown eyes. I immediately took the cow to my heart, it made me so happy to look at her.

Lynx ran about close by me, kept his eye on the cow, drank from the trough at the spring and went off on little hunting expeditions in the bushes. He was his old self again, the old cheerful dog, and seemed to have forgotten his fears of the last few days. He seemed to have got used to the idea that, at least temporarily, I was his master.

At midday I made soup with *erbswurst* and opened a tin of corned beef. After the meal I was overwhelmed with fatigue. I told Lynx to keep an eye on the cow for a while, and lay down on the bed with my clothes on, as if under anesthetic. After everything that had happened I ought not to have been able to sleep at all; but I must say that for the first few days in the hunting lodge I slept particularly well, until my body had got used to the heavy work. Insomnia only began to bother me much later on.

At about four o'clock I woke up. The cow had lain down, chewing the cud. Lynx sat on the bench by the house and watched her sleepily. I relieved him of his guard duties, and he went off exploring again. At that time I always grew worried the minute I couldn't see him. Later, when I knew how much I could rely on him, I completely lost this fear.

When it grew cool, I put water on the stove to heat. I desperately needed a bath.

Toward evening I took the cow into the byre, milked her, poured fresh water into the pot on the bedstead and then left her alone for the night. After my bath I wrapped myself in my dressing gown, drank hot milk and then sat down at the table to have a think. I was amazed that I didn't feel sad and desperate. I grew so sleepy that I had to rest my head on my hands and almost fell asleep in my chair. But since I couldn't think after all, I tried to read; one of Hugo's thrillers. But it didn't seem to be the right thing; I wasn't very interested in the white slave trade at that particular moment. Incidentally, Hugo too had regularly dozed off on the third or fourth page of his hard-boiled thrillers. Maybe he used them as a kind of sleeping potion.

Likewise, I managed only ten minutes at the most, then resolutely got up, switched off the torch, bolted the door and went to bed. The next morning the weather was cool and cheerless and made me realize that I had to get hold of some hay for my cow.

I remembered having seen a barn in the meadow by the stream—perhaps there was still a little hay in it. I had no way of using Hugo's car; he'd taken the key with him when he went away. Only two weeks ago, urged by my daughters, I'd completed a course of driving lessons, and wouldn't have risked driving to the gorge for any price. I found a few old sacks in the garage, and after working in the stable I set off, laden with these, in search of hay.

In the barn in the meadow by the stream I actually did find some hay. I stuffed it into the sacks, which I tied together and dragged behind me. But I soon saw that the sacks weren't going to withstand the journey along the gravel path. So I left two of them lying at the side of the road and carried the other two over my shoulders to the hunting lodge. I cleared the tools out of the garage and lodged them in the room beside the kitchen, then fetched the sacks I'd left behind and emptied them in the garage.

I went to fetch hay twice more in the afternoon, and then again the following day. It was now early May, and around this time it can still get chillingly cold in the mountains. As long as it stayed cool and slightly rainy I was able to graze the cow on the forest meadow. She seemed very happy with her new life and patiently put up with my clumsy milking. Sometimes she turned her great head toward me as if she was watching my efforts with amusement, but she stood there quietly and never kicked at me; she was friendly, often even a little bumptious.

I thought of a name for my cow, and called her Bella. It didn't fit with the landscape, but it was short and sonorous. The cow soon understood that she was now called Bella, and turned her head when I called her. I would love to know what she had been called before; Dirndl, Gretl, or Gray, perhaps. Actually she wouldn't have needed a name at all, as she was the only cow in the forest, perhaps the only cow in the region.

Lynx too had quite an unsuitable name, testifying to the ignorance of the people hereabouts. But all the hunting dogs in the valley had been called Lynx since time immemorial. The real lynxes had been hunted to extinction so long ago that nobody in the valley had any idea of what they were like. Maybe one of Lynx's ancestors had killed the last real lynx, and kept its name as a victory prize.

The gloomy weather merged into rainy days, and later even to snowstorms. Bella stayed in the stall and was given hay to eat, and I suddenly found the time and the peace to think about things. In my diary, Hugo's diary, that is, there's a note for the tenth of May: "Inventory."

That tenth of May was a truly wintry day. The snow, which had at first melted immediately, began to settle, and it was still snowing.

It started when I woke up feeling entirely unprotected and abandoned. I was no longer physically tired and defenseless against the onslaught of my thoughts. Ten days had passed, and nothing in my situation had changed. For ten days I had anesthetized myself with work, but the wall was still there and nobody had come to fetch me. I had no alternative but to face reality. Back then I didn't give up hope, far from it. Even when I finally had to tell myself that I could no longer expect any help, that mad hope stayed within me; a hope against all reason and against my own conviction.

Even then, on the tenth of May, it seemed certain to me that the scale of the catastrophe was enormous. Everything pointed to it: the absence of rescuers, the silence of human voices on the radio, and what little I had seen through the wall.

Much later, when almost all hope had been extinguished in me, I still couldn't believe that my children were dead too, like the old man by the stream and the woman on the bench.

If I think about my children today, I always see them as five-year-olds, and it strikes me that they'd left my life even then. That's probably the age at which all children begin to leave their parents' lives; quite slowly they turn into strangers. But that all happens so imperceptibly that you barely notice it. There were moments when that terrible possibility dawned on me, but like any other mother I very quickly suppressed the thought. I had to live, and what mother could live if she recognized this process?

When I woke up on the tenth of May I thought about my children as little girls, skipping hand in hand across the playground. The two rather unpleasant, loveless and argumentative semiadults that I had left behind in the city had suddenly become quite unreal. I never mourned for them, only ever for the children that they had been many years before. That probably sounds very cruel, but I can't think who I should lie to today. I can allow myself to write the truth; all the people for whom I have lied throughout my life are dead.

Shivering in bed I considered what was to be done. I could kill myself, or try and dig my way under the wall, which would probably only have been a more strenuous kind of suicide. Or of course I could stay here and try to stay alive.

I was no longer young enough to think seriously about suicide. It was chiefly thoughts about Lynx and Bella that kept me from it, and also a certain curiosity. The wall was a riddle, and I would never have managed to leave a riddle unsolved. Thanks to Hugo's solicitude I had a few provisions that might keep me through the summer, a home, a lifetime's supply of wood and a cow, who was also an unsolved riddle—and was perhaps expecting a calf.

I wanted to wait at least for the appearance or nonappearance of this calf before making further decisions. I didn't give too much thought to the wall. I assumed it was a new weapon that one of the major powers had managed to keep secret; an ideal weapon, it left the earth untouched and killed only humans and animals. It would have been better, certainly, if the animals could have been spared, but that had probably been impossible. As long as they got the people, they hadn't given a thought to the animals in the course of their slaughter. Once the poison, at least I imagined a kind of poison, had ceased to be effective, it would be possible to seize the country. Judging by the peaceful appearance of the victims, they hadn't suffered; it all seemed like the most humane piece of devilry ever to have occurred to a human brain.

I had no idea how long the land would remain infertile, and assumed that once it could be entered again the wall would disappear and the victors would move in.

Today I sometimes wonder whether the experiment, if indeed that's what it was, wasn't just that little bit too successful. The victors are such a long time coming.

Perhaps there were no victors. There's no point in thinking about that. A scientist, a specialist in weapons of destruction, would probably have discovered more than I have, but it wouldn't have been much use to him. For all his knowledge, he could do no different from myself: wait, and try to stay alive.

After I'd sorted everything out as well as a person with my experience and my intelligence could do, I threw off my blanket and set about heating the house, for it was very cold that morning. Lynx crept out of the stove door, and then it was time to go into the byre and see to Bella.

After breakfast I started to bring all my supplies down into the bedroom and draw up a list. I have the list in front of me, I don't want to copy it out, because almost everything I owned will be mentioned in the course of this report. I moved the food from the little room into the bedroom, because it's cool there even in the summer.

The house is built against the mountain, and its back is always in the shade.

There were enough items of clothing about, and petroleum for the lamp and spirit for the little stove. There were also a bundle of candles and two torches with extra batteries. The medicine cabinet was fully supplied; apart from bandages and painkillers everything's still there. Hugo had devoted himself to this medicine cabinet with a passion; I think most of the medicines became unusable long ago.

The things that turned out to be essential were a big bag of potatoes, a lot of matches and ammunition. And, of course, the various tools, a shotgun and a Mannlicher rifle, the binoculars, a scythe, a rake and a pitchfork that had been used to cut the forest meadow for fodder for the deer, and a little sack of beans. Without these things, which I owe to Hugo's anxieties and to chance, I would no longer be alive.

I established that I'd already used up too much of the food. Above all it was a waste to feed Lynx on it; it wasn't good for him either, he urgently needed fresh meat. The flour might last another three months, if I was extremely economical with it, and I could no longer rely on being found by then. I could never rely on being found.

My most treasured possessions for the future were the potatoes and the beans. I absolutely had to find a place that I could use as a little plowed field. And above all I had to see about getting hold of some fresh meat. I knew how to use guns, and had often successfully shot clay pigeons, but I'd never shot deer.

Later, at the deer's feeding place, I found three red salt licks, and kept them in the kitchen where it was dry. For a long time now that rough salt has been all the salt I have. In the summer I was also able to catch trout with Luise's fishing rod. I'd never done it before, but it couldn't be all that difficult. I didn't like the idea of that kind of murderous activity at all, but I had no choice if I was to keep Lynx and myself alive.

At lunchtime I cooked rice pudding, making do without sugar. Despite my economies, however, after only eight weeks I hadn't a single piece of sugar left, and in future had to do without sweetness of any kind.

I also resolutely decided to wind the clocks daily, and cross off each day in the diary. At the time it struck me as very important; I was practically clinging to the meager remnants of human routine left to me. Incidentally, I've never abandoned certain habits. I wash myself daily, brush my teeth, do my laundry and keep the house clean.

I don't know why I do that, it's as if I'm driven by an inner compulsion. Maybe I'm afraid that if I could do otherwise I would gradually cease to be a human being, and would soon be creeping about, dirty and stinking, emitting incomprehensible noises. Not that I'm afraid of becoming an animal. That wouldn't be too bad, but a human being can never become just an animal; he plunges beyond, into the abyss. I don't want this to happen to me. Recently that's what has made me most afraid, and it is out of that fear I am writing my report. Once I've reached the end I shall hide it well and forget about it. I don't want the strange thing that I might turn into to find it one day. I shall do all I can to avoid that transformation, but I'm not fool enough to believe with any confidence that what has happened to so many people before me could not happen to me.

If I think now about the woman I once was, before the wall entered my life, I don't recognize myself in her. But even the woman who marked the diary with the word "Inventory" on the tenth of May has become very strange to me. It was very sensible of her to leave notes behind, so that I can awaken her to new life in my memory. It occurs to me that I haven't written down my name. I had almost forgotten it, and that's how it's going to stay. No one calls me by that name, so it no longer exists. Neither would I like it if my name were one day perhaps to appear in the victors' magazines. Unimaginable that there should still be magazines somewhere in the world. But in fact why not? If the catastrophe had taken place in Beluchistan, we'd be sitting completely unmoved in our cafés, reading about it in the paper. This is like Beluchistan now, a very far-off, foreign country, one whose whereabouts are scarcely known, a country inhabited by people who are presumably not real people at all; underdeveloped and insensitive to pain; numbers and statistics in foreign newspapers. Nothing to get bothered about. I remember very clearly how little imagination most people used to have. That was probably their good fortune. Imagination makes people oversensitive, vulnerable and exposed. Perhaps it's a form of degeneracy. I have never held the shortcomings of the unimaginative against them, sometimes I've even envied them. They had an easier and more pleasant life than everyone else.

That doesn't really belong in my report. But I can't avoid sometimes thinking about things that are completely meaningless to me. I'm so alone that I can't always get away from useless thoughts. Since Lynx died that's got a lot worse.

I shall try not to deviate too often from the diary entries.

On the sixteenth of May I finally found a place for the potato field. I'd been looking for it with Lynx for days. The field couldn't be too far from the hut, couldn't be in the shade, and above all it had to have fertile soil. This last requirement was almost impossible to fulfill.

The humus hereabouts only lies like a thin skin over the chalk. I was about to abandon all hope on earth when, in a little clearing on the sunny side of the mountain, I found just the place. The space was almost level, dry, and protected on all sides by the forest, and there actually was some soil. A quite strange, light soil, black, permeated by tiny bits of charcoal. An old charcoal pile must once have stood on this spot, long ago, because the last charcoal burner had disappeared from the forest a long time since.

I didn't know whether potatoes liked sooty soil, but I nevertheless decided to plant them on this spot, since I knew I wouldn't find such deep soil anywhere else.

I fetched my shovel and picks from the hut and immediately set about digging over the ground. It wasn't all that easy, because there were bushes growing on it, and an unbelievably stubborn weed with long roots. This work went on for four days and was excessively tiring. When I'd finished it, I rested for a day, and then immediately set about planting the potatoes. I dimly remembered that you cut them up to do this, and made sure that each piece had at least one eye.

Then I piled the soil on top of them. There was now nothing I could do but wait and hope.

I smeared my sore hands with deer fat, a large piece of which I'd found in the hunting lodge. As soon as I'd recovered I started digging over the ground beside the stable and planting my beans. There was only enough for a tiny garden, and I didn't know whether the beans would even germinate. They might be too old or chemically treated. In any case I had to give it a try.

In the meantime the weather had improved, and sunshine alternated with showers. There was even a slight storm at one point, and the forest turned into a green, steaming basin. After this storm I thought it worth noting that it became as warm as summer and the grass on the forest meadow grew high and lush. It was a remarkably tough, almost thorny grass, very long, and I assume it wasn't much use as cattle feed. But Bella seemed happy with it. She spent every day in the meadow, and it struck me that she was getting rounder. Just to be on the safe side, however, I fetched the last hay out of the barn to have a supply in case the weather suddenly turned. Every second day I cut fresh branches for Bella's bed. I wanted my cow to be able to flourish amid cleanliness and order. I took a lot of trouble looking after Bella. I now had plenty of milk for myself and Lynx, but even if Bella hadn't given any milk I couldn't have helped looking after her so well. She had very quickly become more to me than simply a piece of beef that I kept for my own use. Perhaps that idea was nonsensical; but I couldn't and wouldn't resist it. The animals were all I had now, and I began to feel like the head of our curious family.

The day after the storm, on the thirtieth of May, it rained all day, a warm and fertile rain that forced me to stay in the hut if I didn't want to get soaked to the skin in a few minutes. Toward evening it became unpleasantly cold, and I lit a fire. After I'd done my work in the byre and washed I put on my dressing gown, to read a little by torchlight. I had found a farmer's diary that struck me as worth reading. There was a lot in it about making a garden and raising cattle, and I urgently needed to learn more about these matters. Lynx lay in the stove door and snuffled comfortably in the warmth, and I drank bitter tea and listened to the monotonous sound of the rain. Suddenly I thought I heard children calling. I knew it must be an illusion, and returned to my diary, but then Lynx lifted his head and listened, and there it was again, a quiet, sorrowful wailing.

That evening the cat came into my house. A sopping-wet gray bundle, she was crouched wailing by the door.

Later, in the hut, she plunged her claws into my dressing gown with horror, and hissed furiously at the barking Lynx.

I shouted at the dog, and he crept back into his hole, hurt and reluctant. Then I put the cat on the table. She was still hissing at Lynx, a thin, gray-and-black striped farmer's cat, hungry and soaking, but still capable of defending herself with tooth and claw. She only calmed down once I had banished Lynx to the bedroom.

I gave her warm milk and a little meat, and, looking around her all the time, she hastily wolfed down everything I put in front of her. Then she allowed herself to be stroked, jumped off the table, stalked through the room and slid onto my bed. There she sat down and started to wash herself. When she was dry I saw that she was a beautiful creature, not big, but with unusual markings. The most beautiful thing about her was her eyes, big, round and amber. She might have belonged to the old man by the stream, and bumped into the wall on her way home from her evening hunt. She'd been wandering around for four weeks, perhaps she'd been watching me for ages before she'd dared approach the hut. The enticing warmth and the glimmer of light, and maybe also the smell of milk, had overcome her mistrust.

Lynx whined in his prison, and I led him out by the collar, showed him the cat, stroked first Lynx and then the cat and introduced her as a new member of the household. Lynx seemed to have understood and behaved very well. For a few days the cat remained hostile and cold toward him. She might have had bad experiences, for she would hiss furiously whenever Lynx inquisitively approached her.

At night she slept in my bed, pressed close against my legs. It wasn't very comfortable for me, but as time passed I got used to it. In the morning she ran off and didn't return until dusk started falling, to eat, drink and sleep in my bed. She acted like this for five or six days. After that she stayed with me all the time, and from then on behaved like a true house cat.

Lynx didn't stop trying to get close to her, as he was a very inquisitive dog, and at last the cat came to terms with his behavior, stopped hissing and even allowed herself to be sniffed at. All the same, she didn't seem too happy about it. She was a very nervous and suspicious creature, jumped at the slightest noise and was always tense and ready to make off at any moment.

It was weeks before she calmed down and seemed to stop being afraid that I might kick her out. Strangely, she soon seemed less suspicious of Lynx than of me. She clearly didn't expect any nasty surprises from him anymore, and started to treat him as a moody wife treats her oaf of a husband. She sometimes hissed at him and made to claw him, and then, once Lynx had drawn back, she would approach him and even go to sleep beside him.

Her experiences with people must indeed have been bad, and as I knew how poorly cats are often treated, particularly in the country, I wasn't surprised. I always treated her in the same friendly way, only ever approached her slowly and never without talking to her at the same time. And when, at the end of June, she left where she was sitting, crossed the table to me and rubbed her little head against my forehead for the first time, I saw this as a great success. From then on the ice was broken. Not that she showered me with caresses, but she seemed prepared to forget the harm that people had done her.

Even now she sometimes cowers from me or runs to the door if I move too suddenly. I'm hurt, but who knows, maybe the cat knows me better than I know myself, and knows what I could be capable of. As I write, she's lying in front of me on the table, staring with her big yellow eyes over my shoulder at a patch of wall. I've turned around three times to look, and can see nothing there but the old dark wood. Sometimes she stares at me too, with a long and steady gaze, but never for as long as she looks at the wall: after a certain amount of time she gets uncomfortable and turns her head away or shuts her eyelids.

Lynx too used to have to turn his eyes away if I looked at him for a long time. I don't think that human eyes have a hypnotic effect, but I can imagine that they're simply too big and shining to be agreeable to a smaller animal. I don't like being stared at by eyes as big as saucers, either.

Since Lynx died, the cat has grown closer to me. Maybe she sees that we are entirely dependent on one another, but she was jealous of the dog, without being able to show it. In fact, however, I depend on her more than she does on me. I can speak to her, stroke her, and her warmth seeps across my palms into my body and comforts me. I don't think the cat needs me as desperately as I need her.

Over time, Lynx developed a certain affection for her. For him she was a member of the family or the gang, and he would have gone for any aggressor to protect her.

So there were four of us, the cow, the cat, Lynx and me. Lynx was closest to me, and soon he wasn't just my dog, but my friend; my only friend in a world of troubles and loneliness. He understood everything I said, knew whether I was sad or cheerful and tried, in his simple way, to comfort me.

The cat was entirely different, a brave, hard-nosed animal that I respected and admired, but one who always insisted on her freedom. She hadn't fallen under my spell at all. Of course Lynx had no choice, he was dependent on a master. A dog without a master is the poorest creature in the world; even the most wicked people can send their dog into ecstasies.

The cat soon started to make certain demands on me. She wanted to come and go as she pleased at all times, even at night. I understood that, and as I had to keep the window closed when the weather was cold, I dug a little hole in the wall behind the cupboard. It was hard work, but it was worth it because from now on I had peace at night. The cupboard kept cold drafts out in winter. In the summer I naturally slept with the window open, but the cat always used her own little door. Her life assumed a very regular pattern: she slept by day, went out in the evening and didn't come back until morning, when she warmed herself with me in bed.

I can see my face, small and tight, in the mirror of her big eyes. She has got used to answering when I speak to her. Don't go out tonight, I say, the owl and the fox are in the forest, with me you're warm and safe. Hrr, grrr, meow, she says, and that might mean, we'll see, woman-creature, I mightn't commit myself. And then, soon, comes the moment when she stands up, arches into a bow, stretches herself out twice, jumps from the table, slips into the background and, without a sound, disappears into the dusk. And later I will sleep my quiet sleep, a sleep in which the spruce trees rustle and the stream splashes.

Toward morning, when the familiar little body rubs up against my legs, I shall allow myself to sink a little further into sleep, never very deeply because I have to be very cautious.

Someone might come up to the window, looking like a man and hiding an ax behind his back.

My gun hangs loaded beside the bed. I have to listen out for footsteps approaching the house or the byre. Recently I've often thought about clearing out the bedroom and setting up a byre there for Bella. There are a lot of arguments against this, but it would be a great relief to me to be able to hear her through the door and know that she was close by and safe. I would naturally have to make a doorway leading from the room into the open, and tear up the floor and make a gutter. I could have the gutter leading to the cesspit behind the house, under the little wooden cottage. All that worries me is the matter of the door. I could manage, with the greatest effort, to break open a doorway, but I then would have to fit the byre door into it properly, and I don't think I can do that. Every evening in bed I think about that door, and I could weep at my clumsiness and incompetence. And nevertheless, when I've thought about it for a very long time, I'll give the door a go. In winter Bella will be pleasantly warm next to the kitchen, and she'll hear my voice. As long as it's cold and the snow lies all I can do is think about it.

Bella's byre brought new tasks with it back then, in June. The wooden floor was soaked with her urine, and was starting to rot and stink. That couldn't go on. I tore up two boards and dug a gutter to let the urine flow outside. The hut was on a slight inclination, toward the slope that led down to the stream. The floor might have sunk a little over the years, but that suited my work. Everything could flow unhindered through the porous chalk soil and seep away into the ground.

In the summer it smelled a bit behind the byre, but I never went there anyway; at least the byre was now clean and dry. The slope behind the stable had always been a particularly inhospitable and almost weird area, permanently in shadow, dense with spruce trees, and damp. Whitish mushrooms grew there, and it smelt a little mildewy. I wasn't bothered that the waste might seep into the stream. The spring water came from a source above the hunting lodge, and it was clear and very cold, the best water I've ever drunk.

I find it striking that I've never noted in my diary when I shot a deer. I now recall that the idea of writing it down simply repelled me; it was quite enough that I had to do it. I'd rather not write about it even now, only to say that after a few failed attempts I got quite good at supplying us with meat without using up too much ammunition. I'm a child of the city, but my mother came from the country, in fact from the part I live in now. She and Luise's mother were sisters, and we always used to spend the summer holidays in the country. In those days people didn't normally spend their holidays on the Riviera. If those summers in the country always seemed like a game, a lot of what I learned stayed with me, and made it easier for me to live as I now have to. At least I'm not completely hopeless. Even as a child I practiced clay-pigeon shooting with Luise. I was even better at it than Luise, but she was the one who became a passionate hunter. The first summer here in the forest I often used to catch trout as well. I found killing them less of a problem. I don't know why; killing deer seems particularly despicable even today, almost like a betrayal. I'll never get used to it.

My supplies dwindled much too fast, and I had to tighten my belt a great deal. I was particularly short of fruit, vegetables, sugar and bread. I got by as well as I could with nettles, lettuce and the tops of young spruce trees. Later, when I was waiting with longing for the potato crop, I went through a period of being beset by cravings, like a pregnant woman. Images of good substantial meals pursued me into my dreams. Fortunately this state didn't last too long. I was familiar with it from the war, but I'd forgotten how terrible it is to be dependent on an unsatisfied body. Quite suddenly, when the first potatoes appeared, my wild desires left me, and I started forgetting what fresh fruit, chocolate and iced coffee had tasted like. But I could never quite forget bread. Even today I'm often surprised by a desire for it. Black bread has become a quite unimaginable delicacy for me.

If I think back to that summer I see it as filled with activity and hardship. I could barely do all the work I had set myself. As I wasn't used to hard work I felt constantly exhausted. I hadn't yet found out how to divide it up properly. I worked either too quickly or too slowly, and I had to get everything done however many setbacks there were. I grew thin and weak, and even the work in the stable was excessively exhausting. I don't know how I managed to get through that period. I really don't know; maybe I was only able to do it because I'd got it into my head that I had to, and because I had three animals to care for. The constant overexertion soon left me feeling like poor Hugo; I fell asleep the moment I sat on the bench. On top of that I used to dream of good food, but whenever I tried to eat I could manage only a few mouthfuls. I think I lived on Bella's milk alone. It was the only thing I could take.

I was much too immersed in these tribulations to have a clear view of my situation. As I had decided to stick it out, I stuck it out, but I'd forgotten why it was important and was just living from one day to the next. I can't remember whether I went to the gorge a lot in those days, probably not. I only remember once, at the end of June, going to the meadow by the stream to see how the grass was doing, and while I was there I looked through the wall. The man by the stream had fallen over and now lay on his back, his knees slightly bent, his cupped hand still on the way to his face. He must have been knocked over in a storm. He didn't look like a corpse, more like something excavated from Pompeii. While I was standing there looking at that petrified absurdity, I saw two birds lying in the tall grass under one of the bushes on the other side of the wall. They too must have been blown out of the bushes. They looked pretty, like painted toys. Their eyes shone like polished stones, and the colors of their plumage hadn't faded. They didn't look dead, but rather like things that had never been alive, entirely inorganic. And yet they had once lived, and their warm breath had moved their little throats. Lynx, who was with me as always, turned away and prodded me with his muzzle. He wanted me to go on. He was more sensible than I was, so I allowed him to lead me away from the stone things.

When I had to go to the meadow later on, I usually avoided looking through the wall. The first summer it was almost blocked off. A few of my hazel twigs had miraculously grown roots and soon a green hedge ran along the wall. Maiden pinks, columbines and a tall yellow weed bloomed in the meadow by the stream. The meadow looked cheerful and friendly, in contrast to the gorge, but since it adjoined the wall I could never be friends with it.

Bella kept me tied to the hunting lodge, but I wanted to try to have a look around. I remembered a path that led to a hunting lodge higher up, and thence down into the valley opposite. I wanted to follow it. Since I couldn't leave the cow alone for long, I decided to go at night. There was a full moon, and it was clear and warm. I didn't milk Bella until late in the evening, left hay and water in the stable and put milk for the cat by the stove. At the first glimmer of moonlight I set off with Lynx. I took some provisions with me, the shotgun and the binoculars. It all weighed me down, but I still didn't dare go unarmed. Lynx was excited and very pleased by this late walk. First I went up to the hunting lodge that was still within Hugo's hunting ground. The path had been well looked after and there was enough light from the moon. I've never been scared in the forest at night, while I was always nervous in the city. I don't know why that was, probably because it never occurred to me that I might bump into people in the forest as well. The way up took almost three hours. When I stepped out of the shadows of the forest, the clearing lay in the white light before me, with the little hut in the middle. I wanted to wait until the return trip before examining the hut, and sat down on the bench in front of it to have a brief rest and a drink from the thermos flask. It was much cooler here than in the valley basin, but perhaps this was just an impression caused by the cold white light.

All the numb depression of the past while slipped from me, leaving me feeling light and liberated. If I have ever felt peace, it was that June night in the moonlit clearing. Lynx sat pressed close to me, gazing peacefully and alertly across to the ink-black forest. It was hard for me to stand up and go on hiking. I crossed the dew-drenched meadow and disappeared into the darkness of the forest once more. Now and again there were rustling noises in the darkness; there must have been a lot of little animals on the move. Lynx stayed silently by my side, perhaps still imagining that we were going stalking. The path took us through the forest for half an hour, and I had to walk slowly because the moon cast only a faint light on the path. A screech owl cried, and his call sounded no stranger than any other animal noise. I caught myself walking unusually carefully and quietly. I couldn't help it, something forced me to. When I finally emerged from the forest, dawn was just beginning to break. Its dim glow mingled with the light of the sinking moon. The path now took us between mountain pines and alpine roses, large and small gray clumps in the first light. Sometimes a stone broke away under my feet, and clattered down the scree into the valley. Once I'd reached the highest point I sat down on a little rock and waited. At around half past four the sun rose. A cool wind came up and passed through my hair. The grayish-pink sky turned orange and fiery red. It was my first sunrise in the mountains. Only Lynx was sitting beside me, staring into the light as I did. It was a great effort for him not to start barking with joy, as I could see from the twitching of his ears and muscular spasms rippling across his back. Suddenly it was bright daylight. I stood up and began my descent into the valley. It was a long, thin, densely forested valley. Using the binoculars I could see nothing but forest. A ridge of peaks rising opposite blocked my view. That was disappointing, for I'd hoped I'd be able to see a village at least. Now I knew I'd have to go back along the path through the mountain pines

if I wanted a clear view. There was an Alm* there, and
from that point I would surely be able to see deeper into
the landscape. But I couldn't get to both the Alm and the
valley, so I opted for the valley. It seemed more important
to me. Maybe I was still foolishly hoping I wouldn't find a
wall down there. I'm afraid that was it, because otherwise
I could have spared myself the journey. I was now on the
neighbor's beat, which, as far as I remember, was leased
to a rich foreigner who turned up only once a year, in the
rutting season. Maybe that was the reason for the poor
state of the road; you could see the marks of the spring
thaw everywhere. In Hugo's beat the damage had been
repaired immediately. In places the road looked almost
like a riverbed. There was no gorge here. Wooded slopes
rose on either side of the stream. All in all this valley
had a friendlier face than my valley. I'm calling it "my
valley." The new owner, if he exists, hasn't contacted me
yet. If the road hadn't been so washed away I would have
considered the trip a mere stroll. The closer I got to the
valley floor, the more cautious I grew. I stuck my walking
stick out in front of me and made sure that Lynx wasn't
growing tired. He didn't, incidentally, seem to be troubled
by any dark imaginings or recollections, and trotted along
cheerfully beside me. I was still in the forest when my
stick hit the wall. Here the wall was further from the
nearest houses than it was on the other side. Even the big
hunting lodge, which had been built only two years before
and was said to be fitted with all mod cons, was still out
of sight.

Suddenly I grew very tired, almost exhausted. I almost
keeled over at the thought of the long walk back. I slowly
went back a little way, up to a woodman's hut that I hadn't
noticed. It nestled against the mountain in a little hollow,
and the door was completely overgrown with stinging net-

* Alpine pasture.

tles. There was nothing in the hut apart from a tin bowl and a piece of moldy, mouse-gnawed bacon. I sat down at the rough table and unpacked my supplies. Lynx had gone to the stream for a drink. I could see him through the open door, and that set my mind somewhat at rest. I drank tea from the flask, ate a kind of rice cake and later gave Lynx some as well. The silence and the sun blazing on the roof encouraged sleep. But I was afraid of the fleas in the straw-filled bedsteads, and in any case a brief sleep would only have made me even more tired. It was better not to yield to the desire. So I packed my rucksack and left the hut.

My high spirits of the night and the morning had flown, and my feet ached in my heavy mountain boots. The sun burned down on my head, and even Lynx seemed tired and didn't try to cheer me up. The path upward wasn't steep, but it was very long and monotonous. Maybe it only seemed monotonous to me given the depressed mood I was in. I stumbled up there without noticing my surroundings, and gave myself up to brooding thoughts.

So now I had examined the valleys that I could reach without staying away for days at a time. I could still climb up to the pasture and look out over the landscape, but I couldn't risk going any further into the long mountain range. Of course somebody would find me if there was no wall over there, in fact, I had to tell myself, they would surely have found me long since. I could sit quietly at home and wait. But I kept feeling compelled to do something myself to counteract that uncertainty. And I was forced to do nothing and to wait, a state that I had always particularly disliked. I had waited much too often and much too long for people or events which had never turned up, or which had turned up so late that they had ceased to mean anything to me.

On the long walk back I thought about my former life and found it unsatisfactory in all respects. I had achieved little that I had wanted, and everything I had achieved I had ceased to want. That's probably how it was for everybody else, too. It's something we never talked about, when we used to talk. I don't think I shall have the opportunity to talk to other people about it again now. So I shall have to presume it was so. Back then, walking back into my valley, it still hadn't quite dawned on me that my former life had come to a sudden end; I knew it, that is, but only in my head, so I didn't believe it. It's only when knowledge about something slowly spreads to the whole body that you truly know. I know too that I, like every living thing, will have to die some day, but my hands, my feet and my guts still don't know it, which is why death seems so unreal. Time has passed since that June day, and gradually I'm beginning to understand that I can never go back.

At about one o'clock in the afternoon I reached the path through the mountain pines, and sat down on a stone to rest. The forest lay hazily in the midday sun, and the warm scent from the pines floated up to me. Only now could I see that the alpine roses were in bloom. They stretched in a red ribbon over the scree. It was now much quieter than in the moonlit night, as if the forest lay paralyzed by sleep beneath the yellow sun. A bird of prey circled high in the blue sky, Lynx slept, his ears twitching, and the great silence descended on me like a bell jar. I wished I could sit here forever, in the warmth, in the light; the dog at my feet and the circling bird above. I had stopped thinking long since, as if my worries and memories no longer had anything to do with me. When I walked on I did so with deep regret, and on the way I slowly changed, becoming the only creature that didn't belong here, a person troubled by chaotic thoughts, cracking branches with her clumsy shoes and engaged in the bloody business of hunting.

Later, when I reached the hunting lodge higher up the hill, I was my old self again, keen to find something usable in the hut. A faint hint of regret remained within me for hours.

I remember that expedition very well, perhaps because it was the first one; it rises like a peak from the unchanging months of my daily troubles. Incidentally, I haven't gone that way again since that time. I always wanted to, but I never got around to it, and without Lynx I don't dare go on expeditions anymore. Never again shall I sit above the alpine roses in the midday sun, listening to the great silence.

The key to the hut hung on a nail under a loose tile, and wasn't hard to find. I immediately set about looking through the house. It was naturally much smaller than the hunting lodge, and consisted only of a kitchen and a little bedroom. I found a few blankets, a tarpaulin and two rock-hard wedge-shaped headrests. I didn't need the headrests or the blankets; the tarpaulin was waterproof, and I took it with me. I didn't find any clothes there. In the kitchen, in a little cupboard over the stove, there was flour, fat, biscuits, tea, salt, powdered egg and a little sack of prunes, which the huntsman must have seen as a panacea, for I remember he was always chewing them. Also, in the drawer of the table, I found a pack of dirty Tarot cards. I know the Tarot only from having watched it, but I liked the cards, so I took them with me. Later I invented a new game with them, a game for a lonely woman. I have spent many evenings laying out the old cards. The figures were as familiar to me as if I'd known them forever. I gave them names, and took to some of them more than others. My relationship with them became as personal as those with the characters in a Dickens novel that you've read twenty times. I no longer play that game. One of the cards was devoured by Tiger, the cat's son, and Lynx flicked one into a bowl of water with his ears. I would rather not be constantly reminded of Lynx and Tiger. But then is there anything in the hunting lodge that doesn't remind me of them?

In the hunting lodge up the hill I also found an old alarm clock that became very useful to me. I did still have the little traveling alarm clock and the watch, but shortly afterward I dropped the traveling clock and the watch never showed the right time. Today I still have that old alarm clock from the hunting lodge, but it stopped ages ago. I take my bearings from the sun, or, if it isn't shining, from the crows as they fly away and back again, and various other signs. I'd like to know where the right time is, now there aren't any people left. Sometimes I'm struck by how important it once was not to be five minutes late. An awful lot of people I know seemed to see their watches as little idols, and that always struck me as sensible. If you're already living in slavery, it's a good idea to keep to the rules and not put your master in a bad humor. I did not enjoy being a servant of time, artificial human time, dissected by the ticking of clocks, and that often caused difficulties for me. I've never liked clocks, and after a while each of my own mysteriously broke or disappeared. But I concealed my method of systematically destroying clocks even from myself. Today, of course, I know how it all came about. I have so much time to think that I'll eventually catch on to all my little tricks.

I can manage, it doesn't affect me at all. Even if I were suddenly given the most exciting news it would have no meaning for me. I would still have to muck out the byre twice a day, chop wood and fetch hay up from the gorge. My mind is free, it can do what it likes, but it mustn't lose its reason, the reason that will keep me and the animals alive.

On the kitchen table in the hut up the hill there were two newspapers dated the eleventh of April, a completed lottery slip, half a packet of cheap cigarettes, lighters, a ball of twine, six trouser buttons and two needles. The last traces that the huntsman had left behind in the forest. I should really have burned his possessions in a great flaming fire. The huntsman was a good, orderly man, and he won't ever exist again until the end of time. I had always paid him too little attention. He was a troubled-looking man in middle age, haggard, and, for a huntsman, unnaturally pale-skinned. The most striking thing about him was his very pale, greenish-blue eyes; they were particularly sharp and were apparently a great source of vanity to this modest man. He only ever used the binoculars with a contemptuous smile. That's the only thing I know about the huntsman; apart from the fact that he was very conscientious and liked chewing prunes, and, yes, that he was good with dogs. I used to think about him occasionally in the early days. Hugo could easily have brought him along when he first arrived. Then the last few years would probably have been easier for me. Now, all the same, I'm no longer quite sure. Who knows what imprisonment would have done to that unassuming man. In any case he was physically stronger than I am, and I would have been dependent on him. Perhaps he would now be sitting around lazily in the hut, sending me off to do the work. The possibility of delegating work must be a great temptation for any man. And why should a man, without the fear of criticism, go on working at all? No, it's better that I'm alone. And it wouldn't be good for me to be with a weaker partner, either; I'd reduce him to a shadow and kill him with care. That's the way I am, and the forest hasn't changed matters. Maybe only animals can put up with me. If Hugo and Luise had stayed behind in the forest there would certainly have been endless friction as time passed. I can't see anything that could have made our co-existence a happy one.

There's no point thinking about it. Luise, Hugo and the huntsman no longer exist, and basically I don't want them back. I'm no longer the person I was two years ago. If I did wish to have anyone with me, it would have to be an old woman, someone shrewd and witty, someone I could laugh with sometimes. But she would probably die before me, and I'd be left on my own again. It would be worse than never having known her. That would be too high a price to pay for laughter. Then I'd have to remember her too, and that would be too much. Even now I'm nothing but a thin skin covering a mountain of memories. I don't want to go on. What will happen to me if that skin gets torn?

I will never get to the end of my report if I allow myself to be sidetracked into writing down every thought that goes through my head. But now I've lost the desire to write anything else about my expedition. I can't even remember what the walk up to the hut was like. In any case I came back with a fully laden rucksack, saw to Bella and went straight to bed.

The following day, and it's noted down in my diary, the toothache started. My tooth hurt so terribly that the diary entry doesn't surprise me. Never before and never again have I had so much pain from a tooth. I had never given that tooth a thought, probably because I was too aware that there was something far from right about it. It had been drilled, and there was a filling in it, and the dentist had told me to come back in three days, without fail. The three days had turned into three months. I used up a huge number of Hugo's painkillers and felt so depressed on the third day that it was only with the greatest effort that I could do the work I had to do. Sometimes I thought I must be going mad; it was as if the tooth had grown long, thin roots that were now boring their way through my skull. On the fourth day the tablets stopped working at all, and I sat at the table, my head on my arms, listening to the raging racket in my skull. Lynx lay gloomily beside me on the bench, but I wasn't able to say a kind word to him. I sat at the table all night, because the pain was even worse in bed. On the fifth day I got an ulcer, and in an attack of despair and rage I cut my gums open with Hugo's razor. The pain that came when I cut myself was almost pleasant, because it extinguished the other pain for a moment. The wound oozed badly, and I was so miserable that I groaned and cried, and I thought I was going to faint.

But I didn't faint; it's not something I do, I've never fainted in my life. Finally, while I still had my senses about me, I stood up shakily, washed the blood, pus and tears off my face and lay down on the bed. The hours that followed were the purest bliss. I went to sleep with the hut door wide open, and slept until Lynx woke me in the evening. Then I got up, still quite shaky, drove Bella to her byre, fed and milked her, doing everything very slowly and carefully, because I stumbled if I had to make a sudden movement. Later, after I'd drunk a bit of milk and fed Lynx, I went to sleep straightaway, sitting at the table. Since then the boil has come to a head every so often, burst and healed again. But I no longer have any pain. I don't know how long a thing like that can go on without causing me any problems. I desperately want some false teeth, but I still have twenty-six of my own teeth in my mouth, including some that should have been taken out long ago, but which were crowned for reasons of vanity. Sometimes I wake up at three o'clock in the morning, and the thought of those twenty-six teeth enfolds me in a cold despair. They're fixed in my jaw like time bombs: I don't think I'll ever be capable of pulling one of my own teeth. If pain comes, I shall have to bear it. It would be funny if, after years of never-ending troubles in the forest, I were to die from an abscess on my tooth.

I recovered very slowly from the business of the tooth. I think it was because of all the tablets I'd taken. When I went for my next roebuck I used up too much ammunition because my hands were shaking. I was hardly eating anything, but I drank a lot of milk, and I think the milk finally cured me of the poison.

On the tenth of June I went to the potato field. The green leaves were very high, and almost all the tubers had grown. But the weeds had shot up as well; and since it had rained the previous day I started hoeing straightaway. I realized I would also have to protect my field. I don't think deer eat potato leaves if they can find the finest plants round about, but there was still a possibility that some other animal would go for the delicious tubers. So I spent the next few days fencing off the field with strong branches, weaving them together with long brown vines. It wasn't particularly hard work, but it called for a certain amount of skill that I had to learn.

Once this work was done, my little field looked like a fortress in the middle of the forest. It was protected on all sides; there were just the mice I couldn't do much about. Of course I could have filled their holes with petrol, but I couldn't bring myself to waste it like that; in any case, the potatoes might have tasted of petrol. I have no idea, of course, but I can't allow myself all that many experiments, for obvious reasons.

Only half of the beans near the stable had grown. Maybe they'd been too old. But here too, if the weather stayed promising, I could hope for a little harvest. In fact it was pure chance that I'd planted the beans, on a whim more than from serious thought. It was only later that I realized how important the beans were for me, as they had to take the place of bread. Today I have a great big bean garden.

I fenced off the bean garden as well, because I could imagine that Bella, in an unsupervised moment, would not have turned her nose up at the bean leaves. If I had a little time over from my work, on rainy days, for example, I immediately lapsed into a state of worry and anxiety.

Certainly, Bella was still giving just as much milk, and had become decidedly rounder. But I didn't yet know if she was expecting a calf.

And if she did have a calf? I sat at the table for hours, my head in my hands, and thought about Bella. I knew so little about cows. What if I wasn't capable of helping the calf into the world, if Bella didn't survive the birth, if she and the calf both died, if Bella ate poisonous grass in the meadow, broke a leg or got bitten by an adder? I dimly remembered hearing gruesome stories about cattle during my summer holidays in the country. There was an illness for which you had to stick a knife into the cow's body at a particular point. I didn't know where that point was, and even if I had I would never have been able to stick a knife into Bella's body. I'd rather have shot her. There might be nails or bits of glass in the meadow as well. Luise had always been careless about that. Nails and bits of glass could tear open one of Bella's countless stomachs. I didn't even know how many stomachs a cow has; you learn things like that for your exams and then forget them again. And it wasn't only Bella, even if she was my biggest headache, who was in that kind of danger; Lynx might get stuck in an old trap, or adders might bite him. I don't know why I was so afraid of adders in those days. In the two and a half years that I've been here, I haven't even seen a single snake in the clearing. What might happen to the cat was beyond thinking about. I couldn't protect her either; she ran into the forest at night and escaped me entirely. The owl could catch her, or the fox, and she was more likely to get caught in a trap than Lynx was.

However hard I tried to get away from these ideas I never really succeeded. I don't think they were fantasies either, since it was far less likely that I could help the animals to survive in the middle of the forest than that they would die. I've suffered from anxieties like these as far back as I can remember, and I will suffer from them as long as any creature is entrusted to me. Sometimes, long before the wall existed, I wished I was dead, so that I could finally cast off my burden. I always kept quiet about this heavy load; a man wouldn't have understood, and the women felt exactly the same way as I did. And so we preferred to chat about clothes, friends and the theater and laugh, keeping our secret, consuming worry in our eyes. Each of us knew about it, and that's why we never discussed it. That was the price we paid for our ability to love.

Later I told Lynx about it, for no particular reason, just so that I wouldn't forget how to talk. For every ill he knew only a single cure, a nice little race in the forest. The cat listens to me attentively, but only as long as I don't get at all excited. She mistrusts even the merest hint of hysteria, and simply wanders off if I let myself go. Bella responds to everything I have to say by simply licking my face; that's a comfort, certainly, but it's no solution. In fact there is no solution, even my cow knows that, but I keep on arming myself against suffering.

At the end of June the cat changed in a very suspicious way. She grew fat and ill-tempered. Sometimes she crouched for hours in an ugly and brooding posture on a single spot, and seemed to be listening to something within her. If Lynx went near her he got a good clout around the ear, and with me she was either exaggeratedly unfriendly or more tender than before. Since she wasn't ill and was eating, her condition seemed to me quite unambiguous. While I'd only ever thought about the calf, tiny kittens had been growing in the cat. I gave her a lot of milk, and she was thirstier than before.

On the twenty-seventh of June, a stormy day, I heard a faint whimpering from the cupboard. I'd left the cupboard open when I went to the stable, and there were a few of Luise's old magazines in it. It was on these that the cat had chosen to go into labor, on the front page of *Elegant Lady*.

The cat was purring loudly, looking up at me, proud and happy, with big, moist eyes. I was even allowed to stroke her and look at her young. One of them had gray tiger stripes like its mother, and one was snow-white and tousled. The gray one was dead. I took it away and buried it beside the stable. The cat didn't seem to miss it, and devoted herself entirely to caring for the white tousled thing.

When Lynx poked his head inquisitively into the cupboard he was furiously hissed at, and fled outside, scared and indignant. The cat stayed in the cupboard, and refused to be moved to any alternative accommodation. So I left the door open and tied it with a piece of string so that it wouldn't open wide, and the kitten lay protected in the semidarkness.

The cat turned out to be a passionate mother, and only went out for a short time at night. She didn't have to go hunting now, since I fed her enough meat and milk.

On the tenth day the cat introduced us to her offspring. She carried it into the middle of the room by the scruff of its neck, and put it on the floor. It looked very pretty already, white and pink; but it was still more tousled than any other cat I had ever looked after. Whimpering, it escaped back to the warmth of its mother, and the introduction was over. The cat was very proud, and any time she brought the little cat out of the cupboard after that I had to stroke and praise her immediately. She was, like all mothers, filled with awareness of having created something unique. And that was how it was, because not even two young cats are as alike as peas in a pod: not outwardly, and certainly not in their independent little souls.

Soon the little cat was crawling out of the cupboard by itself, and running under our feet, first mine, then Lynx's.

It showed not the slightest sign of fear, and Lynx watched it and sniffed it interestedly as soon as the cat had left the vicinity. But the cat was almost always around, and observed the incipient relationship through suspicious eyes.

I called the little cat Pearl, because she was so white and pink. You could even see the blood shimmering through the skin of her little ears. Later great tufts of hair grew on them, but when she was still quite small you could see the skin gleaming through the fluffy fur in many places. At that time I still didn't know that she was a female, but something in her gentle, rather flat face looked somehow feminine to me. Pearl was very attracted by Lynx, and began lying with him in the stove door playing with his long ears. But at night she slept in the cupboard with her mother.

In a few weeks I realized that Pearl, a scruffy little thing, was on the point of turning into a beauty. She grew quite long, silky hair and was, judging by her appearance, an angora cat. Only judging by her appearance, of course; some longhaired ancestor had been reincarnated in her. Pearl was a little miracle, but even then I knew that she'd been born in the wrong place. A longhaired white cat, in the middle of the forest, is condemned to an early death. She hadn't a chance. A new burden of worries had been laid on my shoulders. I shuddered to think of the day when she would go outside. That didn't take long, and she played in front of the hut with her mother or with Lynx. The old cat was very concerned for Pearl, perhaps feeling what I knew, that her child was in danger. I ordered Lynx to keep an eye on Pearl, and when we were at home he didn't let her out of his sight. The old cat, finally worn out by the strenuous duties of motherhood, was happy that Lynx assumed the role of Pearl's protector. The little one's nature was rather different from other house cats; more peaceful, gentle and tender. She would often sit for ages on the bench in front of the house watching a butterfly. Her blue eyes had turned green after a few weeks, and glowed like jewels in her white face. Her nose was blunter than her mother's, her neck embellished with a magnificent ruff. I was always put at my ease when I saw her sitting on the bench, her front paws on her bushy tail, staring alertly into the light. Then I would reassure myself that she would turn into a house cat though the most she would ever do, as now, was to sit under the veranda leading a contemplative life.

If I think back to the first summer, it is shadowed more by the concern for my animals than by my own desperate situation. The catastrophe had relieved me of a great deal of responsibility yet, although I failed to notice it straightaway, placed a new burden upon me. When I was finally able to assess the situation a little, I had long ceased to be able to change anything about it.

I don't think my behavior was due to any weakness or sentimentality—I was simply following an instinct that had been implanted in me and which I could do nothing to fight against if I didn't want to destroy myself. Our freedom is in a sorry state. In all probability it's only ever existed on paper. External freedom has probably never existed, but neither have I ever known anyone who knew inner freedom. And I have never found this fact shaming. I can't see what should be dishonorable about bearing, as all animals do, this burden that is laid upon us; in the end, we die as all animals do. I don't even know what honor is. It isn't honorable to be born and to die, it happens to all creatures and has no meaning beyond that. Even the wall's inventors didn't obey a free decision of the will, but simply followed their instinctive curiosity. They should only have been prevented, in the interest of the greater order, from making their invention a reality.

But I would rather turn to the second of July, the day I

realized my life depended on the number of matches I had left. That thought struck me, as all disagreeable thoughts do, in the early hours of the morning.

Until then I had lived very recklessly in that respect, without considering that every burned-out match could cost me a day of my life. I jumped out of bed and fetched my supplies from the storage space. Hugo, who was a heavy smoker, had thought of matches, and had even bought a box of flints for his lighter. Unfortunately I could never get that table lighter to work. But I still had ten boxes of matches, about four thousand altogether. According to my calculations I could last five years with these. Today I know I calculated more or less correctly; my supplies will last another two and a half years, if I'm very economical. Back then I heaved a sigh of relief. Five years seemed an impossibly long time. I didn't think I would use up all the matches. Now the day of the last match seems palpably close. But even today I still tell myself it will never come to that.

Two and a half years will pass, then my fire will go out, and all the wood that surrounds me will not be able to save me from starving or freezing. And yet I still nurture an insane hope. I can only smile upon it indulgently. With the same stubborn independence, as a child I had hoped that I should never have to die. I see this hope like a blind mole, crouched within me, brooding over his delusion. As I can't drive him from me, I have to endure him.

One day the final blow will fall upon both of us, and then even my blind mole will know, before we both die. I'm almost sorry, I would have granted him a little success for his persistence. On the other hand he is insane, and I shall be happy if I can keep him under control.

There is, incidentally, another crucial question, the question of ammunition. I can last another year with what I have. With Lynx's death, a lot less meat is needed. In the summer I'll catch trout now and again, and also hope for a good potato and bean harvest. If necessary I could even live on potatoes, beans and milk. But there will only be milk if Bella has another calf. In any case, I'm much less afraid of hunger than I am of cold and darkness. There's no point in brooding so much about the future, I just have to make sure that I remain healthy and adaptable. Actually I haven't been very worried for the last few weeks. I don't know if that's a good or a bad sign. Maybe everything would be different if I knew that Bella was expecting a calf. Sometimes I think, too, that it would be better if she didn't have one. It would only put off the inevitable end, and load me with a new burden. But it would be nice if there was something new, something young here again. Above all it would be good for poor Bella, who now stands waiting so forlornly in her dark byre.

In fact I enjoy living in the forest now, and I'll find it very difficult to leave it. But I shall come back, if I stay alive over on the other side of the wall. Sometimes I imagine how nice it would have been to bring up my children here in the forest. I think that would have been paradise for me. But I doubt whether my children would have liked it that much. No, it wouldn't have been paradise. I don't believe that paradise has ever existed. A paradise could exist only outside nature, and I can't imagine that kind of paradise. It bores me even to think about it: I have no desire for it.

On the twentieth of July I started to harvest the hay. The weather was summery and warm and the grass in the meadow by the stream was tall and lush. I carried my scythe, rake and fork to the barn, and from then on I left the tools there, since there was nobody who could have taken them.

When I was standing by the stream like this, looking up at the mountain pasture, I had the feeling that I would never be able to get my task completed. I learned to scythe as a young girl, and then it had been enjoyable, after sitting for ages in stuffy classrooms. But that was more than twenty years before, and I was sure I had forgotten how to do it long since. I knew that you can only scythe in the early morning, or in the evening, when there is dew on the ground, and so I'd set off from the hut at four o'clock. As soon as I'd cut the first few swathes I realized that the rhythm hadn't left me, and relaxed my cramped muscles. The work went very slowly, of course, and was excessively exhausting. On the second day I managed much better, and on the third day it rained, and I had to take a break. It rained for four days, and the hay was rotting in the meadow; not all of it, only the part that lay in the shade. Back then I didn't know the various signs from which I can now predict the weather to a certain degree. I never knew whether it was going to be fine, or whether it would rain the next day. All through the hay harvest I had to fight against changeable weather. Later I always managed to recognize the most promising time to work, but that first summer I was entirely at the mercy of the weather.

It took me three weeks to harvest the meadow. This wasn't only the fault of the changeable weather, but also of my clumsiness and physical weakness. When the hay was finally dry in the barn in August, I was so exhausted that I sat down in the meadow and wept. I was overcome by a wave of despair, and for the first time I understood quite clearly the hard blow that had hit me. I don't know what would have happened if responsibility for my animals hadn't forced me at least to do the most necessary things. I don't like remembering that time. It lasted for fourteen days, before I was finally able to pull myself together and start living again. Lynx had suffered deeply from my bad moods. He was entirely dependent on me. He kept trying to cheer me up, and if I didn't respond he grew completely helpless and crept away under the table. I think I was so sorry for him in the end that I started feigning a good mood until I finally slipped back into a peaceful equanimity.

I'm not moody by nature. I think it was simply the physical exhaustion that left me with so little resistance back then.

In fact I had every reason to be pleased. The heavy work of the hay harvest was behind me. What did it matter that it had cost me too much strength? To make a new start I hoed the potato field and then set about cutting wood for the coming winter. I went about this work quite sensibly. It was probably simply my weakness that forced me to do so. A big pile of timber, exactly seven cubic yards, stood just above the hut at the side of the road. It was the winter supply of a certain Herr Gassner, as blue chalk markings attested. Herr Gassner, whoever he might have been, had no more need of firewood.

I placed the timber on a sawhorse from the garage, and immediately discovered that I had a lot of difficulty with the saw. It kept sticking in the wood, and I had to slave away to get it out again. On the third day I finally got the hang of it, that is, my hands, arms and shoulders got the hang of it, and suddenly it was as if I'd spent my whole life doing nothing but sawing wood. I worked slowly, but consistently. My hands were soon covered with blisters, which suddenly came to a head and wept. Then I stopped for two days and treated them with deer fat. I enjoyed working with the wood, because I could do it close to the animals. Bella stood in the forest meadow, and sometimes looked over at me. Lynx always ran about not far away, and Pearl sat on the bench in the sun, watching the hornets through half-closed eyes. And inside the house the old cat slept on my bed. For the time being everything was fine, and I had nothing to worry about.

Sometimes I brushed Bella with Hugo's nylon brush.

She was very partial to that, and stood quite still. Lynx was brushed too, and the cats were examined for fleas with an old dust comb from the hunting lodge. Like Lynx, they always had a few fleas and were grateful for the treatment. Fortunately they were fleas that didn't seem keen on human blood, big yellowish-brown creatures that looked almost like little beetles and were very bad at jumping. Hugo hadn't anticipated them and hadn't laid in any flea powder. He probably didn't even know his own dog had fleas.

Bella was free of vermin. She was, incidentally, a very clean animal, and was always careful not to lie down in her own cowpats. Of course I kept her byre painstakingly clean as well. The dung heap slowly grew beside the byre. I intended to spread it on the potato field in the autumn. Huge nettles grew around the dung heap, an ineradicable nuisance. On the other hand I always needed young nettles to cook as spinach. They were the only vegetable I had. But I didn't want to use the nettles from the dung heap. I think that was a stupid prejudice; even today I can't rid myself of it.

The young tips of the spruce trees were now dark green and tough, and didn't taste as good as they had done in the spring. But I still chewed them. My hunger for greens was insatiable. Sometimes, in the forest, I found pleasantly sour-tasting wild sorrel. I don't know what its real name is, but I enjoyed eating it when I was a child. My diet was very monotonous, of course. I had only a few supplies left, and waited with longing for the harvest. I knew that the potatoes, like everything in the mountains, would ripen more slowly than in the open countryside. I was very stingy with the rest of my supplies, and lived chiefly on meat and milk.

I had grown very thin. I sometimes looked with amazement at my new appearance in Luise's dressing table mirror. As my hair had grown a great deal, I had cut it short with the nail scissors. Now it was quite flat, and bleached by the sun. My face was thin and tanned, and my shoulders angular, like those of a half-grown boy. My hands, always covered with blisters and calluses, had become my most important tools. I had taken off my rings ages ago. Who would decorate their tools with gold rings? It struck me as absurd, even laughable, that I had done so before. The womanliness of my forties had fallen from me, along with my curls, my little double chin and my rounded hips. At the same time I lost the awareness of being a woman. My body, more skillful than myself, had adapted itself and limited the burdens of my femininity to a minimum. I could simply forget I was a woman. Sometimes I was a child in search of strawberries, or a young man sawing wood, or, when sitting on the bench holding Pearl on my scrawny lap watching the setting sun, I was a very old, sexless creature. Today the peculiar charm that emanated from me back then has left me entirely. I am still scrawny, but muscular, and my face is crisscrossed with tiny wrinkles. I'm not ugly, but neither am I attractive, more like a tree than a person, a tough brown branch that needs its whole strength to survive.

If I think today of the woman I once was, the woman with the little double chin, who tried very hard to look younger than her age, I feel little sympathy for her. But I shouldn't like to judge her too harshly. After all, she never had the chance of consciously shaping her life. When she was young she unwittingly assumed a heavy burden by starting a family, and from then on she was always hemmed in by an intimidating amount of duties and worries. Only a giantess would have been able to free herself, and in no respect was she a giantess, never anything other than a tormented, overtaxed woman of medium intelligence, in a world, on top of everything else, that was hostile to women and which women found strange and unsettling. She knew a great deal about many things, and nothing at all about many others; all in all her mind was governed by terrible disorder, a reflection of the society in which she lived, which was just as ignorant and put-upon as herself. But I should like to grant her one thing: she always had a dim sense of discomfort, and knew that all this was far from enough.

For two and a half years I have suffered from the fact that this woman was so ill armed for real life. I still can't hammer a nail in properly to this very day, and the idea of the doorway I want to break open for Bella sends shivers down my spine. Of course nobody had anticipated that I would have to make a doorway. But I know practically nothing else either, I don't even know the names of the flowers in the meadow by the stream. I learned them in science lessons, from books and drawings, and I've forgotten them again like all the other things I couldn't get into my head. I did sums with logarithms for years, and have no idea what they're for or what they mean. I found it easy to learn foreign languages, but for want of opportunity I never learned to speak them, and I've forgotten their spelling and grammar. I don't know when Charles IV lived, and I don't know exactly where the Antilles are, or who lives there. Nevertheless I was always a good pupil. I don't know; there must have been something wrong with our educational system. People from an alien world would see in me the idiocy of my age. And I'm pretty sure that most of my acquaintances fared no better.

Never again shall I have the opportunity to make up for these losses, for even if I manage to find the many books stacked up in the lifeless houses, I will never be able to retain what I read. When I was born I had a chance, but neither my parents, my teacher nor myself was able to spot it. It's too late now. I shall die without having used the chance that I had. In my first life I was a dilettante, and here in the forest, too, I shall never be anything else.

My only teacher is as ignorant and untrained as I am, for my only teacher is myself.

Over the last few days I have realized that I still hope someone will read this report. I don't know why I wish that, it makes no difference, after all. But my heart beats faster when I imagine human eyes resting on these lines, and human hands turning the pages. But mice will eat the report long before that. There are so many mice in the forest. If I didn't have the cat, the house would have been overrun with them long ago. But one day the cat will have ceased to be, and the mice will eat my supplies and finally every last scrap of paper. They probably like eating paper with writing on just as much as blank sheets. Perhaps the lead of the pencil will disagree with them; I don't even know whether it's poisonous or not. It's a strange feeling, writing for mice. Sometimes I simply have to imagine I'm writing for people, which is a bit easier.

August brought fine, steady weather. I decided to put off the harvest a little longer the following year, and that later proved sensible. I remembered finding a patch of wild raspberries on one of my hunting expeditions. It was a good hour away from the house, but back then the prospect of something sweet would have sent me on a two-hour walk. As I'd always heard that raspberry patches were the ideal playground for adders, I left Lynx at home. He obeyed only reluctantly and slunk, downcast, back to the house. Over my shoes I pulled on some old leather leggings that had belonged to the huntsman and which, since they reached above my knees, slowed me down a lot. Of course I didn't see a single adder among the raspberries. I'm not at all afraid of them today. Either there are very few snakes here, or they avoid me. They probably find me just as dangerous as I do them.

The raspberries had just ripened, and I picked a big bucket full of them and carried it home. As I had no sugar and couldn't make preserves, I had to eat the berries straightaway. I went to the patch every other day. It was the purest joy; I was bathed in sweetness. The sun warmed the ripe berries, and a wild aroma of sun and maturing fruits enveloped and intoxicated me. I was sorry that Lynx wasn't with me. Sometimes, if I got up from a bush and had a stretch, I was struck by the knowledge that I was alone. It wasn't fear, just apprehension. In the raspberry patch, quite alone among thorny plants, bees, wasps and flies, I understood how much Lynx meant to me. Then I couldn't imagine living without him. But I never took him with me to the raspberry patch. I was still plagued by the idea of adders. I couldn't expose Lynx to such a danger just to feel comfortable myself.

Only much later, up in the pasture, did I actually see an adder. It lay sunning itself on a scree slope. From that point on I was never afraid of snakes again. The adder was very beautiful, and when I saw it lying there like that, entirely devoted to the yellow sun, I was sure it had no intention of biting me. Its thoughts were remote from me, it didn't want to do anything but lie in peace on the white stones and bathe in sunlight and warmth. I was still happy that Lynx had stayed behind that time. But I don't think he would have gone near the snake. I never saw him attack a snake or a lizard. He would sometimes dig for a mouse; but in the stony ground he rarely managed to catch one.

The raspberry harvest lasted ten days. I was lazy, sat on the bench and popped one raspberry after the other into my mouth. I was amazed that my flesh hadn't turned into the flesh of raspberries. And then, quite suddenly, I had had enough. I wasn't sick, I had just had enough of the sweetness and the smell of raspberries. I strained the last two bucketfuls of berries through a cloth, poured the juice into bottles and put the bottles into the trough at the spring, where the water stayed ice-cold even in summer. Sweet though the berries were, the juice tasted sour and refreshing, and I was sorry that it wouldn't keep for an unlimited time. I never tried it, but without sugar the juice would probably have started fermenting even in the spring. As I had no tight stoppers I couldn't steam it, either. At first my hunger for sweet things was assuaged for a bit, and over the course of the next few months it remained within bearable limits. Today I no longer suffer from it. You can live very well without sugar, and over time the body loses its addictive desire for it.

When I was in the raspberry patch for the last time the sun was particularly hot on my back. The sky was still clear, but also leaden, and the air lay hot and dense like a thick paste over the bushes. It hadn't rained for a fortnight, and I had to expect a storm. I had been spared violent storms until then, but I was a little afraid of them, knowing how wild they could be in the mountains. My life was quite difficult and arduous enough without natural disasters.

At about four o'clock in the afternoon a black bank of clouds suddenly rose behind the spruce trees. My bucket wasn't quite full, but I decided to stop there. The wasps and flies had been bothering and tormenting me all day, and circled my head buzzing poisonously. There were also a few hornets in the patch, but they had always kept themselves to themselves; today they too became intrusive, and shot through the air like furious shuttles on a loom. They looked as if they were made of pure gold. Although the hornets were so beautiful, I thought it safer to leave the raspberry patch to them.

The wasps pursued me into the forest for a while, and only then did they leave my raspberries alone. The heat hung beneath the spruce trees and beeches as if trapped under a big green bell jar. The bank of clouds came menacingly closer, and the sun was veiled. I almost ran the last part of the way. All I wanted was to get home, lead Bella to the byre and then barricade myself in the house.

Lynx came whining to welcome me, and looked up at the sky, worried and concerned. He could sense the coming storm. Bella trotted along immediately, drank at the stream and then willingly allowed herself to be led to the byre. The flies and horseflies had been annoying her all day, and she seemed happy to get to her byre. I milked her, closed the shutters and turned the key in the lock; the bolt didn't strike me as secure enough in a storm.

Then I went to the hut, fed Lynx and the cats, strained the berries and poured the juice into bottles. But I didn't put the bottles into the spring just yet, lest they be broken in a storm. By now it was six o'clock or half past. The sky was completely dark, and its grayish black was showing an ugly hint of sulfurous yellow. That could mean hail or a storm; it looked worrying. Although the sun now cast only a diffuse light on the valley, the terrible bell jar of heat still hung over the clearing. It was hard to breathe. There wasn't the slightest breath of air. I drank a little cold milk and, quite without any appetite, ate a piece of rice cake. Then there was nothing more I could do. So I went upstairs and tried the shutters in the rooms. Then I fastened the window in the bedroom too. The kitchen window was still open, as was the door, but there wasn't the slightest draft.

The old cat had gone into the forest after being fed. Pearl was sitting on the windowsill staring into the black and yellow sky. She had drawn back her ears and hunched her shoulder blades, and her whole posture expressed discomfort and fear. Lynx lay in the doorway with his tongue hanging out, panting loudly. I stroked Pearl, and her white fur crackled and sparkled under my hand. My hair crackled too, if I ran my hand through it, and I felt as if ants were running over my arms and legs. I decided to stay quite still, and sat down on the bench in front of the hut. I was sorry for poor Bella in her gloomy, dark prison, but she would have to put up with it; there was nothing I could do. The storm could break at any minute. But it was still quiet.

It's never entirely silent in the forest. You only imagine it's silent, but there is always a whole host of noises. A woodpecker taps in the distance, a bird calls, the wind hisses through the grass in the forest, a big branch knocks against a tree trunk, and the twigs rustle as little animals scurry around. Everything is alive, everything is working. But that evening it really was almost silent. The silencing of the many familiar noises frightened me. Even the splashing of the stream sounded restrained and muted, as if the water too was only moving lethargically and unwillingly. Lynx stood up, jumped miserably up on the bench beside me and nudged me gently, intimidated by the terrible silence.

I couldn't understand what was stopping the storm from finally breaking. It was as dark as it is late in the evening, and it occurred to me how harmless and almost cozy the storms in the city had been. It had been so comforting to watch them through thick panes of glass. Usually I had barely noticed them.

Then, with no transition, it grew as black as night. I stood up and went into the house with Lynx. I was somewhat at a loss, and didn't know what to do. So I lit a candle. I didn't want to light the lamp, probably because of the old superstition that light attracts lightning. I locked the door, but left the window open and then sat down at the table. The candle was burning vertically and quietly, not stirred by a breath of air. Lynx went to the stove door, stopped hesitantly, turned around and jumped back up beside me onto the bench. He didn't want to leave me alone with this danger, although everything encouraged him to creep into the stove door, into the security of that cave. I too would have liked to creep into a secure cave more than anything else, but I didn't have one. I felt the sweat running over my face and collecting in the corners of my mouth. My shirt stuck to my skin. Then the first clap of thunder broke the silence. Pearl jumped terrified off the windowsill and fled for the stove door. I closed the window and the shutters, and it grew suffocatingly close. Then a thundering arose among the clouds. Through the slats of the shutters I saw the lightning jerk down, gleaming yellow. The old cat emerged again from the darkness, stopped in the middle of the room, her fur soaking, uttered a plaintive cry and crept under my bed. From there I saw her eyes gleaming yellowish-red in the weak candlelight. I tried to calm the animals, but the next clap of thunder drowned my voice. The drawn-out deep rumbling above us lasted ten minutes, perhaps, but it seemed endless to me. My ears hurt, right inside my head, and even my teeth started to ache. I have always been very bad at putting up with noise, and it felt like a physical pain.

Then, suddenly, it was quite silent for a minute, and that silence was more oppressive than the noise had been. It was as if a giant was standing above us, his legs spread, swinging a fiery hammer to bring it crashing down on our toy house. Lynx whimpered and pressed against me. It was almost a release when the next flash of lightning came and the thunder shook the house. What followed was a violent storm, but the worst was behind us. Even Lynx seemed to feel that, since he jumped off the bench and crawled to Pearl in the stove door. White fur cuddled next to reddish-brown fur, and I stayed alone at the table.

Now the storm had lifted, and swept away hissing over the house. The candle began to flicker, and it immediately seemed to me to get less sultry. The sight of the flickering candle made me think of cool, fresh air. I now began counting the seconds between the lightning and the thunder. By this calculation the storm was still over the valley. The huntsman had once told me about a storm that had been caught in the valley for three whole days. At the time I didn't really believe him, but now I thought differently. The only thing I could do was wait. I had spent the whole day bending over in the raspberry patch, and fatigue was overtaking me. I didn't dare lie down on the bed, but I felt myself growing so tired that the candle flames turned into a watery, wavering ring. It still wasn't raining. That should have worried me, but to my astonishment I started becoming quite apathetic. My thoughts grew sleepily confused. I was very sorry for myself because I was so tired yet was denied sleep; I was very angry and bitter with somebody, but when I started awake I forgot who I'd been arguing with. Poor Bella passed through my mind, and the potato field, and then it occurred to me that the windows in my apartment in the city would be open. I found it hard to convince myself of the absurdity of this thought. I said out loud, "Forget the bloody windows," and woke up.

A crash of thunder rattled the pots on the stove. The lightning must have struck quite close by. I thought about the nights of bombing raids spent in the cellar, and old fears set my teeth chattering. The air too was as thick and bad as it had been back in the cellar. I was about to tear the door open when the wind roared furiously around the house and the shingles on the roof started clattering. I didn't dare lie down, and no longer dared sit at the table, because I didn't want to slip back into that unpleasant half sleep. So I started walking back and forth in the room, my hands folded against my back, staggering with fatigue. Lynx poked his head out of the stove door and looked at me anxiously. I managed to say something comforting to him and he pulled himself back in again. The storm now seemed to have been going on for hours; and it was only half past nine. Finally the gaps between lightning and thunder lengthened, and I breathed more freely. But it still wasn't raining, and the crashing of the wind wasn't letting up. And then I suddenly heard, as if from a long way off, the ringing of bells. It was quite inexplicable, but in the howling of the wind I could clearly hear the bright note of a distant bell. If it wasn't in my head, it had to be coming from the bells in the village. Since there were no people left, the storm must have been ringing the bell. It was a ghostly sound, something that I couldn't be hearing; yet hearing it I was. I have experienced several more storms in the forest, but I've never heard the bell again. Perhaps the storm broke the rope, or the ringing was an illusion in my ears, tormented by noise. Finally the wind died down, and with it died the phantom tinkling. Then there was a sound as of someone tearing a huge piece of material, and water fell from the sky.

I went to the door and opened it wide. The rain whipped into my face and washed the fear and sleepiness from me. I could breathe again. The air tasted fresh and cool and tickled my lungs. Lynx emerged from his cave and sniffed curiously outside. Then he gave a cheerful bark, shook his long ears and walked back with a measured tread to his white friend who, rolled in a ball, had gone peacefully to sleep. I put on a coat and ran with my torch through the wet blackness to the byre. Bella had broken free, and was standing with her forehead against the door. She bellowed pitifully and pressed herself against me. I stroked her flanks, which were rising and falling with fear, and she gladly allowed me to turn her around and tie her to the bedstead again. Then I opened the window. The rain could hardly get in here, as the spruce trees protected the rear slope of the roof. After the terror of that night Bella had earned some air and coolness. Then I went back into the house and at last, at last, I found that I too was allowed to lie down in peace. The cat crept out from under the bed and came to me, and in a few minutes I was fast asleep. I dreamed of a storm and was woken by a thunderclap. It wasn't a dream. The old tempest had returned, or else a new one had reached the valley. It was raining heavily, and I got up to close the window and wipe a pool of water from the floor. It was refreshingly cool in the room. I lay down again and slept again at once. I kept being woken by thunderclaps, and then going back to sleep. There was a constant alternation of real and dream storms; but around morning I'd reached the point where no storm bothered me. I drew the blanket over my head and fell at last into a deep and undisturbed sleep.

I was awoken by a dull crashing, a noise that I had never heard before, and I was immediately wide awake. It was eight o'clock in the morning, and I had slept in. First of all I let the impatient Lynx out and had a look to see what could be crashing, scraping and dragging so loudly. There was nothing to be seen in front of the hut. The storm had ruffled the bushes and bent a few branches, and there were big puddles on the path to the byre. I got dressed, took the milking pail and went to Bella. Everything in the byre was fine. The crashing was coming from the stream. I went a little way down the slope and saw a yellow flood surging along, tearing with it uprooted trees, patches of grass and blocks of stone. I immediately thought of the gorge. The water must have come up against the wall and flooded the meadow by the stream. I decided to go and have a look as soon as possible. But first, as I did every day, I would have to do the work that needed to be done. I let Bella out of the stable. It was cool, the rain was quite light, and the flies and horseflies would leave her in peace. A big oak tree had stood in the meadow by the forest. It had been lightning-scarred from an earlier storm. Finally, however, the lightning had claimed its victim. This time it wasn't just a single mark, the old oak was completely shattered. It was a shame. Oak trees were quite rare hereabouts. When I returned to the house I could hear a distant rumbling. The storm seemed still to be hanging in the mountains. Perhaps it was wandering from valley to valley, round and round, just as the huntsman had described.

After lunch I went to the gorge with Lynx. The path there couldn't be flooded, as it was too high up, but the water had surged over to the other side, tearing trees, bushes, stones and sods of earth with it. My friendly green stream had turned into a yellowish-brown monster. I hardly dared to look. One false step on the slippery stone, and all my worries would have come to an end in the icy water. As I had anticipated, the water couldn't flow away quickly enough once it reached the wall. A small lake had formed; the grasses of the meadow by the stream floated slowly back and forth at the bottom. Along the wall lay a mountain of trees, bushes and stones, piled up in a pyramid. So the wall wasn't just invisible, it was also unbreakable, for the force with which the tree trunks and stones had hit it must have been unimaginable. The lake wasn't as big as I'd feared, though, and would certainly drain away completely within a few days. I couldn't see what things looked like beyond the washed-up piles; probably the yellow floods were streaming happily onward on the other side. The rivers would swell, tearing houses and bridges with them, pushing in windows and doors, and drag the lifeless stone things that had once been people from their beds and chairs. And they would be left on the big sandbanks to dry out in the sun, stone people, stone animals, and between them gravel and bits of rubble that had never been anything but stone.

I could picture all this very clearly before my eyes, and

it made me feel slightly unwell. Lynx prodded me with his muzzle and pushed me sideways. Maybe he didn't like the flood, maybe he also felt that I was miles away and wanted to attract some attention. As always on such occasions I followed him in the end. He knew much better than I did what was good for me. All the way back he walked at my side, pushing me against the wall of the cliff with his flank, away from the crashing, scraping monster that could have swallowed me up. His concern finally made me laugh, and he jumped up with his wet paws on my chest, barking encouragingly, loud and happy. Lynx should have had a strong and cheerful master. I couldn't always cope with his joie de vivre, and had to force myself to look happy, so as not to disappoint him. But if I couldn't give him a very merry life, he must at least have sensed how fond I was of him, and how intensely I needed him. Lynx was extremely friendly, he needed a lot of love and was very fond of people. The huntsman must have been a good man; I never discovered a hint of bad temper or slyness in Lynx.

When we arrived at the hunting lodge we were both soaked to the skin. I lit a fire and hung my clothes up to dry on the rack over the stove. I stuffed my shoes with the driving manual rolled up in little balls, and set them to dry on two wooden planks.

Meanwhile the grumbling in the clouds continued, coming sometimes from the right, sometimes from the left. It sounded angry and a little disappointed, and went on all day. All in all I had suffered little damage from the storm. Some of my trout would surely have perished, and that was the worst loss that the storm had caused me. But in time they too would recover and multiply. A few shingles hung loose on the roof, and I would have to repair that damage as soon as possible. I was a little afraid of that, for I suffer from vertigo to some extent, but vertigo or not, I simply had to get up on the roof and mend it.

In the open space in front of the hut I had stacked a pile of timber that I was going to chop into little pieces. The raspberry harvest and my sweet tooth had interrupted that important work. Now the wood was soaking wet, and I would have to wait until it could dry in the sun. The rain had swept the sawdust into the path in little streams, three narrow, orangey strips that slowly disappeared into the gravel. The path through the gorge was also washed away, but not as badly as I had feared. When it was possible, I would have to sort it out. There was so much that I had to do, chopping wood, harvesting potatoes, digging fields, fetching hay from the gorge, mending the path and repairing the roof. Hardly had I begun to hope that I would be able to relax than I was faced with a new task.

It was already mid-August; the short mountain summer would soon be over. It rained for another two days, and the storm was still grumbling very quietly in the distance. On the third day white mist hung down as far as the meadow. Not a single mountain could be seen, and the spruces looked as if they'd been cut down. I drove Bella back to the meadow, as the cool and damp weather seemed to do her good. I cleaned the hunting lodge, did my sewing for a while and waited for better weather. On the fifth day after the storm the sun suddenly burst through the white veils of mist. I know this precisely, because I noted it in my diary. Back then I was still fairly communicative, and often jotted things down. Later I was more sparing with my notes, and shall have to rely on my memory.

After the big storm it stopped being so warm. The sun was shining, and my wood was able to dry out, but the landscape suddenly assumed an autumnal character. The long-stemmed gentians blossomed on the wet sides of the gorge, and cyclamen grew in the shade of the bushes. Sometimes the cyclamen blossom as early as July in the mountains, and that is said to presage an early winter. In cyclamen flowers the red of summer combines with the blue of autumn into a pinkish purple, and their fragrance recaptures all the sweetness of the past; but as you inhale it for longer, there is a quite different smell behind it: that of decay and death. I have always considered the cyclamen a strange and rather frightening flower.

As the sun was shining again, I set about cutting timber. It was easier for me to chop than to saw, and I made quick progress. But this time I didn't wait until the ground was covered with a mountain of logs, but every evening I cleared the chopped wood under the veranda, and stacked it up neatly there. I didn't want the rain to take me by surprise this time.

Quite gradually I managed to introduce a system into all my tasks, and that made my life a little easier. Disorganization had never been one of my faults, yet I had rarely found myself in a position to carry out one of my plans, because as sure as fate somebody or something had always turned up to ruin them. If I failed now, it would be my own fault, and I could hold only myself responsible for it.

By cutting timber, in fact, I missed a very fine Indian summer. I didn't see the landscape at all, obsessed as I was by the thought of stacking up a big enough supply of wood. Once the last log had been stored under the veranda I had a stretch and decided to treat myself a little. It's strange, in fact, how slight my pleasure is every time I complete a task. Once it's out of the way I forget it, and think about new things to do. Even at that time I didn't allow myself much time to recover. That's how it always was: while I was slaving away I dreamed about how I would rest quietly and peacefully on the bench, but as soon as I finally sat down on the bench I grew restless, and started looking out for new work to do. I don't think this was due to any particular industriousness, since by nature I'm rather lethargic, but was probably through self-protection, for what would I have done otherwise but remember and brood? That was exactly what I mustn't do, so what was there to do but more work? I didn't even have to look for work, it turned up insistently enough of its own accord.

After I'd pottered around in the house for two days, doing my washing and sewing, I set about fixing up the path. Armed with picks and shovel I went into the gorge. There wasn't much that I could do without a wheelbarrow. So I opened up the path with the picks, spread the gravel evenly and tamped it firmly down with the shovel. The next cloudburst would wash out new gullies, and I would fill them up again and beat them down. I could really have done with a wheelbarrow. But Hugo had never thought about wheelbarrows. He had never anticipated having to improve paths with his own hands either. I think he'd have been happiest buying a bunker, and he didn't dare to do that only because it struck him as an unsociable thing to do and he set great store by not seeming to be that way. So he had to settle for half measures which were something of a game, designed to assuage his fears a bit. He was well aware of that, of course, because he was a thoroughly realistic man who sometimes had quite consciously to give his dark fears something to feed on, so that he could work and live his life in peace. Wheelbarrows, as I said, didn't seem ever to have had a place in his dreams of survival. That's why the path is in such bad condition today. All I ever do is distribute the loose stones as best I can, but as time passes they get washed away, and the bare rock shows through. I would be able to mend the path well with gravel from the stream; it's just a question of transport. I suppose I could fill a sack with gravel, and drag it to the path on beech branches. Perhaps fifteen sacks would do it; it's hard to say exactly. Perhaps I'd have taken it on a year ago. Today I don't think it's worth it. Even dragging the hay home in the dry bed of a stream is less hard work than pulling fifteen sacks of gravel up to the path.

On the sixth of September I had a look at the potatoes and found that the tubers were still too small and the plants were still green. So I had to suppress my hunger for a few more weeks; but the sight of the little tubers gave me new hope. The fact that I hadn't wasted the potatoes, but planted them, was the basis of my relative security today. As long as no meteorological disaster destroyed my harvest I would never have to starve.

The beans too were almost ripe, and although not all of them had grown they had multiplied. I intended to plant most of them back as seeds. My work was beginning to bear fruit, and it was high time too, because after mending the paths I felt very downcast. As it rained for a few days, I got up only for the tasks that had to be done, and stayed in bed the rest of the time. I slept in the daytime too, and the more I slept the more tired I grew. I don't know what was wrong with me back then. Maybe I was lacking important vitamins, or it was simply overwork that had weakened me. Lynx didn't like it at all. He kept coming to me and prodding me with his muzzle, and when that got him no-where he jumped up with his front paws on the bed, and barked so loudly that sleep was unthinkable. That time I hated him for a moment as one hates a slave driver. Cursing, I got dressed, took my gun and set off with him. It was high time in any case. We didn't have a scrap of meat in the house, and I had given Lynx the last precious noodles. I managed to shoot a weak roebuck, and Lynx was pleased with me again. I feigned a little enthusiasm, put the buck over my neck and went home. Back then, after giving it a great deal of thought, I shot only weak bucks. I was afraid that the deer, only a little depleted in my hunting ground so far, would increase, and in a few years find themselves caught in the trap of a forest stripped of vegetation. To anticipate that future predicament somewhat, I shot only bucks where possible. I don't think I was wrong back then. Now, after only two and a half years, I see more deer than I did before. If I ever leave here I shall dig the hole under the wall so deep that this forest can never become a trap. My roe deer and red deer will find either an immense, fertile meadow or sudden death. Either would be better than imprisonment in a forest stripped bare of vegetation. Their plight is vengeance for the fact that all beasts of prey have been extinct here for years, and the deer no longer have any natural enemy apart from man. Sometimes, when I close my eyes, I can picture that mass exodus from the forest. But it's just a dream. Evidently people never stop daydreaming.

I jointed the roebuck, a task that caused me a great deal of effort at first, and put the salted meat in buckets which I fastened shut with big lids. Then I carried the buckets to a well and plunged them to the brim in the icy water. This isn't my spring; there are a lot of wells here. It comes out under a beech tree and collects into a little pool in a hollow between the roots, then flows on for a few yards and disappears into the ground again. One of Hugo's hunting guests, a little man with glasses, once claimed that the whole mountain range, even the valley, stood over enormous caves. I don't know whether it's true or not, but I've often seen springs or little streams disappearing into the earth without a trace. The little man was probably right.

The thought of those caves sometimes haunts me for days. All the water gathering down there, absolutely clear, filtered by earth and chalk. Maybe there are animals in the caves as well. Salamanders and blind white fish. I can see them swimming around endlessly under the huge domes of the stalactites. The only sound is the lapping and hissing of the water. Could there be anywhere lonelier? I will never see the salamanders and fishes. They may not even exist. I'd just like there to be a little life in the caves as well. There's something about caves that's at once very attractive and disturbing. When I was still young and still took death as a personal insult, I often imagined withdrawing to a cave to die, never to be found. This idea still holds a certain charm for me; it's like a game you've played as a child, which you still like to think about from time to time. I have no need to withdraw into a cave before I die. Nobody will be with me when I die. Nobody will touch me, stare at me or press their hot and living fingers on my cooling lids. They won't hiss and whisper by my deathbed and force the last bitter drops between my teeth. For a while I thought that Lynx would keen for my death. That's not to be, and it's better that way. Lynx is safe: for me there will be neither human voices nor the howling of animals. Nothing will pull me back into the old torment. I'm still glad to be alive, but one day I'll have lived enough, and I'll be happy that it's over.

But of course everything could happen quite differently. I'm far from safe. They could come back any day and get me. They will be strangers, who will find a stranger. We won't have anything more to say to each other. It would be better for me if they never came. Back then, in the first year, I didn't yet feel that way. Everything has changed almost imperceptibly. That's why I no longer dare to plan too far ahead, because I don't know how I shall be feeling and thinking in two years' time, or in five, or ten. I can't even imagine it. I don't like living day by day, without a plan. I've become a tiller of the soil, and a tiller of the soil has to plan ahead. I was probably never anything but a frustrated tiller of the soil. Maybe my grandchildren would have turned into frivolous butterflies. My children rejected all responsibility. I've stopped giving life and death. Even the solitude that has kept us company for so many generations dies with me. That is not good and it is not bad; it simply is.

And how do I spend my days this winter?

I wake up in the half-light and get up straightaway. If I stayed in bed I would start thinking. I'm afraid of thoughts in the morning gloom. So I go to work. Bella greets me happily. She's had so little pleasure lately. I wonder how she bears it. Being alone day and all night in her dark byre. I know so little about her. Maybe she dreams sometimes, fleeting memories, sun on her back, lush grass between her teeth, a calf pressing against her, warm and fragrant, tenderness, an endless, mute conversation from winter days past. Nearby the calf rustles in the straw, familiar breath rising from familiar nostrils. Memories rise from her heavy body, and sink down in her sluggish bloodstream. I know nothing of how she feels. Every morning I stroke her big head, speak to her and see her huge, moist eyes gazing at my face. If they were human eyes I'd think they were a little mad.

The lamp stands on the little oven. By its yellow light I wash Bella's udder with warm water, and then start milking. She's giving a little milk again. Not much, but enough for me and the cat. And I talk and talk, I promise her a new calf, a long, warm summer, fresh green grass, warm showers of rain that will chase the mosquitoes away; again and again, I promise her a calf. And she looks at me with her gentle, crazy eyes, presses her broad forehead against me and lets me scratch the roots of her horns. I'm warm and alive, and she senses that I mean her well. We will never know anything more about each other. After the milking I clean the byre, and the cold winter air streams in. I never air it longer than necessary. The byre is cool in any case; the breath and warmth of a cow only make it slightly milder. I throw Bella the rustling, fragrant hay, and fill the bowl with water, and once a week I go over her short, smooth coat with the brush. Then I take the lamp back, and leave her alone in the dim-lit byre for a long, lonely day. I don't know what happens when I leave. Does Bella gaze after me for a long time, or does she sink into a peaceful half sleep until evening? If I only knew how to make the door into the bedroom. I think about this every day when I have to leave her on her own. I've told her about it, too, and halfway through my story she licked my face. Poor Bella.

Then I carry the milk into the house, rake the fire and prepare breakfast. The cat gets up from my bed, walks over to her saucer and drinks. Then she retires to her stove door again, and washes her winter coat. Since Lynx died, she's slept all day in his old place under the warm oven. I haven't the heart to drive her away. In any case it's better than having to see the sad, empty cave. In the morning we barely talk to one another; then she's bad-tempered and sullen. I sweep the room and carry wood into the house for the day. It's got bright in the meantime, as bright as it ever gets on an overcast winter morning. The crows fall shrieking into the clearing and settle on the spruce trees. Then I know that it's half past eight. If I have rubbish, I carry it to the clearing and leave it under the spruces. If I have to work outside, chopping wood, shoveling snow or fetching hay, I wear Hugo's lederhosen. It took a lot of effort to make them narrower around the waist. They reach down to my ankles, and keep me warm even on very cold days. After having lunch and clearing up I sit down at the table and write my report. I could also go to sleep, I suppose, but I don't want to. I need to be so tired in the evening that I can go to sleep on the spot. I can't let the lamp burn too long, either. In the coming winter I'll have to make do with candles made of deer fat. I've tried it before and they smell frightful, but I'll have to get used to that as well.

At around four o'clock, when I light the lamp, the cat comes out from under the stove, and jumps up on the kitchen table to where I'm sitting. She patiently watches me writing for a while. She loves the yellow lamplight just as much as I do. We hear the crows rising out of the clearing with their raw shrieks, and the cat gets nervous and puts her ears back. When she's calmed down again, our time has come. The cat gently knocks the pencil from my hand and spreads herself out on the covered pages. Then I stroke her and tell her old stories or sing for her. I'm not a good singer, and only do it quietly, intimidated by the silence of the winter afternoon. But the cat likes my singing. She loves serious, drawn-out notes, especially hymns. She doesn't like high notes, any more than I do. When she's had enough she stops purring and I fall silent immediately. The fire crackles and pops in the oven, and if it's snowing we watch the big flakes together. If it's raining, or if there's a storm, the cat tends to become melancholy, and I try to cheer her up. Sometimes I succeed, but generally we both sink into hopeless silence. And very rarely the miracle happens: the cat stands up, presses her forehead against my cheek and props her front paws on my chest. Or she takes my knuckles between her teeth and bites at them, gently and daintily. It doesn't happen terribly often, for she's sparing with proofs of her affection. Certain songs send her into raptures, and she pulls her claws over the rustling paper with delight. Her nose gets damp, and a gleaming film comes over her eyes.

All cats tend toward mysterious states; then they are far away and entirely impossible to reach. Pearl was in love with a tiny red velvet cushion that had belonged to Luise. For her it was a magic object. She licked it, scratched runnels through its soft nap and finally rested on it, white breast on red velvet, her eyes narrowed to green slits, a magnificent fairy-tale creature. Her half brother, Tiger, born after her, was enraptured by fragrances. He could sit for ages by a scented plant, his whiskers spread, his eyes closed, little drops of saliva on his little bottom lip. In the end he looked as if he was on the point of exploding into a thousand pieces. When that point had been reached, he escaped back into reality with a bold leap and, tail upright, uttering little cries, dashed into the hut. Usually, after these extravagances, he would behave in a truly loutish manner, like a half-grown boy caught reading a poem. You can never laugh at cats, they take it very badly. Sometimes it wasn't easy to take Tiger seriously. Pearl was much too beautiful to laugh at, and I wouldn't dare laugh at her mother. What do I know about her life? I once surprised her playing with a dead mouse behind the hut. She must just have killed the little creature. What I saw that time convinced me that she saw the mouse as a favorite toy. She lay down on her back, pressed the lifeless thing to her breast and tenderly licked it. Then she carefully put it down and gave it an almost loving shove, licked it again and finally turned to me with piteous little cries. I was supposed to make her toy move again. Not a trace of cruelty or malice.

I have never seen eyes more innocent than those of my cat when she had just tortured a little mouse to death. She had no idea that she had caused the little thing pain. A favorite toy had stopped moving, and the cat was lamenting the fact. I shivered in the bright sunshine, and something akin to hatred moved within me. I stroked the cat quite absently and felt the hatred growing. There was nothing and nobody that I could hate for this. I knew I would never understand, and I didn't want to understand, either. I was afraid. I'm still afraid, because I know that I can live only if I fail to understand certain things. That was, incidentally, the only time that I happened upon the cat with a mouse. She seems only to pursue her shocking and innocent games at night, and I am pleased about that.

Now she is lying in front of me on the table, and her eyes are as clear as a lake, with fine-branched plants growing on its bed. The lamp has already been burning too long, and the time is coming for me to go into the stable and spend half an hour with Bella, before I have to leave her alone for a night in the darkness. And tomorrow will be like today, and like yesterday. I shall wake up, get out of bed before my first thought has had time to impinge, and later the black cloud of crows will sink down over the clearing, and their harsh cries will enliven the day a little.

Before, I sometimes used to read old newspapers and magazines in the evening. Today I've lost all feeling for them. They bore me. The old newspapers were the only thing that has bored me here in the forest. They probably always bored me. Only I didn't know that the constant mild unease was boredom. Even my poor children suffered from the same thing, and couldn't stay alone for ten minutes. We were all thoroughly numbed by boredom. There was nothing we could do to escape it, with its uninterrupted droning and flickering. Nothing surprises me anymore. Perhaps the wall was only the last desperate experiment of a tormented person who had to break out, break out or go mad.

The wall has killed boredom too, among other things. The meadows, trees and rivers beyond the wall can't get bored. With a shudder the roaring drum was silenced. On this side all you can hear now is the rain, the wind and the creaking of the empty houses; the despised, bellowing voice is silent now. But there is nobody left to enjoy the great silence.

As September stayed cheerful and warm, and as I had recovered from my fatigue, I decided to go in search of berries again. I knew the people of the village had always fetched cranberries from the Alm. Cranberries had been a blessing for me, because you can preserve them without sugar. Their tannin content means that they don't go off. On the twelfth of September I set off with Lynx after early milking. I left Bella in the byre for safety. My sole concern was for Pearl, who had taken to going off for little trips to the stream. A few days before, she had come home with a trout in her mouth, and lain down to have dinner under the veranda. She was proud and pleased about her first success, and I had to praise and stroke her. So every day she sat on a stone in the middle of the stream, her right paw raised, waiting. Her coat gleamed in the sun from afar, and no one with eyes in their head could fail to see her. There was nothing I could do about it. My dream of a peaceful house cat was over, and in any case I had never really believed it. Neither the old cat nor, later on, Tiger, ever went to the stream. They were both terribly frightened of water. But Pearl was different. The old cat watched the irksome behavior of her daughter with disapproval, but no longer meddled in her affairs. Pearl was barely half grown, yet her mother hardly ever bothered about her now, and had returned to her old way of life. So I locked Pearl with meat and water in the upper room, where I stored bark and kindling. I was sorry for it, but there was nothing else I could do.

The climb to the Alm, and the path wasn't hard to find, took three hours. The path was in good condition, having been used when the cattle were driven up there. If the wall had come up a few days later there would have been a little herd of cattle up there, and a dairymaid. But I wasn't complaining, as everything could have been a lot worse for me.

The hut in the pasture stood in the middle of a large meadow, where the grass was already yellowing a little. While I walked across the soft meadows I thought of Bella who had been eating the hard and scrubby grass in the clearing all summer long, while the tenderest plants were growing here for her. I immediately thought of bringing her up here the following May. At the same time, however, I saw so many difficulties arising before me that I shied away in fear. The hut was in good condition, and if necessary I could live in it for a summer. I found a butter churn, two old diaries and the photograph of a film star I didn't know pinned to the cupboard with drawing pins. So, the dairymaid had been a dairyman. The hut was very dirty, there were brown rings of fat on the pots and pans, and the table looked as if it had never been washed down. I also found a greeny-black, shiny felt hat and a torn weatherproof cape. I was tired, and my desire for cranberries was weakening by the minute. I had to force myself to go on. Finally I found the place where they grew. But they were still pink; so I would have to climb back up to the pasture to fetch them. Before I set off homeward I looked for another vantage point from which to view the countryside. The meadow turned into forest, and then fell suddenly away into a scree slope. I sat down on a tree trunk there and looked into the distance through the binoculars.

It was a fine autumn day, and visibility was very good. I shuddered slightly when I started counting the red church towers. There were five in all, and a few tiny houses. The forests and meadows were not yet changing color. In between there were yellowish-brown rectangles, the still unharvested cornfields. The streets were deserted. I thought I could make out a few little objects as lorries. Nothing was moving down there, no smoke was rising and no flocks of birds descended on the fields. I gazed into the sky for a long time. It remained empty and free of any movement. I hadn't, I suppose, expected to see anything else. The binoculars slipped from my hand and fell into my lap. Now I could no longer make out the church towers.

Lynx was bored, and wanted to go on. I stood up and followed him. I left the empty pail behind in the hut, so that I wouldn't have to carry it back up again, but I took the diaries, a little sack of flour and the butter churn with me. I fastened the churn to my rucksack and it immediately started to rub and stick into me. But I couldn't do without it. It was hard enough beating tiny portions of butter with the whisk. Now that I had a churn I could even think about making clarified butter. Lynx had one of his fits and dashed off across the meadow, his long ears flying. I panted along behind him with the butter churn. I've always had an aversion to heavy loads, and I'd always had to struggle with them. First with my overfull schoolbag, then with suitcases, children, shopping bags and coal scuttles, and now, after bales of hay and logs, a butter churn. I was amazed my arms didn't reach to my knees. Perhaps then the small of my back wouldn't have hurt so much when I bent down. All I lacked now were claws, thick fur and long fangs, and I would have been a thoroughly well-adapted creature. I looked enviously at Lynx, flying light-footed over the meadow, and it struck me that I had only drunk a little water from the stream. I had entirely forgotten to eat. My supplies were under the butter churn. I was quite exhausted when I arrived at the hunting lodge, and my shoulders hurt for days. But the butter churn had been rescued.

I find no entries in my diary for a fortnight now. I barely remember that time. Were things so good or so bad that I didn't want to write? Bad, I think. The monotonous food and the great strain had left me much weaker. But it must have been at that time that I gathered twigs and bark and piled them in the upper room. I had already done that once before. I needed dry wood for kindling. The wood under the veranda was protected when the weather was steady, but when there were storms and rain it sometimes got damp and wouldn't light. The garage would have made a very good storage space for wood, but I needed it for the hay. Incidentally, damp wood has advantages too, it burns much slower and you don't have to add so much to it. In the evening, if I want the fire to stay lit throughout the night, I always put damp wood on it.

On the second of October I came back to life in the diary. The potatoes were harvested. I dragged them home in sacks and spread them out in the bedroom. I didn't dare put them in the little cellar dug into the mountain behind the hut. As an experiment I put a few potatoes in it and they froze when the first frost came. In the bedroom, with the shutters closed, it was dark and cool, and, strangely, not damp. It was now terribly cramped because I'd stored all my supplies in it. My initial capital had multiplied. In the evening, despite being tired, I cooked up a pot of potatoes and ate them with fresh butter. It was a feast, and I was truly satisfied and went to sleep at the table. Lynx too, who had woken me reproachfully after an hour, had been given potatoes, but the cats, pure carnivores, had turned up their noses at them. Lynx, incidentally, liked eating potatoes, but I didn't give them to him often, because I knew they weren't good for him.

I didn't want the field to go to seed: in the first year I could barely control the weeds, so I decided to dig it over immediately. After resting a day, during which I picked the beans, I began to dig the field. I couldn't relax until that had been done. I dried the beans in the sun and stored them as seed crop. After long calculations and reflection I set aside a portion of the potatoes as well. I always held back from touching these. It was better to go relatively hungry for a few weeks than starve in the coming year. When my harvest was brought in, I came upon the fruit trees in the very meadow where I had found Bella. I found an apple tree there, two damson trees and a crabapple tree.

The damson trees bore twenty-four fruits, little spotted things with drops of resin on them, very sweet. I ate them up on the spot and had a stomachache that night. There were about fifty fruits on the apple tree, big, hard-skinned, red-cheeked winter apples, the only kind of apple that really thrives in the mountains. Before, I'd always thought they tasted like turnips. I must have been very choosy and spoiled back then. The crabapple tree was covered from top to bottom with its tiny red apples. You are really supposed to use them only in cider mash. I eat them, with some determination, all year long, for the vitamins. The apples weren't yet ripe, so I left them where they were. It was a magnificent day, the air was already a little cool and sharp and I could see every tree and farmyard very clearly on the other side of the wall. The curtains were still drawn, and the two cows, Bella's companions, lay in their deep and stony sleep. The grass, which had never been mowed, reached up to their flanks and concealed their nostrils from me. A great flood of nettles grew around the little house. It could have been a beautiful expedition, but the sight of the two animals and the forest of nettles unsettled and depressed me.

Autumn was always my favorite season, although I never felt physically very well. In the daytime I was tired yet wide awake, and at night I lay for hours in a disturbed half sleep and my dreams were more confused and vivid than usual. My autumnal malaise didn't spare me in the forest, either, but since I could hardly allow myself to have it, it assumed a less extreme form. Perhaps I didn't have the time to notice it. Lynx was very cheerful, in very high spirits, but an outsider probably wouldn't have noticed the difference. He was, after all, cheerful almost all the time. I never saw him stay sulky for more than three minutes. He simply couldn't resist the urge to be cheerful. And life in the forest was a constant temptation to him. Sun, snow, wind, rain—everything was a cause for enthusiasm. With Lynx nearby I could never stay sad for long. It was almost shaming that being with me made him so happy. I don't think that grown animals living wild are happy or even content. Living with people must have awoken this capacity in the dog. I'd like to know why we have this narcotic effect on dogs. Perhaps man's megalomania comes from dogs. Sometimes I even imagined there must be something special about me that made Lynx almost keel over with joy at the sight of me. Of course there was never anything special about me; Lynx was, like all dogs, simply addicted to people.

At times now, when I walk alone in the wintry forest, I talk to Lynx as I did before. I have no idea I'm doing it until something startles me and I fall silent. I turn my head and catch the gleam of a reddish-brown coat. But the path is empty: bare bushes and wet stones. I'm not surprised that I still hear the dry branches cracking under the light tread of his feet. Where else would his little dog's soul go haunting, if not on my trail? He's a friendly ghost, and I'm not afraid of him. Lynx, beautiful, good dog, my dog, it's probably just my poor head making the sound of your footsteps, the gleam of your coat. As long as I exist you'll follow my trail, hungry and yearning, as I myself, hungry and yearning, follow invisible trails. Neither of us will ever bring our prey to ground.

On the tenth of October I harvested the apples and laid them out on a blanket in the bedroom. It was now so cool in the morning that frost could come any day. It was time to fetch the cranberries.

This time I didn't stop at the vantage point. I could immediately see that nothing had changed. Only the forests glowed in their magnificent new colors. It was windy, and the sun gave so little warmth that my hands grew stiff picking berries. I made some tea in the hut and gave Lynx a little meat, and then I packed the pail full of berries into the rucksack and went down the hill. I boiled jam from the berries and poured it into jars. This little supply, too, was to help me to survive the winter.

I now faced only two more tasks. The straw for Bella had to be cut, and I had to fill the garage with hay before the cold set in. I needn't have hurried, since the weather stayed fine for a long time. I cut the straw with the sickle and raked it together with the dry leaves. It took only a day to dry, and I shifted it to a little space under the roof of the byre. Anything that didn't fit there I stored in a corner of the byre. And finally I'd lugged some hay into the garage as well, and was able to rest.

Now I was actually sitting on the bench in front of the house, in the faint warmth of the midday sun, and it could do me no harm, for I was much too weary to brood.

I sat quite still, my hands hidden under my cape, and held my face up toward the lukewarm light. Lynx rummaged in the bushes and kept coming back to me to satisfy himself that I was all right. Pearl devoured a trout under the veranda, and then sat down next to me on the bench and started washing her long fur. Sometimes she stopped, blinked at me, purred loudly and then yielded once more to her instinct for cleanliness. As the weather was fine I still let Bella into the meadow, but gave her fresh hay in the evening; the grass in the meadow could no longer satisfy her, it had become hard and dry, and I'd cut most of it for straw. Bella had grown plumper, but I still couldn't tell if she was expecting a calf. My hope was strengthened by the fact that for all those months she hadn't once called for the bull. But I still wasn't sure.

Spring, summer and autumn had passed, and I had done everything I could. Perhaps it was absurd, but I was too tired to worry. All my animals were nearby, and I had looked after them as well as I could have done. The sun tingled on my face and I closed my eyes. But I didn't sleep, I was too tired to sleep. I didn't move either, for every movement hurt, and I wanted to sit still in the sun, completely free of pain, and not have to think.

I remember that day very clearly. I can see the spiders' webs stretched glistening between the trees, behind the stable under the spruce trees, in the trembling green-and-gold air. The landscape assumed quite a new depth and clarity, and I wished I could sit there all day, looking.

In the evening, when I went from the byre to the house, the sky had grown overcast, and it seemed to me that it had got warmer. At night, despite being tired, I slept very badly, but it didn't bother me. I lay there quite happily, stretched out, and waited. Once the thought occurred to me that it was a great waste of time to sleep at all. Toward morning the cat came home, snuggled into the backs of my knees and started purring. It was cozy and warm, and I didn't need to sleep. But I must have gone to sleep in the end, for it was late when I woke up, and Lynx was furiously demanding to be let out. It was raining, and after the long period of drought I was very glad. The stream had almost run dry and the trout were in great distress. The rain hung over the forest in a gray veil, and higher up it concentrated into mist. It was warmer than it had been on the fine days, but everything glistened with moisture. I knew this rain meant the end of the autumn. It ushered in the winter, the long period that I feared. I slowly went back into the house to light a fire.

It rained for two days and grew cooler and cooler. On the twenty-seventh of October the first snow fell. Lynx greeted it cheerily, the cat was disgruntled and Pearl stared inquisitively into the white swirl. I opened the door for her, and she cautiously approached the strange white thing that covered the path. Quite slowly she raised one paw, touched the snow, gave a startled shake and fled back into the hut. Ten times a day she would try, but never managed to push her paw into the wet coldness. Finally she sat on the windowsill and dozed off, like her mother. The old cat was tough and brave, but she didn't like treading through the snow while it was still wet. At night she slipped out to relieve herself, but came back straightaway. She is an extremely clean creature, a real angel of domestic hygiene, and she brought up her children to be as clean as possible too. She even ate her prey somewhere out of doors. Before, she probably hadn't been allowed into the house at all. Pearl always brought her trout home, and Tiger laid everything he caught at my feet; he had to be stroked before he would touch it. But I'm very happy that the cat spares my feelings toward these little tokens, and that she is so extraordinarily independent. If she had to, she could get by without any help from me.

All my cats have had a habit of walking around their bowls after eating and then dragging them along the floor. I don't know what it means, but they do it every time, without fail. In general, cats obey a practically Byzantine series of ceremonies and take it very badly if you disturb them during their mysterious rites. In comparison with them, Lynx was a shameless child of nature, and they seemed to hold him rather in contempt for that.

If I put one of my cats on the bench, it would jump down, walk up and down three times and then sit down exactly where I'd just put it. With this gesture the cats were asserting their freedom and independence. It always gave me pleasure to watch them, and my affection was always mixed with a sneaking admiration. Lynx seemed to feel similarly. He was fond of the cats because they belonged to us, and was particularly fond of Pearl because she never spurned him or hissed at him; yet he always seemed to feel a little insecure with the cats.

It was nice sharing a house with Lynx, Pearl and the

old cat that first October. I finally had the time to pay attention to them.

It took only a few days for winter to set in. After that, the foehn* came and licked the young snow from the mountains. It became disagreeably warm, and the wind went hissing day and night around the little house. I slept badly and listened to the baying of the stags, which came down from the heights for the rutting season. Lynx grew restive, and barked and whimpered even in his sleep. He must have been dreaming of hunts long past. Both cats were drawn outside into the warm, damp forest. I lay awake and worried about Pearl. The baying of the stags sounded sad, threatening and sometimes even desperate. Maybe it only seemed to sound that way to me; I've read quite different accounts of it in books, where it's always described in terms of nothing but challenge, pride and pleasure. It may have something to do with me that I couldn't hear any of that in it. To me it always sounded like a terrible urge that drove them running blindly into danger. They couldn't know that nothing threatened them that year. The meat of a rutting stag is thoroughly un- pleasant. So I lay awake and thought about little Pearl, so inexperienced and in such danger with her little white coat in a world of owls, foxes and martens. I only hoped the foehn wouldn't last too long, and that winter would fi- nally bring us peace. The foehn actually lasted only three days, just long enough to kill Pearl.

On the third of November she didn't come home in the morning. I looked for her with Lynx, but we couldn't find her. The day slipped slowly and mercilessly onward. The weather was still dominated by the foehn, and the warm wind unsettled me. Lynx too kept wandering up and down; when he was let out he wanted to come back

---

* The warm, dry wind that blows down the northern slopes of the Alps.

into the house and looked up helplessly. Only the old cat lay on my bed and slept. She didn't seem to miss Pearl. Evening fell; I looked after the cow, cooked a few potatoes and fed Lynx and the cat. Darkness had suddenly fallen, and the wind rattled the shutters. I lit the lamp, sat down at the table and tried to read a diary, but my glance kept wandering through the gloom to the cat door. And then there was a scraping noise and Pearl crept around the corner of the cupboard.

The old cat sat upright, gave a loud cry and jumped down off the bed. I think it was this cry that startled me so much that I couldn't get up immediately. Pearl came slowly closer, a terrible blind creeping and sliding, as if all her bones were broken. She tried to stand up by my feet, uttered a strangled noise and fell with her head hard against the floor. A stream of blood poured from her mouth; she trembled and stretched out. When I knelt beside her, she was already dead. Lynx stood beside me and started back from his bleeding playmate. I stroked the clammy fur, and felt as if I'd been expecting this day since Pearl had been born. I wrapped her in a cloth, and in the morning I buried her in the forest meadow. The dry wooden floor had thirstily sucked up her blood. The stain has faded, but I'll never get rid of it. Lynx looked for Pearl for days, then he seemed to understand that she had gone forever. He had seen her dying, but he didn't seem to understand the connection. The old cat ran away for two days and then resumed her usual life.

I haven't forgotten Pearl. Her death was the first loss I suffered in the forest. Whenever I think of her, I rarely see her sitting on the bench in her white glory staring at the little blue butterflies. I generally see her as a pathetic, bloodstained pelt, her eyes half open, broken, her pink tongue gripped between her teeth. There is no point resisting images. They come and go, and the more I resist them, the more horrible they become.

Pearl was buried, and the foehn died overnight, as if it had accomplished its task. New snow fell from the sky, the baying of the stags grew weaker and after a few days it fell entirely silent. I set about my work and tried not to yield to the sadness that had fallen upon me. Now a wintry peace had set in, but not the peace that I would have wished for. A victim had been taken, and not even the warmth of the stove and light of the lamps could create comfort in the hut. In any case I was no longer interested in that comfort, and to Lynx's delight I often went to the forest with him. It was cold and hostile there, and that was easier to bear than the false coziness of my warm, gently lit home.

I found it hard to shoot a deer. I had to force myself to eat, and grew thin again, as I had after the hay harvest. I never lost this abhorrence of killing. It must be innate in me, and I had to overcome it over and over again whenever I needed meat. I now understand why Hugo left the shooting to Luise and his business colleagues. Sometimes I think it's a shame that Luise didn't stay alive; at least she wouldn't have any problems getting hold of meat. But she would never take the back seat in anything, and so she forced poor Hugo into decline. Maybe she's still sitting at the table in the inn, a lifeless, rigid thing with painted lips and strawberry-blonde hair. She loved life so much, and always did everything wrong, because in our world you can't love life as much as that with impunity. When she was still alive I found her very strange, and sometimes repulsive. But I've almost grown fond of the dead Luise, perhaps because I now have so much time to think about her. In reality I never knew anything more about her than I know about Bella or the cat today. But it's much easier to love Bella or the cat than it is to love a human being.

On the sixth of November I went on a long walk with Lynx, and took a path that was new to me. My sense of direction is very underdeveloped. I tend always to go the wrong way. But Lynx always brought me home safely when I got lost. Today I go only along the old familiar paths, otherwise I'd have to carve signs into the trees to find my way back. But I have no reason to stray wild in the forest; the deer still use their old trails, and I could find the paths to the potato field and the meadow by the stream in my sleep. Even if I don't want to admit it, though, without Lynx I'm a prisoner of the valley.

On that sixth of November, a cool, sunny day, I was still able to allow myself an expedition into new territory. The snow had melted again, and reddish-brown leaves, smooth and glistening with moisture, covered the paths. I climbed up a hill and clambered over a tree, a fallen giant, that pointed, wet and dangerous, into the valley. Then I reached a little level plateau, densely covered with beeches and spruces, where I rested for a while. At around midday the sun penetrated the mist and warmed my back. Lynx went into raptures about this, and jumped up at me with enthusiasm. He knew that this wasn't a hunting trip, as I hadn't brought the gun with me, and that he could take a few liberties. His paws were wet and dirty, and bits of leaf and sand stuck to my coat. Finally he calmed down again and drank from a tiny stream that probably only carried water from the little thaw of snow.

As always when I walked in the forest with Lynx a certain peace and cheerfulness came over me. I had no intention of doing anything but giving the dog a little exercise and keeping myself from fruitless thoughts. Walking in the forest distracted me from myself. It did me good to walk along slowly, to look around and breathe in the cool air. I followed the little stream downhill. The water thinned to a thread, and I finally walked on in the bed of the stream, because the track was overgrown and when I walked between the branches and held them apart I always got a shower of cold water down my neck. Lynx began to get worried and put on his working expression. He was following a trail. Silently, his nose close to the ground, he ran ahead of me. He stopped in front of a little cave washed out by the water on the shore, half hidden by a hazel bush, and showed me what he had found. He was excited, but not as happy as he was when he had sniffed out a deer.

I bent back the dripping branches, and there in the gloom of the cave, pressed close to the wall, I saw a dead chamois. It was an adult animal which now, in death, looked strangely small and thin. I could clearly see the whitish leprosy of mange that covered its forehead and eyes like a poisonous fungus. An ostracized and lonely animal that had come down from the scree slopes, the mountain pines and alpine roses to creep, dying and blind, into this cave. I let the branches fall back and shooed away Lynx, who didn't seem averse to further examination. He obeyed reluctantly, and hesitantly followed me downhill. I suddenly felt tired and wanted to go home. Lynx realized that the dead, mangy thing had upset me, and hung his head despondently. Our trip, which had begun so well, ended with us both trotting along in silence, until the streamlet miraculously opened out into our familiar stream and we went home through the gorge. A trout lay motionless in the greenish-brown pond, and I started to shiver at the sight of it. The rocks in the gorge looked cold and dark, and I didn't notice any more sun that day, for once we reached the hunting lodge it had long since disappeared behind veils of mist. The dampness of the gorge lay like a wet cloth on my face.

The crows sat on the spruce trees. When Lynx barked at them, they flapped into the air and then settled again on trees further away. They were well aware that this barking didn't threaten them in any way. Lynx didn't like the crows and was always trying to drive them off. Later he reluctantly came to terms with them and grew a little more tolerant. I have nothing against the crows, and leave them meager scraps from the kitchen. Sometimes, too, there were substantial meals for them, whenever I'd shot a deer. They are actually beautiful birds, with their shimmering plumage, their fat beaks and their brilliant black eyes. I often come across a dead crow in the snow. It's already gone next morning. Perhaps a fox has taken it. Maybe the fox that fatally injured Pearl. I found bite marks on her, but what had killed her had been an internal injury. She'd survived the bites.

Once, it must have been in the first winter, I saw a fox standing drinking at the stream. It was clad in its grayish-brown winter coat covered with a layer of whitish frost. In the sleepy silence of the snowy landscape it looked very much alive. I could have shot it; I had the gun with me, but I didn't do it. Pearl had to die just because one of her ancestors was an overbred angora cat. From the start she had been destined as a victim for foxes, owls and martens. Was I to punish the beautiful living fox for that? Pearl had suffered an injustice, but that same injustice had also befallen her victims, the trout; was I to pass it on to the fox? The only creature in the forest that can really do right or wrong is me. And I alone can show mercy. Sometimes I wish that burden of decision-making didn't lie with me. But I am a human being, and I can only think and act like a human being. Only death will free me from that. Whenever I think "winter," I always see the white, frost-covered fox standing by the snow-covered stream. A lonely adult animal going his predetermined way. Then it seems that this image means something important to me, as if it is only a sign for something else, but I can't get to the meaning of it.

That expedition on which Lynx had found the dead chamois was the last of the year. It was starting to snow again, and soon the snow was ankle-deep. I busied myself with my little household and Bella. She was now giving less milk and growing visibly fatter. I often lay sleeplessly considering all the possibilities. If anything happened to Bella my survival prospects were much smaller. Even if a cow calf was born they were very limited. Only a bull calf could give me hope of staying alive longer in the forest. Back then I still hoped that somebody would find me one day, but I repressed all thoughts of the past and the distant future as best I could, and only concerned myself with immediate things: the next potato harvest and the lush meadows of the Alm. I spent whole evenings thinking about a summer move there. Because I had been sleeping worse since working less outdoors, I stayed up longer in the evening (a criminal waste of oil) reading Luise's magazines, the diaries and thrillers. The magazines and novels bored me to death very quickly, and I always got more pleasure from the diaries. I still read them today.

Everything I know about rearing cattle, and it isn't much, comes from those diaries. I even like the stories in them better; they just make me laugh, some of them are touching, some gruesome, particularly the one in which the king of the eels chases a farmer who's been torturing animals and finally, in dramatic circumstances, strangles him. This story is really excellent, and I get very frightened whenever I read it. But back then in the first winter I still couldn't get on too well with those stories. In Luise's magazines there were page-long articles about face masks, mink coats and porcelain collections. Some of the masks were made of a honey and flour paste, and I always got very hungry when I read about them. What I liked best were the gorgeously illustrated recipes. But one day, when I was very hungry, I got so furious (I have always had a short temper) that I burned all the recipes in a single go. The last thing I saw was a lobster in mayonnaise, which curled as the fire swallowed it up. That was very stupid of me, as I could have lit the fire with it for three weeks. Instead, I wasted it all in a single evening.

I stopped reading in the end, and preferred to lay my Tarot cards. It calmed me down, and contact with the familiar, dirty characters diverted me from my thoughts. Back then I was simply afraid of the moment when I would have to turn off the light and go to bed. That fear sat next to me at the table all evening. Around that time the cat had already gone out, and Lynx was asleep in the stove door. I was quite alone with my cards and my fear. And yet every evening I had to go to bed in the end. I was almost falling under the table with fatigue, but the minute I lay in bed in the darkness and silence I was wide awake, and thoughts fell upon me like a swarm of hornets. Then, when I finally went to sleep, I dreamed and woke up in tears, then was plunged again into one of those terrible dreams.

My dreams had been empty up until then; from that winter onward they were cluttered. I only dreamed about dead people, for even in my dreams I knew there were no more living people. The dreams always started out quite safely and deceitfully, but I knew from the first that something bad was going to happen, and the plot slipped inexorably along to the moment when the familiar faces took shape and I awoke with a groan. I wept until I went to sleep again and sank back down to the dead people, deeper and deeper, faster and faster, and again awoke with a cry. In the daytime I was tired and dejected, and Lynx made desperate attempts to cheer me up. Even the cat, who had always struck me as entirely self-absorbed, gave me abrupt little caresses. I don't think I'd have survived the first winter without them both.

It was a good thing that I was obliged to devote more time to Bella, who had grown so fat that I had to be prepared for the arrival of the calf any day. She had grown ponderous and short of breath, and I talked to her every day to cheer her up. Her beautiful eyes had assumed an anxious, intense expression, as if she was worrying about her condition. But maybe I only imagined that. So my life was divided into terrible nights and sensible days during which I could barely stand up for fatigue.

The days slipped by. In the middle of December it grew warmer and the snow melted. I went to the hunting ground with Lynx every day. Then I could sleep a little better, but I still dreamed. I realized that the composure with which I had adapted to my situation from the first day had only been a kind of anesthetic. Now the anesthetic was wearing off, and I was reacting quite normally to my loss. I felt that the worries that beset me during the day, about my animals, the potatoes and the hay, were appropriate to the circumstances, and hence bearable. I knew I would overcome them, and was prepared to deal with them. The fears that gripped me at night, on the other hand, struck me as entirely futile; fears of the past and dead things that I couldn't bring back to life, which held me at their mercy in the darkness of night. I probably made things worse for myself by so stubbornly refusing to examine the past. But I didn't yet know that. Christmas was approaching, and I dreaded it.

The twenty-fourth of December was still, gray and overcast. In the morning I went to the hunting ground with Lynx, and was glad to see that there was at least no snow. It was silly of me, but Christmas without snow struck me as more bearable back then. As I was walking up the familiar slopes the first flakes broke away and fell, slowly and silently. It was as if even the weather was conspiring against me. Lynx couldn't understand why I didn't go into raptures when more and more flakes floated from the gray and white sky. I tried to be cheerful for his sake, but I couldn't manage it, so he trotted anxiously beside me, his head lowered. When I looked out of the window at midday the trees were already dusted with white, and toward evening, when I went into the byre, the forest had turned into a real Christmas forest, and the snow crunched crisply under my feet. While I was lighting the lamp I suddenly knew I couldn't go on like this. I was seized by a wild desire to give in and let things slide. I had grown tired of constant flight, and wanted to stay put. I sat down at the table and abandoned my resistance. I felt the tension easing in my muscles, and my heart beating slowly and evenly. Even the simple decision to give in seemed to be helping. I remembered past times very clearly, and tried to be just, to distort nothing, and to run nothing down.

It's terribly hard to do justice to one's own past. In that distant reality, Christmas had been a beautiful and mysterious celebration, while I was still small and believed in the miracle. Later, Christmas turned into a jolly feast, at which I got presents from everybody and imagined I was the center of the house. I didn't for a moment consider what Christmas might mean to my parents or grandparents. Something of the old magic had crumbled away, and its gloss went on fading. Later, when my children were small, the celebration came into its own again, but not for long, since my children weren't as susceptible to mysteries and miracles as I had been. And then Christmas became a jolly feast again, at which my children got presents from everybody and imagined everything was happening for their sakes alone. That's actually how it was. And yet another while later, Christmas was no longer even a feast, but just a day on which people habitually gave each other things they had had to pay for in some way or another. Even then Christmas had already died for me, not on that twenty-fourth of December in the forest. I realized I'd dreaded it since my children had stopped being children. I hadn't had the strength to bring the dying feast back to life. And today, after a long series of Christmas Eves, I was sitting alone in the forest with a cow, a dog and a cat, and I no longer had any of the things that had gone to make up my life for forty years. The snow was on the spruce trees and the fire crackled in the stove, and everything was as it originally should have been. But the children weren't there anymore, and no miracles happened. I would never have to run through the department stores again buying unnecessary things. There was no enormous, decorated tree slowly fading in the heated room instead of flourishing and burgeoning in the forest; no flickering of candles, no gilded angel and no sweet songs.

When I was a child we always sang "Ihr Kinderlein kommet." It has always remained my private Christmas carol, even when people stopped singing it at all, for some reason, or sang it only rarely. All the little children, where had they gone, seduced by the seduced into the stony void? Perhaps I was the only person in the world who remembered that old carol. Something conceived for the best had gone wrong and turned out for the worst. I couldn't complain, because I was just as guilty or innocent as the dead. So many feasts had been created, and there had always been one person with whose death the memory of a feast had died. With me dies the feast of all the little children. In the future, a snowy forest will mean nothing but a snowy forest, and a crib in the stable nothing but a crib in the stable.

I stood up and walked to the door. The lamp cast its glow onto the path, and the snow on the little spruce trees gave a yellowish gleam. I wished my eyes could forget what that scene had so long meant to them. For something quite new lay waiting behind it all, which I was unable to see because my head was crammed full of old things and my eyes were unreceptive. I had lost the old without finding anything new; the new was closed to me, but I knew it was there. I don't know why that thought filled me with a very faint, almost imperceptible joy. I felt better than I had done for several weeks.

I put on my shoes and went back to the byre. Bella had lain down and gone to sleep. Her warm, clean fragrance floated around her. Gentleness and patience flowed from her heavy, sleeping body. So I left her again and stamped back through the snow to the house. Lynx, who had gone outside with me, came out from under a bush, and I closed the door from inside. Lynx jumped onto the bench and put his head on my knee. I talked to him and saw that it made him happy. He had earned some attention from me over the last dreary weeks. He understood that I had come back to him completely, and that he could reach me by yapping, whimpering and licking my hand. Lynx was very contented. At last he got tired and fell fast asleep. He felt he was safe, because his human had come back to him, from a strange world where he couldn't have followed her. I laid my cards and stopped being afraid. Whether the night was going to be bad or good, I wanted to take it as it came, and not resist it.

At ten o'clock I carefully pushed Lynx away from me, packed the cards up and went to bed. I lay stretched out in the darkness and looked sleepily at the rosy glow that fell from the stove onto the dark floor. My thoughts came and went quite unhindered, and I still wasn't afraid. The lights on the floor stopped dancing, and my head was a little dizzy from all the thinking I had done. I now knew what had been wrong, and how I could have done it better. I was very wise, but my wisdom had come too late, and even if I'd been born wise I couldn't have done anything in a world that was foolish. I thought about the dead, and I was very sorry for them, not because they were dead, but because they had all found so little joy in life. I thought about all the people I had known, and I enjoyed thinking about them; they would be mine until the day I died. I would have to clear a safe place for them in my new life if I was to live in peace. I went to sleep, and slipped down to my dead people, and this time my dream was different from the dreams I had had before. I wasn't frightened, just sad, and this grief filled me to the brim. I was woken by the cat jumping onto my bed and curling up against me. I was going to reach my hand out to her but I went back to sleep and slept dreamlessly until morning. When I woke up I was tired but contented, as if I'd put a hard task behind me.

From then on my dreams improved; they gradually faded, and the day reclaimed me. The first thing I noticed was that my wood supply had dwindled. The weather, though dreary, was not too cold so I decided to make use of the fine days and attend to the wood. I carted the logs across the snow and started sawing. I felt like working and I had no way of knowing what the weather was going to do next. I might fall ill, the weather could turn cold and hold up my woodcutting. My hands were soon covered with blisters again, but after a few days the blisters turned into calluses and stopped hurting.

After I'd sawed up enough wood I set about cutting it into smaller pieces. Once, when my attention had wandered, I cut myself above the knee with the ax. The wound wasn't deep, but it bled a lot and I realized how careful I would have to be. It wasn't easy for me, but I got used to it. People who live alone in the forest have to be careful if they want to stay alive. The wound above my knee needed stitches; it left a wide, bulging scar that hurt every time the weather changed. Otherwise, however, I was very lucky. All the wounds that I inflicted on myself healed quickly, without suppurating. I still had sticking plaster back then; now I simply tie a piece of material around it and it heals that way too.

I didn't fall ill once throughout the winter. I had always been susceptible to colds, and suddenly I seemed to be thoroughly cured of them, even though I couldn't afford the time to rest and sometimes came home exhausted and soaked. The headaches from which I had often suffered before hadn't appeared since early summer. My head hurt now only when logs flew up and hit it. In the evening I could very often feel all my muscles and bones, particularly after I'd been woodcutting or when I'd been pulling hay up to the gorge. I was never very strong, just stubborn and resilient. I gradually worked out all the things I could do with my hands. Hands are wonderful tools. Sometimes I imagined that Lynx, if he had suddenly grown hands, would soon have started thinking and talking as well.

Of course there are still a lot of tasks that I can't manage, but then it wasn't until I was forty that I discovered I had hands. I can't cope with too much. My greatest triumph would be to fix the door to Bella's new byre properly. I still find carpentry particularly difficult. I'm not so clumsy, on the other hand, when it comes to agriculture and animal husbandry. I've always found anything to do with plants and animals quite straightforward. I just never had the opportunity to make the most of that natural talent. And that kind of work satisfies me the most. Throughout the whole of Christmas week I sawed and chopped wood. I felt good and slept deeply and dreamlessly. On the twenty-fourth of December it grew very cold overnight, and I had to stop and go back into the house. I sealed the cracks in the doors and windows of the byre and the house with strips I'd cut from an old blanket. The byre was solidly built, and it wouldn't be too cold for Bella yet. Also the straw that I'd put down in the byre and on top of it kept out the worst of the cold. The cat hated the cold, and in her little round head she started making me responsible for it. She chastised me with sulky and reproachful looks, and whiningly demanded that I finally put a stop to this nonsense. The only one who wasn't bothered by the cold was Lynx. But he cheerfully welcomed all kinds of weather. He was just a little disappointed that I didn't want to go walking in the crisp cold, and kept trying to rouse me to go on little expeditions. I was worried about the deer. The snow lay more than three feet deep, and there was no longer anything for them to eat. I had two sacks of horse chestnuts left over from the previous year's feed, which I wanted to keep for myself as an emergency supply. I might reach the point where I was glad of horse chestnuts. But when the sharp frost came to an end I dithered, and kept thinking about the two sacks in the bedroom. On the sixth of January, Epiphany, I could no longer stand it in the hut. The cat still treated me with the greatest contempt, showing me her striped backside, and Lynx was feverishly excited about the idea of going out. So I put on everything I had to keep me warm, and set off with the dog.

It was a brilliant and beautiful frosty day. The snow-covered trees glittered painfully in the sunlight, and the snow crunched crisply under my feet. Lynx ran off, enveloped in a cloud of luminous dust. It was so cold that my breath froze immediately, and it hurt to draw breath into my lungs. I wrapped a cloth over my mouth and nose and drew my hood tight across my forehead. My first path took me to the deer's feeding place. There were countless tracks there. A shiver went through my bones when I saw that they'd all gone there in desperation, and found the feed racks empty.

I suddenly hated the blue, swirling air, the snow and myself, because I couldn't do anything for the animals. In this time of need my chestnuts weren't much better than nothing at all. It was extremely foolish to give them all out, but it was all I could do. I went back straightaway, lugged the two sacks out of the room, tied them together and dragged them behind me in the snow. Lynx was excited about all this, and jumped around me, barking encouragingly. The feeding place was only twenty minutes away, but the path led uphill, and it was also heavily covered in snow. I arrived at the top completely exhausted and with my hands quite rigid. I emptied the sacks into the racks and felt like an idiot. As it was so cold and I didn't dare sit down I slowly went back up the hill. I found their tracks everywhere. The red deer had come down from the mountains to join the roe deer. When twilight fell they would all come to the feeding place and be able to eat their fill at least one more time.

The bark of the young trees had been gnawed at, and I decided to set aside a little supply of hay from the forest meadow for the deer. It wasn't hard for me to make this decision, since summer was far away. When I actually got down to cutting the forest meadow with the sickle I felt differently about it. In any case, however, I always have enough hay now so that in the worst emergency the deer have enough to feed on for a week. In fact it might make more sense not to feed them, since they are multiplying too quickly in any case, but I can't simply let them starve and perish so miserably.

After a quarter of an hour I realized I couldn't bear the cold any longer, and turned back. Even Lynx seemed to agree; his enthusiasm had cooled quickly. On the way back I found, half-hidden in a snowfall, a roe deer that had broken its back leg and couldn't move. The leg was so badly broken that the splinters of bone were sticking out of the skin. I knew that I had to put an end to that torment straightaway. It was a young roe deer, and very emaciated. I didn't have my rifle with me and had to kill the animal with my jackknife, giving it a jab in the neck. The deer raised its head miserably and looked at me, then gave a sigh, shuddered and fell back into the snow. I'd hit the right spot.

It was only a small deer, but it was a heavy burden on the way home. Later, after I'd thawed out my hands in the hut, I gutted it. Its coat was already ice-cold, but when I broke it open a little steam rose from the flesh. Its heart still felt quite warm. I laid the meat in a wooden tub and carried it into one of the upper rooms, where it would be frozen stiff by the following morning. I gave Lynx and the cat some of its liver. I only wanted a glass of hot milk. In the night I heard the cold creaking in the wood. I'd put on a lot of extra logs, but I was shivering under the blanket and couldn't get to sleep. Sometimes a log would crackle into life, and then go out again; I felt sick. I knew it was because I had to keep on killing. I imagined what a person who enjoyed killing might feel. The hair stood up on my arms, and my mouth grew dry with disgust. You would probably need to be born to it. I could bring myself to do it as quickly and skillfully as possible, but I would never get used to it. I lay awake for ages in the crackling darkness thinking about the little heart freezing to a clump of ice in the room above me.

That was in the night of the seventh of January. The cold continued for another three days, but the chestnuts had disappeared by the morning.

I found three more frozen roe deer and a red deer calf, and who knows how many I didn't find.

After the great chill a wave of damp, warmer air set in. The path to the byre turned into a shining sheet of ice. I had to scatter ashes and chop up the ice. Then the west wind turned and came from the south and hissed around the hut day and night. Bella grew nervous, and I had to see to her ten times a day. She wasn't eating much, and shifted from foot to foot and jerked away painfully when I milked her. Whenever I thought about the impending birth I was seized by panic. How was I to get the calf out of Bella? I had once been present at the birth of a calf and more or less remembered what had happened. Two strong men had pulled the calf out of its mother's body. It had struck me as very barbaric, and I'd felt terribly sorry for the cow, but maybe that's really how it had to be. I didn't know a thing about it, after all.

On the eleventh of January Bella bled a little. It was after her evening feed, and I decided to set myself up in the byre for the night. I filled the thermos flask with hot tea, kitted myself out with a heavy rope, some string and a pair of scissors, and put a pot of water on the stove. Lynx desperately wanted to be there as well, but I shut him in the house, as he'd only have caused chaos in the byre. I'd already set up a little log partition for the calf, and filled it with fresh straw. Bella greeted me with a dull moo, and seemed pleased to see me. I could only hope that this wasn't her first calf and that she had some experience behind her. Then I stroked her and began to speak to her encouragingly. She was in pain, and entirely preoccupied by the processes at work in her body. She walked nervously back and forth and refused to lie down again. It seemed to calm her down when I spoke to her, so I said the same things to her that the midwife in the clinic had said to me. It'll be fine, it won't be much longer now, it'll hardly hurt and that kind of nonsense. I sat down on the seat that I'd carried over from the garage. Later I fetched the water from the hut; it was steaming hot, but it had time to cool down. The steam rose, and I was as apprehensive as if I was going to have a child myself.

Nine o'clock came. The foehn rattled the roof, and I began to shiver with nerves and poured myself some hot tea. And once more I promised Bella an easy birth and a lovely strong calf. She had turned her head toward me and looked at me, pained and patient. She knew I wanted to help her, and that gave her a little confidence.

Then nothing happened for a long time. I had to clear dung away again, and put down a little fresh straw. The foehn subsided and it suddenly grew quite still. The lamp burned quiet and yellow on the little stove. On no account was I to knock it over. I had to pay attention to so many things. There was also the possibility that the light wouldn't be strong enough at the birth.

Suddenly I was terribly tired. My shoulders hurt and my head lolled from side to side. I would have been happiest lying down in the fresh straw in the calf's partition and going to sleep. I nodded off a few times, and jerked awake again with a start. Bella was bleeding again and going into heavy labor. Her flanks were writhing and working violently. Sometimes she groaned quietly, and I spoke encouraging words. Once she drank a little water. And then, at last, one wet leg appeared and, immediately after it, another one. Bella was struggling away. Trembling a little with excitement, I tied the two brown legs together and pulled on the rope. I had no luck at all. I didn't have the strength of two men. As I looked at Bella everything fell into place. I could imagine precisely how the calf lay inside her. It made no sense at all to pull on the front legs, which would have pulled the calf's head backward rather than pushing it forward. I washed my hands and felt around inside Bella's warm body. It was more difficult than I'd thought. I had to wait until each contraction died away before I could push my hand any further in. I managed to grab the head and push it downward with both hands. The next spasm caught my hand, but the head slid forward. Bella gave a great groan and stepped to one side. I reassured her and pressed the head down until the sweat ran into my eyes. The pain in my arms grew unbearable. But then the head started coming. Bella snorted with relief.

I waited until the next contraction and pulled on the rope, and there was the calf, so suddenly that I had to jump forward and catch it on my knees. I let it slide gently to the floor; the umbilical cord had already torn. I laid the little one by Bella's front legs, and she immediately started to lick it. We were both overjoyed to have managed so well. It was a bull calf, and we had brought it into the world together. Bella couldn't get enough of licking her son, and I admired the damp curls on his forehead. He was grayish-brown, like his mother, and looked as though he might turn a little darker. After only a few minutes he tried to get to his feet, and Bella looked as if she wanted to eat him up with love. Finally, when I thought he'd had enough licking, I lifted the little bull and carried him to his partition. Bella could lean over and lick his nose as much as she wanted. Then I gave her lukewarm water and fresh hay. But I knew that the birth wasn't quite over yet. I was drenched in sweat. It was midnight. I sat down on the chair and drank hot tea. As I couldn't go to sleep I got up again and walked up and down in the byre.

After an hour Bella got nervous and the contractions began again. This time there was only a few minutes to wait, and then the afterbirth was there too. Bella lay down exhausted. I cleaned the byre, scattered fresh straw and had another look at the calf. It had gone to sleep and crawled into the straw. I took the lamp, bolted the byre door and went back into the house. Lynx greeted me excitedly, and I told him how it had been. Even if he didn't understand my words, he definitely understood that something pleasant had happened to Bella, and crept contentedly into his stove door. I washed myself thoroughly, put fresh wood on the fire and went to bed.

That night I didn't even feel the cat jumping onto my bed, and awoke only at the light of dawn. My first journey was to the stable. Heart beating, I drew back the bolt. Bella was busy licking her son's nose, and I heaved a sigh of relief at the sight of that. He was already standing solidly on his powerful legs, and I led him to his mother and pressed his mouth against her udder. He understood straightaway and drank his fill. Bella shifted from one leg to the other when he bumped into her body with his round head. When he had had enough I milked Bella dry. The milk was yellow and fatty and I didn't like the taste of it. Bella now looked a little haggard and anxious, but I knew that would pass if she was well looked after. I could read in her soft, shining eyes that she was bathed in warm delight. I felt quite strange, and had to escape from the stable.

The foehn was still blowing, and the weather stayed windy and rainy. Later a moist blue sky broke through the flying clouds, and black shadows flitted across the clearing. I felt nervous and tense. The cat looked electric. Her hair stood on end and sparked when I ran my hand over it. She was unsettled, and followed me about, complaining, bored her hot, dry nose into the palm of my hand and refused to eat anything. I was afraid that some unknown feline disease had struck her, when I suddenly realized that she was calling for a tomcat. She went into the forest hundreds of times, came back again and showered me with pitiful caresses. Even Lynx, who was hardly aware of the foehn, was infected by her agitation and ran helplessly around the house. At night I was awoken by a strange animal crying in the forest: Ka-au, ka-au. It sounded a little like a tomcat, but it wasn't the same call. I was worried about my cat. She stayed away for three days, and I almost lost hope of ever seeing her again.

The weather turned, and it started snowing. I was pleased, because I knew I was tired and incapable of working. The warm wind had taken a lot out of me. I imagined that it had brought with it a faint odor of decay. Perhaps that wasn't my imagination. Who knows what might have thawed after being frozen stiff in the forest? It was a relief not to have to hear the wind anymore, and to watch the light flakes floating past the window.

That night the cat came back. I lit the candle, and the cat jumped onto my knee. I felt her wet, cold fur through my nightshirt and hugged her in my arms. She cried and cried and tried to tell me what had happened to her. She kept pushing her head against my forehead, and her cries lured Lynx out from the stove door to come and sniff joyfully at the homecomer. At last I stood up and warmed a little milk for them both. The cat was completely starving, unkempt and neglected, just as she had been when she had first cried at my door. I laughed, scolded and praised her in one breath, and Lynx was extremely confused when she honored him by pushing her head against him. Something extraordinary must have happened to the cat. Maybe Lynx understood more of her cries than I did, but at any rate what he understood seemed to please him, for he trotted contentedly back to his sleeping place. The cat couldn't settle down so quickly. With her tail in the air she swaggered up and down and twined herself around my legs, uttering little cries. Only when I had lain down again and blown out the candle did she come to me in bed and start giving herself a thoroughly good wash. For the first time in days I felt peaceful and relaxed. The silence of the winter night was a sweet miracle after the hissing and groaning of the foehn. Finally I went to sleep, with the contented purring of the cat in my ear.

In the morning the new-fallen snow lay four inches thick. There was still no wind, and a muted white light lay over the forest meadow. In the byre Bella greeted me impatiently and let me lead her to her hungry son. From one day to the next he was getting stronger and livelier, and Bella's haggard body had already rounded out a little.

Soon there would be nothing left to recall that January night of the foehn when we had brought the little bull into the world.

They were both entirely absorbed in one another, and I felt a little lost and excluded. I realized that I envied Bella, and got out of the byre. All they needed me for there now was for feeding, milking and mucking out. As soon as I had pulled the door shut behind me the gloomy byre became a little island of happiness, bathed in tenderness and warm animal breath. It was better for me simply to look for something to do rather than giving the matter any thought. There wasn't much hay left in the garage, and after breakfast I went to the gorge with Lynx to fetch hay. The cat, very thin, her coat dull, lay on my bed and slept an exhausted sleep. I fetched hay twice in the morning and again in the afternoon, and I did the same the next day. It wasn't cold, and snowed from time to time in little dry flakes. It stayed windless. It was just the kind of winter I like. Lynx, who had finally grown tired from all that running back and forth between the meadow by the stream and the hunting lodge, didn't stir from the stove, while the cat slept for days, only getting up to eat and go off on her short nocturnal expeditions. She drank in sleep like a medicine, her eyes grew clear again and her coat shone. She seemed very content, and I began to assume that the strange animal in the forest had been a tomcat after all. I called him Mr. Ka-au Ka-au, and imagined he must be very proud and brave, or he wouldn't have survived in the forest. I wasn't looking forward to the kittens; they would only bring trouble again, but I allowed the cat her happiness.

So much had happened recently. Pearl had been killed, a little bull had come into the world, the cat had found a mate, roe deer had frozen and the carnivores had had a rich winter. I myself had had a lot of excitement, and now I was tired. I lay on the bench, and when I closed my eyes I saw snowy mountains on the horizon, white flakes dropping onto my face in a big, bright silence. I had no thoughts, no memories, there was only the big, silent, snowy light. I knew this feeling could be dangerous for a lonely person, but I couldn't muster any strength to resist it.

Lynx didn't leave me in peace for long. He kept coming to me and prodding me with his nose. I turned my head with difficulty and saw the life shining warm and imperious out of his eyes. Sighing, I got up and set about my daily work. Now Lynx, my friend and guardian, has ceased to be, and sometimes the desire to go into the white and painless silence is very great. I must take care of myself and be stricter with myself than I was before.

The cat stares into the distance with yellow eyes. Sometimes she suddenly comes back to me, and her eyes compel me to stretch out my hand and stroke her round head with the black M on the forehead. If the cat enjoys this she purrs. Sometimes she finds my touch irritating. But she's too polite to spurn it, and just stiffens under my hand and stays quite still. And I slowly draw back my hand. Lynx was always delighted when I stroked him. It is true that he couldn't help dying, but I miss him all the same. He was my sixth sense. Now that he's dead I feel like an amputee. I miss something and will always miss it. It isn't only that I miss him when I'm hunting and following trails, and have to spend hours clambering after a deer I've shot. It isn't that alone, although that's made my life more difficult. The worst thing is that without Lynx I feel truly alone.

Since his death I dream about animals a lot. They talk to me like people, and it strikes me as quite natural in the dream. The people who used to populate my sleep in the first winter have all gone away. I never see them anymore. In my dreams people were never kind to me; they were indifferent at best. My dream animals are always kind and full of life. But I don't think that's very remarkable, it only shows how people and animals always seemed to me.

It would be much better not to dream at all. I've been living for so long in the forest now, and I've dreamed about people, animals and things, but not once about the wall. I see it every time I go to fetch hay, or rather I see through it. Now, in the winter, when the trees and bushes are bare, I can clearly make out the little house again. When the snow settles you can hardly see any difference, a white landscape both here and beyond, slightly disturbed on my side by the tracks of my heavy shoes.

The wall has become so much a part of my life that often I don't think about it for weeks. And even if I do think about it, it strikes me as no more strange than a brick wall or a garden fence that stops me going any further. What's so special about it? An object made of material whose composition is unknown to me. There was always more than enough of that kind of thing in my life. The wall forced me to make an entirely new life, but the things that really move me are still the same as before: birth, death, the seasons, growth and decay. The wall is a thing that is neither dead nor alive, it really doesn't concern me, and that's why I don't dream about it.

One day I'll have to reckon with it, because I won't be able to live here forever. But until then I don't want to have anything to do with it.

Since this morning, I'm convinced that I shall never meet another human being again, unless there's someone else living in the mountains. If there were still people outside, they would have flown over in airplanes long ago. I've seen that even low clouds can float across the boundary. And they don't bring any poison with them, or else I wouldn't still be alive. So why do no airplanes come? It should have struck me long before. I don't know why I didn't think of it before. Where are the victors' reconnaissance planes? Are there no victors? I don't think I'll ever get to see them. I'm actually pleased that I never thought about the airplanes. Even a year ago that reflection would have cast me into great despair. Not anymore.

For a number of weeks my eyes haven't seemed to be quite right. I can see excellently into the distance, but when I'm writing, the lines often swim before my eyes. Perhaps it's due to the weak light, and to the fact that I have to write with a hard pencil. I was always proud of my eyes, although it's stupid to be proud of a physical asset. I could imagine nothing worse than going blind. I'm probably only getting a bit farsighted and shouldn't worry about it. My birthday's coming around again soon. Since I've been living in the forest I don't notice myself getting older. There's nobody there to draw my attention to it, after all. Nobody tells me how I look, and I never give it a thought myself. Today is the twentieth of December. I shall write until work starts in the spring. Summer will be less of an effort for me this year, because I'm not moving to the Alm again. Bella will graze the forest meadow, as she did last year, and I'll spare myself those long and arduous journeys.

The February of the first year is quite empty in my diary. But I still remember a few things about it. I think it was warm and damp rather than cold. The grass in the clearing started to go green at the roots, while autumn's yellow stalks remained above them. There was no foehn, only a mild westerly wind. Not unusual weather for February, in fact. I was pleased that there were leaves and old grass everywhere for the deer, so that they could recover a little. The birds were faring better as well. They stayed away from the hut, which meant they no longer needed me. Only the crows stayed faithful to me until spring began in earnest. They sat in the spruce trees waiting for scraps. Their lives followed strict rules. At the same time every morning they descended on the clearing and, after circling about for a long time, shrieking excitedly, they settled on the trees. In late afternoon, when twilight fell, they rose up and left, circling and shrieking above the forest. I have no idea where they spent the night. The crows led an exciting double life. As time passed I came to feel a certain affection for them, and couldn't understand how I hadn't liked them before. When I saw them on dirty dumps in the city they always struck me as miserable, dirty creatures. Here, in the glistening spruce trees, they were suddenly quite different birds, and I forgot my old antipathy. Today I wait for them to come every day, because they tell me the time. Even Lynx got used to them and left them in peace. He got used to everything I was fond of. He was a very adaptable creature. But for the cat the crows remained a constant source of frustration. She sat on the windowsill staring across at them with her hair on end and her teeth bared. Once she had got herself excited and roused herself to fury she lay down crossly on the bench and tried to drown her irritation in sleep. An owl used to live above the hut. Since the crows had come it had left. I had nothing against the owl, but as the cat might be expecting kittens I was quite pleased that the crows had sent it packing.

Toward the end of February the cat's condition became impossible to ignore. She had grown fat, and alternated between moodiness and outbursts of affection. Lynx was baffled by this change. Only when he got a good clout around the ear did he grow cautious, and avoided disturbing his moody friend. He seemed to have forgotten that exactly the same thing had happened before. This time there wouldn't be a Pearl, and it was much better that way. Of course you couldn't say for sure, with such a mixed pedigree. Against all reason I'd started looking forward to the new litter. The thought of it distracted me and occupied my mind. My mood in general improved the longer it stayed light in the evening, and the closer spring came. Winter in the forest is hardly bearable, particularly if one has no companions.

Even in February I spent as much time as possible out of doors. The air made me tired and hungry. I had a look at my supply of potatoes and found I would have to economize to make it through to the next harvest. The seed stock couldn't be touched on any account. In the summer I would probably have to live almost exclusively on meat and milk. But this year I could enlarge my field. I ate the potatoes in their skins, for the vitamins. I don't know whether it really did any good, but the very idea of it cheered me up a little. Every second or third day I allowed myself an apple, and in the meantime I chewed on the tiny crab apples, so bitter that I could hardly swallow them. I had enough of these to do me for the whole winter. Bella was now giving so much milk that the bull couldn't drink it all, and I even had a little surplus of butter and was able to make clarified butter. Keeping food supplies was easier in winter than in summer, because the meat stayed edible for longer. All I lacked was fruit and vegetables. I didn't know how long the bull was supposed to suckle his mother, and scoured all the diaries for enlightenment but didn't find a word on the subject. They were written specially for people familiar with the basic rules of agriculture. My uncertainty sometimes made life exciting for me. Everywhere I sensed dangers that I couldn't recognize in time. I had to be constantly prepared for unpleasant surprises, and all I could do was to bear them with equanimity.

For the time being I let the bull drink as much as he wanted. After all, everything depended on his being big and strong soon. I had no idea how old a bull would have to be to sire a calf, but I hoped he would give a sign of his manhood in time. I was well aware that my plan was a little adventurous, but all I could do was wait for its success. I didn't know how that kind of incest would work out. Perhaps in this instance Bella wouldn't conceive at all, or a deformity would grow within her. There was nothing about that in the diaries, either. It probably hadn't been usual to mate a bull with his mother. As I don't like living day by day without a plan, feeling my way around in the dark, it was hard for me to stay calm. Impatience has always been one of my worst faults, but in the forest I have learned to control it to a certain extent. The potatoes don't grow any quicker if I wring my hands, and even my little bull didn't grow up overnight. When he was fully grown I sometimes wished he'd stayed a little round calf. He presented me with problems that made my life much harder.

I had to wait and wait. Everything takes its time here, a time that isn't agitated by a thousand clocks. There's no haste or urgency, I'm the only disturbance in the forest, and I still suffer from that.

March brought a setback. It snowed and froze, and overnight the forest turned into a gleaming winter landscape. But the chill stayed mild, for in the afternoon the sun shone warmly on the slope and water dripped from the roof. The deer weren't threatened by any danger; on the sunny side there were enough places free of snow, with grass and leaves. I didn't find any more dead roe deer that spring. When the sun shone I went to the hunting ground with Lynx or fetched hay from the barn. Once I felled a weak buck and froze it. Finally the thaw came, and there were a few days of rain and storms. I couldn't see further than from the house to the stable, the mist lay so thick. I lived on a warm little island in a moist sea of mist. Lynx began to get melancholic, and constantly trotted between the hut and the clearing. I couldn't do anything to help him, as the cool wet weather wasn't doing me any good and I didn't want to catch a cold. My throat was already starting to get rough and I had a slight cold. But it didn't turn into anything more serious and went away the next day. What was much worse was that I got rheumatic pains in all my limbs. My fingers suddenly grew fat and red, and hurt when I moved them. I had a slight fever, swallowed Hugo's rheumatic pills, sat crossly in the hut and imagined that in the end I wouldn't be able to move my hands at all.

Finally the rain turned into hail and then into snow again. My fingers were still swollen, and it hurt every time I gripped anything. Lynx saw that I was ill, and smothered me with gestures of love. Once he made me cry, and afterward we both sat depressed on the bench. The crows sat in their spruce trees waiting for scraps. They seemed to see me as a marvelous institution, a kind of social security, and got lazier by the day.

On the eleventh of March the cat jumped off the bed, walked to the wardrobe and urgently demanded to be let in. I took an old cloth, put it in the wardrobe and the cat slipped inside. In the meantime I set about my work, and it was only in the evening, when I came out of the byre, that my thoughts returned to the cat and I looked into the wardrobe. It was all over already. She purred loudly and happily licked my hand. There were three young this time, and all three were alive. Three tabby cats, from the lightest to the darkest gray, all licked clean and in search of food. The cat hardly had time to drink and immediately turned to her young. I left the wardrobe door half open and shooed the inquisitive Lynx away. This time the cat wasn't as wild as she had been with Pearl, she hissed at Lynx but, it seemed to me, more for form's sake. It was strange how interested Lynx was in the joyful event. As he couldn't express his elation any other way he ate a double portion of food. I noticed as a general rule that any mental excitement unleashed in him a compelling desire to eat. The cat was the same; when she'd been annoyed by the crows, she often went to her feeding bowl. That night the cat didn't come to my bed, and I lay awake thinking about Pearl. The bloodstain on the floor refused to fade. I'd decided not to cover it up. I had to get used to it and live with it. And now there were three kittens again. I resolved not to grow fond of them, but I could foresee that I would be unable to keep my resolution.

The weather slowly improved. Over the open countryside it had doubtless been fine for a long time, but in the mountains the mist often brewed for another week before lifting. And then, very quickly, it became almost as warm as summer, and grass and flowers sprouted from the damp earth almost overnight. The spruce trees put out new shoots, and the stinging nettles around the dung heap started to burgeon cheerfully. The change happened so quickly that I couldn't grasp it. I didn't feel better immediately, either, and for the first warm days I was more depressed than I had been in the winter. Only my fingers got better straightaway. The cat's offspring flourished, but still stayed in the wardrobe. The old cat wasn't as concerned about them as she had been about Pearl. At night she liked to go off for an hour or so. Perhaps she trusted me more, or she felt that the little tigers were less threatened. She drank Bella's milk by the bowlful and turned it, in her body, into milk that the kittens could feed on. On the twentieth of March she introduced me to her young. All three were fat and shiny, but none of them had Pearl's longhaired coat. One of them had a slightly narrower face than the others, and I concluded from this that it was a female. It's almost impossible to establish the sex of such small cats, and I had very little experience of it. From then on the cat played with her children in the room. They were a special source of amusement for Lynx, who behaved as if he was their father. Once they realized he was harmless they started to pester him just as much as they did their mother. Sometimes Lynx tired of these pests and felt they should be in bed. Then he carefully carried them to the wardrobe. Hardly had the last one been transported than the first tumbled back into the room. The cat watched him, and if I have ever seen a cat smiling with malice, she was the one. Finally she got up, distributed a few clouts and drove her brood into the wardrobe. She was much less gentle with them than she had been with Pearl. But this was necessary, too, because they were irrepressibly keen on playing and on rough and tumble. Mr. Ka-au Ka-au seemed to have won through entirely. They spent the whole day charging about the hut, and I had to be very careful not to tread on them.

I don't know how it happened, but at noon one day, during a wild game of tag, the smallest cat, the one with the narrow face, went into convulsive spasms and died within a few minutes. I hadn't been paying attention to her, and couldn't think what had happened. She seemed to be completely unhurt. The old cat immediately ran over to her and licked her, moaning tenderly, but by then it was all over. I buried the little cat near Pearl. The old cat spent an hour looking for her and then turned her attention to the other two as if there had never been a third kitten. Her brothers didn't seem to miss her either. Lynx hadn't been in the house, and when I came back he hesitated, gave me a questioning look and went to the wardrobe to have a look. Something distracted him, and he forgot why he'd gone there. But I'm sure he realized one of the cats was missing. I'm the only creature, even today, that sometimes thinks about the narrow-faced lit- tle animal. Had it banged its head against the wall, or do kittens have infant spasms too? I'm happy that it didn't have to suffer long, and that I know what happened to it. Of course I didn't grieve as I did for Pearl, but I missed it a little nevertheless.

The ones who were left were, as it gradually turned out, actually tomcats. Since it was so warm they played outside by the door as well, and worried me by constantly wanting to creep into the bushes. Early on they started catching flies and beetles, and made painful acquaintance with the big wood ants. Their mother kept a close eye on them at first, but I noticed that the business of rearing children was starting to wear her out. In any case the clouts she distributed were increasingly violent. I couldn't hold it against her, as the kittens were both wild and disobedient. I called them Tiger and Panther. Panther had light gray and black stripes, and Tiger dark gray and black stripes on a reddish background. When I had a little time I liked to watch them playing their predatory games. That's how it happened that the two tomcats got names while the little bull was still nameless. No name for him had occurred to me. The old cat was nameless as well, after all. Of course she had a hundred pet names, but she never got a name that lasted. I don't think she'd have got used to it anyway.

The crows, which might have been a danger to the kittens, had left for their unknown summer hunting ground when the weather turned warm, and there was no sign of the owl either. Sometimes, when I sat on the bench in the sun thinking about Panther and Tiger's origins, I thought they had a chance of survival. I hadn't managed simply to ignore them, of course. I was already starting to worry about them. I wished they would both quickly grow big and strong and learn all the tricks from their sly mother. But before they had learned anything more than catching flies Panther disappeared in the bushes and never came back. Lynx looked for him, but he was never found. Perhaps a predator carried him off.

Tiger stayed behind on his own. For a long time he searched and cried for his brother, and when he didn't find him he played with his mother again, or with Lynx, or with me. If nobody was paying him any attention he would dash after a fly, play with twigs or little balls of paper that I tore from a thriller for him. It hurt me to see him so alone. He was so beautifully marked and fully lived up to his name. I've never known a wilder and livelier cat. Over time he became my cat, because his mother wouldn't have anything to do with him anymore, and Lynx was afraid of his sharp claws. So he attached himself entirely to me, and treated me alternately as a surrogate mother and as a companion in his rough and tumble. I took a lot of scratches before he finally understood that he had to draw in his claws when playing. He shredded everything he could get hold of in the hunting lodge, and sharpened his claws on the legs of the table and the bedposts. I didn't mind that, though. I had no valuable furniture, after all, and even if I had, a living cat would have been more important to me than the most beautiful piece of furniture. Tiger will crop up a lot in my report. I couldn't keep him for even a year. It's still hard for me to understand that such a lively creature is dead. Sometimes I imagine that he went and joined Mr. Ka-au Ka-au in the forest and is leading a free and wild life. But those are only daydreams. I know, of course, that he's dead. Or he would have kept coming back to me, at least for a while.

Perhaps, in the spring, the cat will run back into the forest and have kittens again. Who knows. The big forest tomcat may well be dead, or, after her serious illness last year, the cat may never be able to have kittens again. But if there are young cats, it will all happen all over again. I shall make my mind up not to care for them, then I'll grow fond of them, and then I'll lose them. I often look forward to a time when there won't be anything left to grow attached to. I'm tired of everything being taken away from me. Yet there's no escape, for as long as there's something for me to love in the forest, I shall love it; and if some day there is nothing, I shall stop living. If everyone had been like me there would never have been a wall, and the old man wouldn't have had to lie petrified by his spring. But I understand why the others always had the upper hand. Loving and looking after another creature is a very troublesome business, and much harder than killing and destruction. It takes twenty years to bring up a child, and ten seconds to kill it. It took the bull a year to grow big and strong, and a few strokes of an ax were enough to dispatch him. I think about the long time that Bella carried him patiently in her body, the arduous hours of his birth and the long months during which he grew from a little calf to a big bull. The sun had to shine and grow the grass for him, water had to spring from the earth and fall from the sky to slake his thirst. He had to be combed and brushed, and his dung had to be cleared away so that he could lie in a dry bed. And it had all been in vain. I can only see it as a hideous muddle and extravagance. Perhaps the person who killed him was mad; but even his madness betrayed him. The secret wish to murder must have been dormant within him. I'm even inclined to pity his state of mind, but again and again I try to obliterate him from my memory because it is unbearable to think that someone like that could go on murdering and destroying. I don't think anyone else of his kind is living in the forest, but I've become as suspicious as my cat. My rifle always hangs loaded on the wall, and I never set foot outside the house without my sharp jackknife. I've given these things a great deal of thought, and perhaps I've reached the point where I can understand even murderers. Their hate for everything capable of creating new life must be terrible. I understand it, but I, personally, have to resist it. There is no longer any human being to protect or work for me so I can devote myself to my thoughts undisturbed.

As the weather in April stayed reasonably fine I decided to spread dung on the potato field. The dung heap had grown, and I filled two sacks and lugged them to the field on birch branches. I spread the dung in the furrows and distributed the earth on top. I put dung on the little bean garden as well; then there was hay to be fetched from the gorge again, and then wood was in short supply and I spent a week sawing and chopping. I was tired, but pleased that the work had started again, and that it already stayed light for a long time in the evenings. The question of moving to the Alm occupied my mind more with every passing day. The task struck me as terribly arduous, even if I were to take only necessities with me and live quite primitively in the pasture. I was also worried about the cats. It's always been true that they're more attached to a house than a human being. I was hell-bent on taking them with me, but that too could end unhappily. The longer I thought about it, the more the difficulties seemed insuperable. After all, I couldn't neglect the meadow by the stream and the potato field. The hay harvest had to be brought in, and that meant a seven-hour journey every day, and the work on top of that. I had to put off cutting logs for the winter until the autumn, and there wouldn't be any trout for the whole summer. While I turned it around in my head and found it impracticable, I was already aware that I'd already decided long before to go up to the pasture. It was a good idea for Bella and the bull, and I simply had to be able to do the work. We were all too dependent on the survival of those two for me to be able to consider myself. The forest meadow probably wasn't enough for two cattle, and I would have to save the hay from the meadow by the stream for the winter. Once I realized that I'd decided to move long before, when I'd first seen the green pastures, I grew calmer, but also a little depressed. I wanted to stay until I'd planted the potatoes, and also try to lay in a supply of wood by then. So I set about cutting wood. I worked slowly, but every day, and piled up the logs around the hut. And finally there came a Sunday when I only worked in the byre and spent the rest of the time asleep. I was so tired that I imagined I wouldn't be able to get up again. On the Monday, however, I did go back to the log pile and dragged wood to the house.

Spring was blossoming around me, and all I could see was wood. The yellow pile of sawdust grew daily. Resin stuck to my hands. Splinters pierced my skin, my shoulders hurt, but I was as if possessed by the wish to cut as much wood as possible. It gave me a feeling of security. I was much too tired to be hungry, and looked after my animals like a robot. I was actually living on milk alone, I'd never drunk so much milk before. And then, quite suddenly, I knew I had to stop. I had no strength left. I emerged from my working frenzy and went around in my nightshirt and slippers and took care of myself. I also slowly began eating again, nettle spinach and potatoes.

In the meantime the cat had entirely ceased to care for her wild son. If he clumsily approached her she gave him a clout and let him know in no uncertain terms that his childhood was at an end. Tiger had assumed the manners of a proper little rogue. He didn't dare go near his mother, but he tormented poor Lynx throughout the day. And that dog was so patient! With one bite he could have killed the little tomcat, and yet how carefully he treated him. One day, however, the moment seemed to have arrived, even for Lynx, when Tiger had to be taught a lesson. He took the little one by the ear, dragged him struggling and squawking through the room and hurled him under my bed. Then he walked evenly to the stove, where he was finally able to go to sleep in peace. Even Tiger understood. But as it was impossible for him to be nice and quiet, he chose me as his next victim to pounce on.

I was very tired from cutting wood, but he wouldn't leave me in peace. I had always to be throwing him little balls, or running after him. He particularly enjoyed hiding and, when I walked innocently past, biting my legs. All he lacked was little hands to clap with when I jumped aside with a start. His mother watched all this with visible disapproval. I think she despised me for not retaliating. And really, Tiger often was a pest. But when I thought about his sister's fate I couldn't spurn him. He thanked me in his own way, by settling to sleep on my lap, rubbing his head against my forehead, or standing on the table, propping his front paws against my chest and looking at me attentively with honey-colored eyes. His eyes were darker and warmer than his mother's, and his nose was speckled with a fine, brownish rime, as if he'd just been drinking coffee. I grew very fond of him, and he returned my affection with something akin to passion. No human being had ever hurt him, after all, and he hadn't shared his mother's unhappy experiences. He was always wanting to go with me to the byre. There he sat on the stove and watched, attentively and with his whiskers sticking out, as I looked after Bella and the bull. It didn't take him long to understand that Bella was the source of the sweet milk, and immediately after milking I had to fill his little dish. He only ever approached the two big animals cautiously, ready to dash away.

Since Tiger had become so attached to me, Lynx had become a little jealous. One day I took him aside, stroked first him and then the little tomcat, and explained to him that nothing in our friendship had changed. I don't know what he really understood, but from then on he put up with the little tomcat, and as he could see that Tiger mattered to me he became his protector. The minute Tiger went into the bushes Lynx fetched him back by the scruff of the neck. The old cat paid no attention to these matters. She had returned to her own way of life, slept during the day and went hunting at night. Toward morning she would come back and go to sleep purring, pressed up against my legs. Tiger had retained a childlike affection for the cupboard and slept in his old bed. He still hadn't worked out that he was actually a nocturnal animal, and much preferred playing in the sunshine. I was happy about this, for during the day it was possible to keep an eye on him, and when I went off with Lynx I would shut him up in one of the rooms.

I hadn't been mistaken in my dark apprehensions. May started out cold and wet. There was even snow and hail, and I was pleased that the apple blossom had already faded. I had only three wrinkled apples left, and once when I was very hungry I ate all three in one go. The nettles were snowed under again, and all the spring flowers along with them. I didn't have much time to worry about flowers.

Once in the spring, when I was fetching hay from the barn, I saw three or four violets. I absently reached out my hand and leaned against the wall. I'd imagined I could smell their scent, but when my hand touched the wall the scent had gone as well. The violets held their little purple faces to me, but I couldn't touch them. Slight though this experience was, it had a profoundly disturbing effect on me. In the evening I sat by the lamp for a long time with Tiger in my lap, trying to calm down. While I slowly stroked Tiger to sleep I gradually forgot the violets and started to feel at home again. That's all that's left me of the first spring's flowers, the memory of those violets and the cool smoothness of the wall against my palms.

Around the tenth of May I started drawing up a list of

the things I wanted to take up to the Alm. There wasn't a lot, but there was still much too much, bearing in mind that I would have to carry everything up there on my back. I weeded things out, weeded yet more things out, but there was still too much. Finally I divided everything, for making separate trips. I would have to spend several days on the move, as I couldn't lug too much uphill at once. That day I considered how I could get everything done in the best, most rational way. On the fourteenth of May the weather finally turned clement and mild again, and I had to plant the potatoes. I was late already, and couldn't put it off any longer. I'd enlarged the field in the autumn; while I was working on it, however, I noticed that it was still too small, and dug over another patch of land. I stuck branches into the ground there, because I wanted to know whether the dung would have any effect on the harvest. I'd had to remove one side of the fence, and fixed it up again with branches and vines. I didn't have many potatoes left now, but I was pleased not to have touched the seed stock.

On the twentieth of May I began the move. I packed Hugo's big rucksack and my own, and set off with Lynx. The meadow at the Alm was free of snow, and the young grass was green and glistened moistly beneath the blue sky. Lynx charged impetuously off across the soft grass. For some reason he kept rolling over, and looked very gauche and funny. At the hut I unpacked the rucksacks, drank tea from the flask and then lay down in bed on the pallet to rest a little. There was a kitchen with a bed and a small bedroom. I couldn't bear to stay on the pallet for long; I had to have a look at the byre. It was, of course, much bigger than my byre, and had been kept much cleaner than the hut, and it seemed to be in working order, even if the wooden pipes had already rotted a bit. There was a little pile of wood in the stable, which was perhaps enough for two weeks. I wanted to get by with sticks throughout the summer. There was an ax as well, and that was all I needed. The important thing was the dairy implements, a few pails and barrels in which cheese had probably been made in the past. I didn't need to bring any pots and pans either, as there were enough there for one person. I was struck by the fact that the dairy things, in contrast to the pots and pans, had been kept scrupulously clean, just as the byre had been kept so much cleaner than the hut. The dairyman seemed to have made a clear distinction between private and business matters.

I decided to leave the lamp in the hunting lodge as well, and make do with candles and a torch. But I did want to bring the little spirit stove so that I wouldn't have to heat the oven on warm days. The move was certainly worthwhile as far as Bella and the bull were concerned. It was light and sunny up here, and there was enough fodder for a few months. Also, summer would soon be at an end, and perhaps the sun and the dry air would cure my rheumatism completely. Lynx sniffed inquisitively at each object, and seemed thoroughly to concur with all my intentions. It was one of his most lovable aspects, the fact that he approved of everything I did, but it was dangerous for me too, and often encouraged me to do things that were stupid or foolhardy.

In the days that followed I gradually brought to the pasture everything I considered to be absolutely necessary, and on the twenty-fifth of May came the day of departure from the hunting lodge. For the previous few days I had grazed Bella and the bull in the clearing, so that the little one could get used to walking out in the open a bit. The change had made the bull cheerfully excited. After all, the only thing he had ever known was the constant gloom of the stable. The first day in the meadow was perhaps the happiest day in his life. I left a note on the table: "Gone to the Alm," and then locked up the hunting lodge. While I was writing the note, I was surprised at the absurd hope that it expressed, but I simply couldn't help it. I carried the rucksack, the shotgun, the binoculars and the alpenstock. I led Bella beside me on the rope. The little bull stayed close to his mother, and I wasn't afraid that he might run away. In any case I had ordered Lynx to keep an eye on him.

I had put the two cats in a box with air holes, which I tied on to the rucksack. I didn't know how else I could have transported them. They took terrible umbrage at this treatment, and cried furiously in their prison. At first Bella was a little unsettled by their caterwauling, then she got used to it and walked peacefully along by my side. I was very nervous, and afraid that either she or the bull might fall or break a leg. But the journey went better than I had imagined. After an hour the old cat acquiesced in her fate, and only Tiger's pitiful cries echoed in my ears. Sometimes I would stop to allow the little bull to have a break, as he wasn't used to walking. He and Bella used these respites to pull the young leaves peacefully from the trees. They were much less nervous than I was, and seemed quite happy with this expedition. I gave the persistent Tiger a good talking-to, with the sole result that the old cat started vociferating furiously again as well. So in the end I let them both go on screeching, and tried not to listen.

The path was quite well maintained, but laid in serpentine curves, and it was still four hours before our curious procession reached the pasture. It was already approaching midday. I let Bella and the bull graze beside the hut, and ordered Lynx to keep an eye on them. I was completely exhausted, less from physical effort than from nervous tension. The screeching of the cats finally became unbearable. In the hut I closed the door and the window and let out the two squallers. The old cat ran hissing under the bed, and after a last plaintive cry Tiger fled for the stove door. I tried to comfort them, but they would have nothing to do with me so I let them stay where they were. I lay down on the pallet and closed my eyes. Only after a half hour did I feel capable of getting up and going outside. Lynx stood drinking at the stream, without taking his eyes off his charges. I praised and stroked him, and he was visibly pleased to be released from his guard duty. Bella had lain down, and the bull lay close by her side, looking so exhausted that I started to get worried again. I offered both of them a bowl of water. In future they could drink from the stream. There was no danger of their daring to wander too far away in their weary state. We had all earned a little peace. I lay down on the bed again. I had to close the hut door for the sake of the cats. Lynx had lain down under a shady bush beside the hut for a little snooze. In a few minutes I had gone to sleep too, and I slept until evening and awoke still tired and irritable. The hut was thick with dirt, and that disturbed me a great deal. It was by now too late to start spring cleaning. So I only washed the necessary pots with the wire brush and sand, and put a little pot of potatoes on the spirit stove. Then I dismantled the bed and carted the musty pallet to the meadow and beat it with a stick. A cloud of dust arose. I couldn't do anything more for the time being, but resolved to lay the pallet outside to air on every fine day.

The sun sank behind the spruce trees behind the gentle grassy slopes, and it grew cool. Bella and the bull had revived, and were grazing peacefully in their new meadow. I would have liked to leave them outside overnight, but then I didn't dare and drove them into the stable. I had no straw, and they had to sleep on the wood floor. I poured more water into the trough and then left the two of them on their own. Meanwhile the potatoes had cooked long enough, and I ate them with butter and milk. Lynx was given the same supper, and while I was eating, Tiger crept from his hiding place too, enticed by the sweet smell of milk. He drank a bit of warm milk and then, seized with curiosity, investigated everything in the hut. Just as I was opening the wardrobe he crept straight in. I think it was a stroke of luck that, in the Alm hut as well as in the hunting lodge, there was a wardrobe in the kitchen. From that moment on Tiger came to terms with the move. He had his cupboard, and he was reconciled to life once more. He slept in it all summer long. His mother wouldn't be enticed out from under the bed, so I put down some milk for her, washed myself in cold water at the stream and went to bed. I left the window open, and the cool air wafted over my face. I had brought only a little pillow and two woolen blankets with me, and missed my warm, soft quilt. The straw rustled beneath me, but I was still tired enough to be able to go to sleep quickly.

In the night I was woken by the moonlight falling on my face. It was all very strange, and to my astonishment I realized I was homesick for the hunting lodge. Only when I heard Lynx snoring quietly in the stove door did my heart lighten a little, and I tried to go back to sleep, but didn't manage to for a long time. I got up and looked under the bed. The cat wasn't there. I looked for her all through the hut, but without success. She must have jumped out of the window while I was asleep. There was no point in calling her, she never came. I lay down again, staring at the sky, waiting for the little gray shape to appear again. That made me so tired that I went back to sleep.

I was woken by Tiger taking a stroll on me and brushing my cheek with his cold nose. It wasn't yet light, and for a few moments I was confused and couldn't work out why my bed was the wrong way around. But Tiger was fully rested, and in the mood for a little game. Then I realized where I was, and that the old cat had run off in the night. I tried to escape back into sleep from all the unpleasantnesses of the new day. This infuriated Tiger, and he stuck his claws into the blanket and screeched so loudly that sleep became unthinkable. I sat up resignedly and lit the candle. It was half past four, and the first cold glimmer of dawn mingled with the yellow candlelight. Tiger's morning euphoria was one of his most tiresome qualities. I got up with a sigh and looked for the old cat. She hadn't come back. Depressed, I heated up a little milk on the cooker and tried to bribe Tiger. He drank the milk, but then got into a state of cheerful frenzy and pretended he thought my ankles were big white mice that he wanted to put out of their misery. Of course it was all show; he bit and scratched, purring wildly, but without scratching my skin. But it was enough to drive the last hint of sleepiness from my mind. Lynx too had been woken by the scuffle, crept out from the stove door and barked encouragingly in accompaniment to Tiger's mock battles. Regular sleeping hours were unknown to Lynx; the minute I attended to him he was wide awake; if I failed to pay him attention and he couldn't make me do so, he simply went to sleep. I couldn't share the high spirits of the other two because I was thinking about the old cat. So I opened the door, and Lynx dashed outside while Tiger went on with his wild dancing exercises.

The sky was pale gray, turning rosy in the east, and the meadow was thick with dew. A fine day was dawning. It was strange to be able to survey a wide area, unimpeded by mountains and trees. And it wasn't immediately pleasant and liberating. My eyes had to get used to the distance first, after a year spent in the narrow basin of the valley. It was disagreeably cool. I grew chilly and went into the house to put on some warm clothes. The cat's continued absence depressed me a great deal. I knew straightaway that she wasn't anywhere nearby, but had run back to the valley. But had she actually managed to get there? I had betrayed her trust, which was not yet very well established in any case. Her disappearance cast a gloomy shadow over the dawning summer day. I couldn't do anything about that, and so I went about my work as I did every day. I milked Bella and drove her and the bull to the meadow. Tiger showed no signs of running away, he was still young and adaptable. Perhaps he didn't yet feel strong enough to stand on his own two feet.

That morning I drowned my anxiety in tea (I like to remember the time when I still had tea). Its aroma cheered me up, and I began to persuade myself that the old cat would spend the summer in the hunting lodge and greet me happily when I returned in the autumn. Why should that not be possible? She was, after all, a crafty female, familiar with every danger. For a while I sat quite peacefully at the dirty table, watching the sky grow red through the little window. Lynx was taking a look about his surroundings, Tiger had interrupted his game and dragged himself off to the cupboard for an extended snooze. It was quite quiet in the hut. Something new was beginning. I didn't know what it would bring me, but my homesickness and worries about the future gradually left me. I saw the expanse of the alpine meadows, behind them a strip of forest and above them the great, curved bow of the sky, the moon hanging, a pale circle, at its western edge while the sun rose in the east. The air was sharp and I breathed more deeply. I began to find the pasture beautiful, strange and dangerous, but, like everything strange, full of mysterious enticement.

Finally I tore myself from the bewitching view and set about cleaning the hut. I lit the stove for hot water, and then rubbed the table, the bench and the floor with sand and an old brush that I'd found in the bedroom. I had to repeat the process twice, and great streams of water flowed to that purpose. Afterward the hut was still not especially inhabitable, but at least it was clean. In places I had to scrape off the dirt with a knife. I don't think the floor had ever come in contact with water before, at least not during the time of the pinup-worshipping dairyman. I left the picture hanging on the wardrobe, incidentally. As time passed I even grew quite fond of it. It reminded me a little of my daughters. Cleaning the hut was a task that I liked. I left the door and window open and let the clean air pass through the house. When the floor dried in the course of the morning it began to take on a reddish sheen, and I was proud of this success. I had laid the pallet on the meadow, and Lynx immediately made his bed there. When I chased him from it, he withdrew, disgruntled, behind the hut. He disliked domestic cleaning work, because I had forbidden him to march about on the wet floor. After the water and air baths the hut lost its sour smell, and I started to feel a bit better. There were milk and potatoes for lunch, and I realized that I would have to get hold of some meat for Lynx's sake. I decided, since it had to be done, to do it as soon as possible, particularly since the area was still unfamiliar to me and I couldn't count on immediate success. It was only on the second day, after four futile hunting expeditions, that I managed to shoot a young stag, and a very disagreeable problem arose. I didn't have a spring here to cool the meat, so I had to use up the perishable parts promptly and store the rest either boiled or fried in the cool bedroom. Consequently we spent the whole summer alternating between lean and very fat times, and I was forced each time to throw away a part of the meat because it had gone off. I left it far from the hut in the forest, and it regularly disappeared overnight. Some wild animal must have had a very good summer. The food situation was not at all good, as I had only very few potatoes left; but we never really had to starve. During my time in the Alm I wrote no diary entries. I had taken the diary with me and dutifully ticked off each day, but I didn't even enter such important events as the hay harvest. The memory of that time has remained fresh, however, and it isn't hard for me to write about it. I shall never forget the fragrance of summer, the rainstorms and the evenings glittering with stars.

On the afternoon of the first day I sat on the bench in front of the hut warming myself in the sun. I had tied Bella to a post. The little bull never wandered far from his mother. Only a week later I abandoned this precautionary measure. Bella was by nature agreeable and even-tempered and never caused me the slightest trouble, and her son was at that time a happy and impetuous calf. He grew considerably larger and stronger, and I still hadn't found a name for him. Of course there were lots of names for a bull, but I didn't like them, and they all sounded a bit silly. In any case he was already used to being called Bull, and followed me about like a big dog. So I left it at that, and in time I stopped even thinking about giving him another name. He was an innocent, trusting creature, and, as I could clearly see, considered life to be one long pleasure. Even today I'm glad that Bull's youth was spent so happily. He never heard an angry word, was never pushed or beaten, was allowed to drink his mother's milk, eat tender plants in the pasture and sleep at night in Bella's warm aura. There is no finer life for a little bull, and that's how well he lived for a while. Born at another time and in the valley he would long since have been sent to the slaughterhouse.

After the first week spent working in the byre and the stable and collecting fallen wood, I wanted to have a little look at the surrounding region. The hut in the pasture nestled in the broad green trough of the meadows between two steep mountain ridges, which I couldn't climb because I had a touch of vertigo and didn't feel up to clambering along the paths of the chamois. I visited the vantage point again, and surveyed the countryside with the binoculars. I never saw any smoke rising or any movement in the roads. In fact the roads only looked hazy now. They must have been overgrown with weeds in places. I tried to find my bearings with Hugo's road map. I was at the northern end of an extended massif that stretched toward the southeast. I'd visited both valleys that led from my hut to the foothills of the Alps; I lived in one of them, after all. But that area was only a small part of the massif. I had no way of finding out how far the free area extended toward the southeast. I couldn't stray too far from the house, and even with Lynx such an undertaking would have struck me as dangerous. If the whole massif was free, it could only contain hunting grounds, all of them leased and not freely accessible, for otherwise right on the first of May a load of tourists would have arrived and happened upon me long ago. For hours I studied the mountain ridges and valley clefts that lay before me, but I could detect no trace of human life. Either the wall crossed the mountains diagonally or I was the only person in the whole massif. The latter possibility sounded a little unlikely, but it wasn't unthinkable. On the eve of a holiday all the woodcutters and hunters could well have stayed at home. In any case it struck me that new stags which I hadn't seen before kept appearing in my hunting ground. Before, all stags had looked the same to me, but in the course of a year I'd learned to tell my stags from strangers. These strangers had to come from somewhere. At least a part of the mountain must have been free. In the chalk cliffs I sometimes saw chamois, but not many, since the mange had gained ground.

I decided to make little reconnaissance expeditions, and found a slope in the pine forest that I dared to climb. If I took a break after early milking at six o'clock I would be able to go out for four hours into the mountains and still come back in daylight. On days like that I tethered Bella and Bull, but concern for them followed me wherever I went. I invaded entirely unfamiliar hunting grounds, and found a few hunting lodges and woodcutters' huts from which I took things that were still serviceable. The luckiest find was a little sack of flour that had stayed miraculously dry. The hut I found it in was in a very sunny clearing, and in any case the flour had been kept shut up in a cupboard. I also found a little packet of tea, tobacco, a bottle of paraffin, old newspapers and a moldy, flyblown side of bacon that I left behind. All the huts were overgrown with bushes and stinging nettles, and the rain had come through some of the roofs, leaving them in a bad state.

There was something ghostly about the whole endeavor. Mice rustled in the pallets where men had slept a year before. They were now the masters of the old huts. They had gnawed and eaten all the supplies that hadn't been kept shut away. They'd even nibbled at old coats and shoes. And there was a smell of mice; a disagreeable, sharp smell that filled every hut and had driven away the old familiar smell of smoke, sweaty men and bacon. Even Lynx, who had set off on these reconnaissance expeditions very eagerly, seemed depressed the minute we went into a hut, and hurried to get outside again. I couldn't overcome my resistance to the idea of eating in one of the huts, so we had our modest, cold meals on a tree trunk, and Lynx drank from the streams that always flowed near the huts. Very soon I had had enough. I knew I would never find anything but a wilderness of nettles, the smell of mice and sad, cold fireplaces. One hot, still day I spread out the flour, that precious discovery, on a cloth in the sun. It wasn't damp, but it seemed to me that the smell of mice hung about it, too. After it had lain in the sun and air for a day I found it edible. That flour helped me make it through to the next potato harvest. I used it, with milk and butter, to bake thin dough cakes in an iron frying pan, the first bread I had had for a year. It was a holiday; Lynx too seemed to remember past pleasures as the scents arose, and of course I couldn't let him go hungry.

Once, when I was sitting at the vantage point, I thought I could see smoke rising from the spruce trees a long way off. I had to put down the binoculars because my hands started to tremble. When I had got a grip on myself and looked again, there was nothing to be seen. I stared through the binoculars until my eyes watered and everything flowed together into a green mist. I waited for an hour, and went back there for the next few days, but I never saw the smoke again. Either I had conjured something up for myself or the wind—there was a foehn that day—had blown the smoke down. I will never know. In the end I went home with a headache. Lynx, who had waited beside me all afternoon, must have thought I was a boring fool. He didn't like the vantage point at all, and always tried to persuade me to go on different walks. I say persuade, because I can't think of a better word for what he did. He would get in front of me and push me in a different direction, or temptingly run a few steps ahead and look back at me encouragingly. He would keep on until I gave in or until he understood that I wasn't to be persuaded. He probably didn't like the vantage point because he had to sit still there and I didn't pay him any attention. It's also possible that he noticed the gloomy mood I sank into when I looked through the binoculars. Sometimes he sensed my mood before I was aware of it myself. He certainly wouldn't have liked to see me now, sitting at home every day, but his little shade no longer has the strength to push me on to new paths.

Lynx lies buried in the Alm. Beneath the bush with the dark green leaves that exuded a faint fragrance when I rubbed them between my fingers. The very place where he had his first nap when we arrived at the pasture. Even if he had no other choice, he couldn't have laid down more than his life for me. It was all he owned, a short and happy dog's life: a thousand stimulating scents, the sun's warmth on his fur, cold spring water on his tongue, breathless hunts for deer, sleep in the warm stove door when the winter wind blew around the hut, a caressing human hand and a beloved, wonderful human voice.

After I had abandoned the expeditions into unfamiliar hunting grounds I sank very slowly into a sort of paralysis. I stopped worrying and tended to sit on the bench in front of the hut, simply gazing into the blue sky. All my energy and competence slipped from me, making way for a peaceful lethargy. I knew that this state could become dangerous, but even that didn't matter much to me. It no longer disturbed me that I had to live on a kind of primitive summer holiday; the sun, the high and distant sky above the meadow, and the fragrance that rose from it, gradually turned me into a stranger. I probably didn't make any entries about this in my diary because it all struck me as a little unreal. The Alm lay outside of time. Later, during the hay harvest, when I returned from the underworld of the damp gorge, I seemed to be coming back to a land which mysteriously released me from myself. All my fears and memories stayed behind beneath the dark spruces, to attack me every time I went down there. It was as if the big meadow exuded a mild narcotic called oblivion.

After I'd been living up at the Alm for three weeks I roused myself to pay a visit to the potato field. It was the first cool and dull day after a long period of fine weather. I left Bella and Bull in the stable with green fodder and locked Tiger in the hut. To be on the safe side I'd filled his little box with earth and left meat and milk for him. Lynx came with me, as always. At around nine o'clock I reached the hunting lodge. I don't know what I'd hoped or feared. Everything was quite unchanged. The nettles had grown and engulfed the dung heap. When I went into the house, I immediately saw the familiar little hollow on the bed. I went around the house and called the cat, but she didn't come. Neither was I sure that the impression hadn't been left in May. So I carefully brushed the bed smooth and left a little meat in the cat's bowl. Lynx sniffed at the floor and the cat door. But he might have been following old scents. I opened all the windows, including the one in the store cupboard, and let the fresh air sweep through the house. I did the same in the byre as well. Then I investigated the potato field. The potatoes had grown beautifully, and the ones that hadn't been fertilized were actually a little smaller and not such a dark green. Thanks to the long drought the field wasn't very overgrown, and I decided to wait for a fall of rain before hoeing. The beans, too, were already twisting up the sticks. The grass in the meadow by the stream wasn't as lush as it had been the previous year, and desperately needed rain. But there were still a few weeks left before the harvest, and a chance that it might recover quickly after a fall of rain. While I looked at the big, steep meadow I grew quite despondent. The idea that I would get it done was inconceivable, with a long walk on top of everything else. The previous year, when I hadn't had a long journey to get there, the meadow had almost finished me off. I couldn't understand why I hadn't even thought about that in the Alm. It was strange; as soon as I was in the valley I thought about the Alm almost with fear or revulsion; but from the pasture I couldn't imagine living in the valley. It was as if I consisted of two quite different people, one of whom could exist only in the valley, while the other was beginning to flourish in the Alm. It all scared me a little, because I couldn't understand it.

I looked through the wall. The little house was completely covered with shrubs. I couldn't see the old man; he must have been lying behind a wall of nettles that covered the stream. The world, it seemed to me, was slowly being swallowed by nettles. The stream had grown quite small in the drought. There were a few trout in the ponds, barely moving. That summer they were having a honeymoon period, and might recover.

The gorge was as gloomy and damp as ever; nothing had changed. It was drizzling a little, and light mist hung in the beech trees. Not a single salamander showed its face; they were probably sleeping under the damp stones. I hadn't seen any so far that summer, only green and brown lizards in the pasture. Once Tiger had bitten one to death and laid it at my feet. He had the habit of laying all his trophies at my feet: enormous grasshoppers, beetles and gleaming flies. The lizard had been his first big success. He looked up at me expectantly, the light reflecting golden yellow in his eyes. I had to praise and stroke him. What should I have done? I'm not the god of lizards, nor the god of cats. I'm an outsider, who shouldn't get involved. Sometimes I can't help it, and play Providence a little; I save an animal from certain death or shoot a deer because I need meat. But the forest copes easily with my confusion. A new deer is born, another runs headlong to its doom. I'm not a troublemaker worth taking seriously. The nettles beside the byre will go on growing, even if I exterminate them a hundred times, and they will survive me. They have so much more time than I do. One day I shall no longer exist, and no one will cut the meadow, the thickets will encroach upon it and later the forest will push as far as the wall and win back the land that man has stolen from it. Sometimes my thoughts grow confused, and it is as if the forest has put down roots in me, and is thinking its old, eternal thoughts with my brain. And the forest doesn't want human beings to come back.

Back then, in the second summer, I hadn't reached that point. The demarcation lines were still rigidly drawn up. I find it hard to separate my old self from my new self, and I'm not sure that my new self isn't gradually being absorbed into something larger that thinks of itself as "We." It was the Alm's fault. It was almost impossible, in the buzzing stillness of the meadow, beneath the big sky, to remain a single and separate Self, a little, blind, independent life that didn't want to fit in with a greater Being. Once my major source of pride had been that I was just such a life, but in the Alm it suddenly struck me as pathetic and absurd, an overinflated Nothing.

From my first expedition to the hunting lodge I brought the last rucksack full of potatoes and Hugo's flannel pajamas back to the pasture. The nights were bitterly cold, and I missed my warm quilt. I got to the hut at about five o'clock; there it was in front of me, gray and glistening with rain. Suddenly I had the uncomfortable feeling that I didn't really belong anywhere, but after a few minutes it went away, and I was quite at home in the pasture again. Tiger cried furiously at me, and whisked past me into the open. The box of earth was untouched, and he had turned his nose up at the food. He must have been in terrible torment. When he came back he was still profoundly annoyed, sat down in a corner and showed me his rounded backside. His mother used to express her contempt for me in the same way. But Tiger was still a child, and after ten minutes he yielded to the temptations of companionship. Once he was well fed and placated he would finally walk to the wardrobe. I did the work in the byre, drank a little milk with my dough cakes, and crept into bed in Hugo's colossal pajamas. I had been pleased to see that everything was in good order in the valley. The hunting lodge was where it had always been, and there was even cause to hope that the old cat was still alive. As a child I had always suffered from the foolish fear that everything I could see disappeared as soon as I turned my back on it. No amount of reason could completely banish that fear. At school I would think about my parents' house and suddenly I would be able to see nothing but a big, empty patch where it had previously stood. I was later prey to nervous anxieties when my family wasn't at home. I was only really happy when they were all in bed or when we were all sitting around the table. For me, security meant being able to see and touch. And that's how it was for me that summer. When I was in the Alm I doubted the reality of the hunting lodge, and when I was in the valley the Alm dissolved to nothing in my imagination. And were my anxieties really so idiotic? Was the wall not a confirmation of my childhood fears? Overnight my former life, everything I was fond of, had been mysteriously stolen from me. If that had been possible, then anything could happen. In any case, I had been taught so much reason and discipline at an early age that I fought against every such impulse the minute it showed its face. But I don't know whether that kind of behavior is sane; perhaps the only sane reaction to all the things that have happened would be madness.

A few wet days followed. Bella and Bull were in the meadow, covered with delicate little gray drops, grazing or resting side by side. Lynx and Tiger slept through the days, and I sawed up the sticks in the stable. I had to heat the hut. I can go more easily without food than without warmth, and there were enough sticks. The winter storms had torn the branches from the trees, and uprooted the smaller trees. The saw had seen better days and cut very badly, but sticks are easy to saw up and it didn't cost me a lot of effort. I carried the wood to the hut and stacked it in the little bedroom. I was sorry that there were no twigs to lay down for Bella and Bull, but at that altitude there was no deciduous wood. The byre was clean and dry, though, and they didn't have to freeze. Having lugged the butter churn down to the valley, I had had to lug it back up even more laboriously. I couldn't do without it. Bella was giving so much milk that I intended to lay in a supply of clarified butter through the summer. In the pasture her milk became particularly tasty; Tiger seemed to think so too, and gorged himself until he had a little paunch.

When I combed Bella I sometimes told her how important she was to us all. She looked at me with moist eyes, and tried to lick my face. She had no idea how precious and irreplaceable she was. Here she stood, gleaming and brown, warm and relaxed, our big, gentle, nourishing mother. I could only show my gratitude by taking good care of her, and I hope I have done everything for Bella that a human being can do for their only cow. She liked it when I talked to her. Perhaps she would have liked the voice of any human being. It would have been easy for her to trample and gore me, but she licked my face and pressed her nostrils into my palm. I hope she dies before me; without me she would die miserably in winter. I no longer tie her up in the stable. If something should happen to me she will at least be able to batter down the door and have no need to die of thirst. A strong man could loosen the weak bolt, and Bella is stronger than the strongest man. I have to live with these fears; even if I resist them they constantly flow disruptively into my report.

After the short rainy spell I still had a few weeks until the hay harvest. During this time I wanted to recover my strength. It grew warm again, but it was hot only at midday. The nights at this high altitude were bitterly cold. It seldom rained, only after storms, but it rained violently and copiously. After a storm the sun would return to the pasture while the mists hung for days in the valley basin. All the animals flourished and were happy in their freedom, so I could be content as well. Only the thought of the old cat sometimes tormented me. It hurt me that she preferred to stay in the lonely hunting lodge, rather than being here with me and the creamy milk, stalking through the tall grass at night in search of abundant prey. A short time later I was able to persuade myself that she actually had found her way back to the hunting lodge. After a heavy rain shower I went to the valley to hoe the potato field. When I went into the hunting lodge I immediately saw the little hollow in the bed. There was no sign of the cat. I stroked the cool bedspread and hoped she would recognize my smell. I don't know whether she was capable of it, for according to my observations the feline sense of smell isn't particularly keen. Hearing is their sense. The meat that I'd left behind was untouched and dried up. I might have expected that, as she was much too suspicious to touch a strange piece of meat.

The potatoes bore pale purple blossoms, and had grown considerably after the rain. The weeds were easy to pull from the loose earth. I heaped the earth up a little around the plants, so it was three o'clock before I got back to the hunting lodge, made some tea and prepared something to eat for myself and Lynx. I didn't get to the pasture until around seven o'clock, and still had to see to Bella and Bull. Once again, Tiger hadn't touched his little box or his food, and fled furiously into the open. I realized that it was cruel to lock him in. He would never be a house cat. In future I would leave the bedroom window open for him. Perhaps he would stay calmly at home if he noticed that he was free to come and go as he pleased. Bella and Bull always had to go into the byre, however, if I stayed away for a day. I was afraid they might break the rope if something frightened them, and fall down the scree slope at the edge of the meadow. After I'd done my work in the stable, and Tiger's mute scorn had made way for a conciliatory mood, I was finally able to lie down.

The nights in the pasture were always too short. I didn't dream. The cool night air brushed over my face, everything seemed light and free, and the nights were never entirely dark. As it stayed light for a long time I went to bed later than I did in the valley. Every fine evening I sat on the bench in front of the house wrapped in my loden coat and watched the red glow of evening spread across the western sky. Later I saw the moon rising and the stars flashing. Lynx lay beside me on the bench, Tiger, a little gray shadow, flitted from tussock to tussock in pursuit of moths, and when he was tired he rolled up on my lap under my cape and started purring violently. I didn't think, I didn't reminisce, and I wasn't afraid. I just sat quite still, leaning against the wooden wall, tired and awake at the same time, and looked at the sky. I got to know all the stars; although I didn't know their names they soon grew familiar. The only ones I knew were the Plow and Venus. All the others remained nameless, the red, green, bluish and yellow ones. If I narrowed my eyes to slits I could see the infinite abysses opening up between the constellations. Huge black hollows behind dense star clusters. Sometimes I used the binoculars, but I preferred to look at the sky with my naked eye. That way I could see it all at once, while the view through the binoculars was rather confusing. The night, which had always frightened me, and which I had often defied with blazing lights, lost all its terror in the Alm. I had never really known it before, locked in stone houses behind blinds and curtains. The night wasn't dark at all. It was beautiful, and I started to love it. Even when it rained and a layer of clouds covered the sky, I knew that the stars were there, red, green, yellow and blue. They were always there, even during the day, when I couldn't see them.

When it grew cold and the dew fell I finally went into the hut. Lynx followed me sleepily, and Tiger stalked to his bed in the cupboard. I turned my back to the wall and went to sleep. For the first time in my life I was calm, not content or happy, but calm. It had something to do with the stars and the fact that I suddenly knew they were real, but why that was so I couldn't explain. It just was. It was as if a big hand had stopped the clock in my head. And immediately after that it was morning, Tiger went for a stroll over my body, the light of dawn fell on my face and further away, in the forest, a bird called. At first I'd missed the sleepy chorus of birds that had awoken me in the valley. The birds didn't sing and twitter in the pasture, they only had bright, hard calls.

I was awake, and ran barefoot in the dawning day. The meadow was quite still, covered with transparent drops which later, when the sun rose over the forest, gleamed in rainbow colors. I went into the byre to milk Bella and let her and Bull into the meadow. Bella was already awake and waiting for me. Her lazybones of a son still slept, head lolling, the hair on his forehead curled into locks that were damp with sleep. After that I cleaned the byre and then went into the hut to wash, change my clothes and have my breakfast. Lynx and Tiger drank milk still warm from the cow and then ran into the open. All day long the hut door stood open and the sunlight fell onto my bed. If the weather was cool and wet the hut felt uncomfortable to me. It was not much more than a roof over my head then, not a home like the hunting lodge. But it didn't rain often, and never for longer than one or two days. Tiger played with little balls of paper, and Lynx slept through in the stove door. I paid a lot of attention to the little tomcat. He wasn't little anymore, though, he'd grown a lot, and his muscles were very well-developed. His coat gleamed with health and his whiskers grew thick and magnificent. He was quite unlike his mother: stormy, in need of affection and always in a mood to play. His great passion was theater, always playing the same leading roles: the furious predator, terrible and frightening; the gentle, very young kitten, helpless and pitiful; the silent thinker, elevated above everyday matters (a role that he couldn't keep up for more than two minutes), and the severely offended tomcat, his manly honor wounded. His only audience was myself, for Lynx immediately went to sleep during these performances, since they didn't involve him. Nor was there the slightest recognizable trace of the gloomy and melancholic brooding that sometimes afflicts adult cats. In the pasture, of course, I had a lot of time to pay attention to Tiger, and that's how he came to be my playmate. But he was much fonder of his freedom than he was of me. He couldn't bear to be closed in and went twenty times a day to check that the door or the window was open. It was generally enough for him to make sure, and then he went back to the wardrobe and slept. Lynx had long ceased to be jealous. I don't think he took Tiger seriously. He did sometimes play with him, he would devote himself to the little one's games, but he was afraid of his temper tantrums. Whenever Tiger had one of his tantrums and raged through the hut, Lynx looked at me with the expression of a helpless adult, slightly irritated and uncomprehending. But I had to praise him without fail. He lived on my praise and wanted to hear over and over again that he was the best, the most beautiful and the cleverest of dogs. It was as important for him as eating or moving.

During those weeks in the Alm we all put on a bit of weight; but after the hay harvest I grew thin again, brown as wood and dried by the sun. But it hadn't come to that yet. I'd stopped imagining the problems that this hay harvest would cause me, and felt secure as a somnambulist does. When the time came, everything that needed doing would be done. And like a somnambulist I drifted through the warm and fragrant days and the star-spangled nights.

Sometimes I had to shoot a deer. It was still an ugly, bloody business, but I managed it without unnecessary misgivings. I very much missed the cold spring. I had to cook the meat, and then put it in earthenware pots in a tub full of cold water in the cool bedroom. I couldn't put it in the stream, because Bella and Bull drank from that. Tiger preferred raw meat, and when I didn't have any raw meat left for him he went hunting for mice. He had got to the point where he could look after himself if it came to it. That was a good thing, for there was a chance he might at some point have to get by all on his own and without my help. Back then I was constantly in search of green vegetables. I ate every little plant that smelled pleasant and edible. I made a mistake only once, and got violent stomach pains. I missed the nettles, and could hardly find any. They didn't seem to like it in the pasture. In the lowlands it must have been hot and dry all summer. There were three or four violent storms, and storms in the pasture struck me as much more severe than they were in the hunting lodge, where I felt somewhat sheltered by the tall trees and the mountain rising behind the house. In the Alm we lived in the midst of the raging cloud masses. I was frightened, as I always am when bombarded by loud noises, and also had a curious feeling of dizziness that I had never felt before. Tiger and Lynx crept shivering into the stove door, something that never occurred to them otherwise. I had to tie Bella and Bull up in the byre and close the shutters. It was a comfort to me that they were together, and could seek refuge in one another if they were frightened.

Violent as these storms were, the sky was clear the next morning, and the mists billowed only in the valley. The meadow seemed to be floating along on the clouds, a green and damply gleaming ship on the white foaming waves of a turbulent ocean. And the sea subsided very slowly, and the tips of the spruces rose from it wet and fresh. Then I knew the sun would have reached as far as the hunting lodge as well, and I thought of the cat, living all on her own in the damp basin.

Sometimes when I watched Bella and Bull I was glad they had no foreboding of the long winter in the byre. They knew only the present, the tender grass, the spread of the meadow, the warm air caressing their flanks, and the moonlight that fell on their bed at night. A life without fear and without hope. I was afraid of the winter, of cutting wood in the cold and damp. I no longer felt any traces of my rheumatic attack, but I knew that it might return in the winter. And still I had to stay mobile at all costs if I wanted to stay alive with my animals. I spent hours lying in the sunshine, trying to store it up for the long cold spell. I didn't get sunburned, my skin had toughened much too much for that, but my head ached and my heart beat quicker than it should have done. Although I immediately came down to earth and stopped my sunbathing, it had enfeebled me so much that I had to spend a week recuperating.

Lynx was very discontented because I wouldn't go into the forest with him, and Tiger complained and tried to tempt me to play. July had come, and I was weak and apathetic. I forced myself to eat and did everything to make myself strong again in time for the hay harvest. Around the twentieth of July the moon was waxing, and I decided to wait no longer and exploit the good weather. One morning I got up at three o'clock, milked Bella, who was somewhat indignant about this irregularity, and carried a day's green fodder and water into the byre. With a heavy heart I left the window open for Tiger and put out meat and milk for him, and after a hearty breakfast, at four o'clock, Lynx and I left the pasture.

By seven o'clock I was in the meadow by the stream, swinging the scythe. My scything was still a little stiff, and didn't have the right swing to it. It was a good thing that the sun didn't shine here until around nine o'clock, for by then really it was too late for scything. I scythed for three hours, and I found it went better than I'd thought it would after the long walk; better than the previous year, when I had touched the scythe for the first time in twenty years and hadn't yet grown accustomed to hard work. Then I lay down under a hazel bush and didn't stir. Lynx came back from his little foraging expedition and lay down panting beside me. I sat up again with difficulty and drank tea from the flask, then I fell asleep. When I awoke, ants were running over my bare arms, and it was two o'clock. Lynx looked at me attentively. He seemed relieved that I had woken up, and jumped up cheerfully. I felt terribly weary, and my shoulders ached severely.

The sun cast its full brilliance on the slope. The fresh-cut swathes of hay already lay wilted and dull. I stood up and began to turn them with the fork. The meadow was one great hum of startled insects. I worked slowly, almost drowsily, abandoning myself entirely to the buzzing, hot stillness. Lynx, who had checked that everything was all right with me, trotted to the stream and drank in long, lapping gulps, then lay down in the shade, his head on his paws, his mournfully wrinkled face entirely hidden by his long ears, and dozed away. I envied him.

When I'd finished turning the hay I went to the hunting lodge. The hollow of the cat on my bed put me into a slightly better mood. After I'd fed Lynx and eaten a little cold meat myself, I sat down on the bench in front of the house. I called the cat, but she didn't come. Then I stroked the bed smooth, locked the door and wandered into the mountains.

It was seven o'clock by the time I got to the pasture, and I immediately went to the stable and milked the impatient Bella, who was already restless, discomforted by all the milk that had been building up inside her. Then, since it was such a fine day, I let her and Bull into the meadow and tethered them to a post. Tiger was lying on my bed, and greeted me with affection and reproach. He had eaten and drunk this time, because he hadn't been shut in. I gave him warm milk, had a wash, set the alarm for three o'clock and went to sleep straightaway. The alarm went off immediately and I stumbled out of bed. I had left the hut door half open, because Lynx had still been outside in the evening. The moonlight fell on the wooden floor and flooded the meadow with a cold glow. Lynx lay in the doorway; the poor thing had been watching over me and hadn't dared creep into the stove door. I praised him and stroked him, and together we fetched Bella and Bull from the meadow. I led them to the byre, milked Bella and left water and feed for them. Tiger was still lying in the cupboard, and didn't stir. As on the previous day we climbed down to the valley with the first light of dawn. The stars were fading, and the first red glow was rising in the east.

That morning scything was torture, every movement hurt, and I made slower progress than I had the first day. And again I lay down exhausted under a hazel bush after three hours and slept. I woke at midday. Lynx was sitting beside me, staring fixedly into the valley, where the grass stood wild and high, speckled white with the dust from its flowers. In a land without bees, grasshoppers and birds, a deadly silence grew warm beneath the sun. Lynx looked very serious and lonely. It was the first time I'd seen him like that. I made a very slight movement and he immediately turned his head and gave a joyful bark, and his eyes became animated and warm. The loneliness had passed, and he forgot it straightaway. Then he trotted to the stream, and I started to turn the hay. I was able to bring the previous day's hay to the barn immediately; it was quite dry, apart from some that had been too shaded. This time it was eight o'clock before I got back to the pasture to let out Bella and Bull. Tiger grew tiresome. Since he had been alone all day long he wanted to play now, and I was barely able to move.

The following day I did less scything, for the higher I got the sooner the sun caught up with me. The weather stayed fine for the whole week, and I was pleased to have kept to the old rule about the waxing moon. On the eighth day it rained, and I stayed at home. Half of the meadow was harvested and I needed a rest, as I was just dragging myself along. I was so tired I had hardly eaten anything, and drunk nothing but milk and tea. It was also good for Bella to be milked regularly, as she had been before. She wasn't giving quite as much milk now. It rained quietly and grayly for four days. The rain fell in tiny drops. Resting on the bed I could see the meadow and the mountains as if through spiders' webs. I sawed up a few sticks and got us some meat. Because it had been hot I had been obliged to throw away a third of the last stag, a waste that had cut me to the quick, but I could do nothing about it. I spent most of the four days sleeping or playing with Tiger, who didn't like going into the meadow when it rained. My hands were sore and covered with bites and took a long time to heal. Every muscle and every bone still ached, but the pain barely touched me, as if it didn't have anything to do with me at all.

On the fifth day the weather cleared around midday, and in the afternoon the sun broke through the clouds. The wet coolness still lay in the air, and the water trembled in the grass. Bull galloped boisterously back and forth in the meadow, and Tiger cautiously dipped a paw into the grass before deciding on a little hunting expedition. Lynx brightened up as well, shook the sleep from his coat and set off on little reconnaissance expeditions. I cut some grass (there was a scythe at the Alm, of course), and carried it into the stable. Bella and Bull's halcyon days were almost over. The weather stayed fine for four days, then it grew close and the sky clouded over again.

I had harvested two-thirds of the meadow, and migrated back to the Alm in the dull heat. My heart ached. Perhaps only from overexertion, but some of the rheumatism might have lingered with me as well. Even Lynx trotted behind me ill-temperedly and seemed beset by a paralyzing fatigue. I thought about the fact that the work was getting too hard for me and my food was too monotonous. Walking was painful too, as I'd rubbed a blister on my heel in my hard climbing shoes, and my sock was sticking to the little wound. Suddenly everything I had done seemed a pointless nuisance. I felt I'd have been better off shooting myself long ago. But if I hadn't been able to do that, since it isn't easy to shoot yourself with a rifle, I should have dug my way under the wall. There was either enough food for a hundred years over there or a quick, painless death. In fact, what was I still waiting for? Even if, by some miracle, someone were to rescue me, what use could that be to me, if all the human beings I had loved were dead? I wanted to take Lynx with me, the cats could escape all by themselves, and as for Bella and Bull, well, I would probably have to kill them. They would starve in winter.

The cloud layer was now slate-gray, and a feeble light lay over the mountains. I hurried to get home before the storm. Lynx panted along behind me. I was too tired and too despondent to be able to comfort him. In any case everything was completely meaningless and trivial.

When I emerged from the forest I heard the first rumble above me. I let Lynx into the hut, took my shoes off and ran into the stable to relieve Bella of her burden. While I was working in the byre the storm broke. It swept over the grassy slopes, and the clouds scudded low, gray and yellow and ugly. I was frightened, and at the same time I was furious about the violence to which my animals and I were being exposed. I tied Bella and Bull up and closed the shutters. Bull pressed against his mother, and she tenderly and patiently licked his nose as if he was still a helpless calf. Bella was no less frightened than I was, but she tried to comfort Bull. While I was absently stroking her flank I suddenly knew that I couldn't leave. Perhaps it was stupid of me, but that's just how it was. I couldn't flee and let my animals down. This decision wasn't the result of any thought or emotion. There was something planted deep within me that made it impossible for me to abandon something that had been entrusted to me. I calmed down immediately and stopped being afraid. I bolted the stable door so that the storm couldn't wrench it open and then ran to the hut, taking care not to spill the milk. The wind banged the door shut behind me, and I bolted it with a sigh of relief. I lit a candle and closed the shutters. We were finally secure, in a small and pathetic way, perhaps, but protected from the rain and the storm. Tiger and Lynx already lay snuggled up against one another in the stove door, not stirring. I drank warm milk and sat down at the table. It was stupid to allow the candles to burn down, but I couldn't bring myself to sit in the dark. So I struggled not to hear the rumbling in the clouds, and examined my sore foot. The blister had burst, and was crusted with blood. I took a footbath and then applied iodine to the wound. It was all I could do. Then I extinguished the candle after all, and lay down on the bed with my clothes on. Through the slits in the shutters I could see the bolts of lightning jerking down. Finally the storm subsided a little, and it started to rain over the Alm. The thunder and lightning continued for a long time, but the sound of the rain was a comfort to me. After a long time the thunder became a distant grumble, and straight after that I woke up and saw the sun shimmering through the shutters. Tiger was meowing plaintively, and Lynx was prodding me with his nose. I got up and flung the door open, and the two of them dashed outside. I was cold, because I'd spent the whole night without a blanket. It was eight o'clock, and the sun was already above the forest. After letting Bella and Bull out I took a look around.

The meadow lay in the damp morning brightness; all the terrors of the night had fled. Perhaps it was still drizzling in the valley, and I thought, as I always did when the weather was bad, about the cat. Well, she had chosen this free life of her own accord. But had she really? After all, she couldn't choose. I saw no great difference between her and myself. I could choose, certainly, but only with my mind, and as far as I was concerned that amounted to not being able to choose at all. The cat and I were made of the same stuff, and we were in the same boat, drifting with all living things toward the great dark rapids. As a human being, I alone had the honor of recognizing this, without being able to do anything about it. A dubious gift on the part of nature, if I thought about it. I dismissed these thoughts and shook my head. Yes, I clearly remember that, because I gave it such a shake that something clicked in my neck and I walked around with a stiff neck for days. Having come down to earth I spent the next few days sawing wood and allowing my heel to get better. I walked barefoot and made myself cold poultices and the inflammation actually subsided. I drank a lot of milk, churned butter, scoured out the hut, darned my ragged socks, washed a few clothes and sat on the bench in the sun. Only on the fifth day after the storm did I go back to the valley with Lynx. Over the next few days I brought in the rest of the hay. I finished at around two o'clock and brought the last load from the edge of the forest to the barn on beech branches.

A colossal task was completed; a task that had lain before me for months like an enormous mountain. Now I was tired and happy. I couldn't remember having felt such satisfaction since my children were little. Back then, after the strain of a long day, when the toys were cleared away and the children lay in their beds, bathed and dried, back then I'd been happy. I was a good mother to little children. Once they grew bigger and went to school I failed them. I don't know how it happened, but the bigger the children grew the more insecure I felt with them. I still looked after them as well as I could, but only very rarely was I happy around them. Then I became very dependent on my husband again; he seemed to need me more than they did. My children had gone away; hand in hand, their satchels on their backs, their hair blowing about, and I hadn't known that that was the beginning of the end. Or perhaps I'd had an inkling. Later on I had never been happy again. Everything changed in a wretched way, and I stopped really living.

I put my scythe, rake and fork in the barn and bolted the door. Then I went to the hunting lodge. The stream had risen a little where it met the wall. I waded through the icy water and called Lynx to the shore. Later I boiled up some tea on the stove and shared my lunch with Lynx. The bed bore the impression of the cat, and that was a great comfort to me. Perhaps in the autumn we would all be united again around the warm stove. I stroked the bed smooth and then had a look at the beans. All through the summer they had had white and red blossoms, now they were already covered with little green pods. The storm had scattered the petals of the flowers, but hadn't snapped the vines and canes. I decided to make a big extension to the bean garden, and gradually give myself a filling substitute for bread. August had arrived in the meantime, and in a few weeks we would be returning to our winter quarters. I made sure there wasn't a spark left in the stove, and set off with Lynx on the return journey. I was happy that the great strain was past, that Bella and Bull could go to the meadow in the daytime and that we could keep to our milking times.

This time Tiger didn't welcome us with a cry, but crouched crossly beside the stove with his shoulders hunched, meowing quietly and plaintively. I stroked him, but he didn't move, and when Lynx sniffed at him he gave an angry and irritable hiss. Later, when my work was done, I saw that he was limping on three paws. It isn't very easy to examine an injured cat, still less a tom-cat with Tiger's temperament. I laid him on his back and tickled his stomach until I managed to hold his paw quite gently. He had trodden a thorn or a splinter into the pad. I tried at least ten times to get it out with tweezers. I only managed to do so because a bird swept past the hut door at that moment and distracted Tiger's attention from me and the tweezers. The little operation was successful. Tiger jumped up furiously, knocked the tweezers from my hand and dashed out of the hut.

I later saw him eagerly licking the little wound, sitting on the bench. In fact he had behaved more or less reasonably. Cats panic very easily; any rustle of paper, any sudden movement can send them into a complete twitch. Solitary creatures, they have to be constantly on their guard and ready for flight. The enemy could be lying in wait behind any harmless-looking bush, behind the corner of any house. There is only one thing about them that is stronger than suspicion and caution, and that is curiosity.

Dusk had fallen in the meantime, and I cooked supper. I had brought back the last jar of cranberries from the hunting lodge, and made pancakes without eggs. Even that's all right if you're used to it. The end of the hay harvest seemed to me to be the occasion for such a feast. At that time, however, I had ceased to suffer so much from my desire for unattainable pleasures. There were no longer any external stimuli to feed my fantasies, and the craving slowly passed. I was just happy that I was able to satisfy myself and the animals, and that we didn't have to starve. I hardly missed sugar, either. That summer I went only twice to the raspberry patch and filled a bucket with berries. The journey was too long and arduous for me. There were also fewer berries than there had been the first summer, perhaps because it had been too dry. The fruits were small and very sweet. I saw that the patch was starting to get overgrown. In a few years it will be entirely covered by thickets that will have suffocated the raspberry bushes.

After the hay harvest I stayed quietly at home, and spent a lot of time sitting on the bench. I was tired and a bit exhausted, and the mysterious magic began to cast its spell over me once again. My days now passed very regularly. At six o'clock I got up, milked Bella and let her and Bull into the meadow. Then I cleaned the stable, carried the milk into the hut and emptied it into the earthenware pots in the bedroom so that the cream could settle on the surface. Then I had breakfast and fed Lynx and Tiger. Lynx had his meal in the morning, while Tiger got only milk. For some reason, perhaps because he was a nocturnal animal, Tiger wanted to eat in the evening. Lynx would then have his milk in the evening. Then there came Tiger's morning game: catch-as-catch-can around the hut. I sometimes had to force myself to join in, but it did me some good, and Tiger needed it for his well-being. The game had strict rules, all of them invented and enforced by Tiger; it always had to follow the same route, and the same hiding places were used every time. The corner of the house, an old rain barrel, a stack of fallen wood, a biggish stone, a corner of the house and an old chopping block. Tiger dashed around the corner and I had to play dumb and go looking for him, plaintively and anxiously. I wasn't allowed to see him lowering round the corner until he finally rushed at my legs with a wild leap. Then came the rain barrel, which I had to tap blindly past, and, having been given a powerful, but not too painful bite, I was allowed to let out a yell, while Tiger, tail in the air, disappeared behind the woodpile, which I had to circle around for ages because I simply couldn't see the little cat with his protective coloring, until he emerged again, delicately stepping sideways like a horse on tiptoes, his back in a great arch. Everything was designed to show that he, a proud and clever predator, could terrify a stupid and ridiculous human being. But as the stupid human being was also the agreeable and beloved human being, she didn't get eaten, but was licked tenderly once the game was over. Perhaps I shouldn't have played those games with him. Possibly they induced in him a kind of megalomania that made him incautious in the face of any real danger. Tiger could have managed twenty rounds of the game, while ten at the most was enough for me. All the same, it always left him so satisfied that he went back to the cupboard to sleep for a while. At first Lynx wanted to join in, and circled around us barking and jumping clumsily. But Tiger sharply rebuked him and he now only followed the game from a distance, twitching his tail and yapping loudly. Only if I had no time and absolutely refused to cooperate was Lynx allowed to step in for me. All the same, neither of them seemed to enjoy it much then.

After a little rest I attended to the milk. It always needed something doing to it. The cream was skimmed off, and

Bull got most of the skim milk. Sometimes I was able to churn butter, too, or render clarified butter from the leftovers. Of course my store of clarified butter never grew very big. It took days for me to skim off enough cream. I drank a lot of milk myself so as to stay healthy, given my monotonous diet, and I also needed a little every day for Lynx and Tiger. Then I tidied up the hut, aired the bed, did the washing or cleaning and prepared lunch. It was nothing special, and I usually looked for a few edible herbs in the meadow to spice up the meat a little. There were mushrooms in the meadow as well, but I wasn't familiar with them and didn't dare eat them. They looked very tempting, but since Bella didn't touch them I suppressed my hunger.

After lunch I sat down on the bench and dozed sleepily. The sun shone on my face and my head grew heavy with fatigue. When I realized I was about to fall asleep I got up and went into the forest with Lynx. He needed this daily expedition as Tiger needed his morning game. We generally went to the vantage point, and I looked out over the countryside with the binoculars. I only really did it out of habit. The church towers always gleamed the same red, and only the color of the meadows and fields changed a little. When the foehn came everything looked close enough to touch, quite brightly colored, and when the wind came from the east the countryside was masked by fine bluish veils, and sometimes I couldn't see anything at all when mist lay over the river. I never stayed sitting for long, because Lynx found that too boring. We made a great detour through the forest and usually returned to the hut from the opposite direction at around four or five o'clock. On my peregrinations I saw only red deer; roe didn't come up to this altitude. Through the telescope I could sometimes see a few chamois on the white chalk cliffs. In the course of the summer I found four dead chamois that had crept off into the bushes. When they went blind they came into the valley. These four hadn't got far. Death had claimed them quickly. They should actually all have been shot to eradicate the plague, and to release the poor creatures from their suffering. But I wouldn't have hit them from that distance, and I had to be economical with my ammunition. So there was no alternative but to watch their misery.

Once our expedition was over, Lynx took up his position on the bench and fell asleep in the sun. His coat seemed to protect him, since he could doze for hours in the heat. In the meantime I got busy in the byre, sawed a little wood or mended something.

Often I did nothing at all and watched Bella and Bull, or observed a buzzard gliding and wheeling over the forest. I couldn't tell whether it actually was a buzzard, it might just as easily have been a falcon or a hawk. I'd got used to calling all birds of prey buzzards, because I liked the word so much. I was always a little uneasy about Tiger if the buzzard turned up too often. Fortunately Tiger preferred to stay close to the hut, and seemed to be afraid of crossing the wide meadow to get to the forest. There was enough prey for him around the hut in any case. The fat grasshoppers even jumped over the doorstep, right in front of Tiger's paws. I was very fond of the buzzard, although I had also to be wary of him. He looked very beautiful, and I gazed after him until he disappeared in the blue of the sky or plunged into the forest. His hoarse cry was the only strange voice that reached me up in the Alm.

But what I liked doing best was simply looking out over the meadow. It was always in gentle motion, even if I thought the wind was still. An endless, gentle ripple emanated peace and a sweet fragrance. Lavender grew here. Alpine roses, cat's foot, wild thyme and a host of herbs whose names I didn't know; which smelt just as good as thyme, but different. Tiger would often sit mad-eyed by one of the fragrant plants, and was quite unapproachable. He used the herbs as an opium addict uses his drug. His intoxications didn't have any ill effects on him, though. When the sun had gone down I led Bella and Bull into the byre and did my usual work. Supper generally turned out to be quite meager and consisted of the leftovers from lunch and a glass of milk. It was only when I had shot a deer that we lived quite luxuriously, until the sight of meat filled me with nausea. I had it without bread or potatoes, since I had to save the flour for the days when there was no meat left.

Then I would sit down on the bench and wait. The meadow slowly went to sleep, the stars came out, and later the moon rose high and bathed the meadow in its cold light. I waited for those hours all day, filled with secret impatience. They were the only hours in which I was capable of thinking quite without illusions, completely clearly. I was no longer in search of a meaning to make my life more bearable. That kind of desire struck me as being almost presumptuous. Human beings had played their own games, and in almost every case they had ended badly. And how could I complain? I was one of them and couldn't judge them, because I understood them so well. It was better not to think about human beings. The great game of the sun, moon and stars seemed to be working out, and that hadn't been invented by humans. But it wasn't completed yet, and might bear the seeds of failure within it. I was only an attentive and enchanted onlooker; my whole life would be too short to grasp even the tiniest stage of the game. I'd spent most of my life struggling with daily human concerns. Now that I had barely anything left, I could sit in peace on the bench and watch the stars dancing against the black firmament. I had got as far from myself as it is possible for a human being to get, and I realized that this state couldn't last if I wanted to stay alive. I sometimes thought I would never fully understand what had come over me in the Alm. But I realized that everything I had thought and done until then, or almost everything, had been nothing but a poor imitation. I had copied the thoughts and actions of other people. The hours on the bench by the house were real to me, an experience of my own, yet they were not the whole. My thoughts almost always raced ahead of my eyes and distorted the true picture.

Just after waking, when my mind is still paralyzed by sleep, I sometimes see things before I can categorize and recognize them. The impression is frightening and menacing. It is only knowledge that turns the chair, with the clothes draped on it, into a familiar object. A moment before, it was something inexpressibly strange and set my heart racing. I didn't carry out these experiments very often, but neither was it especially curious that I did carry them out. There was nothing, after all, to distract me and occupy my mind, no books, no conversation, no music; nothing. Since my childhood I had forgotten how to see things with my own eyes, and I had forgotten that the world had once been young, untouched and very beautiful and terrible. I couldn't find my way back there, since I was no longer a child and no longer capable of experiencing things as a child, but loneliness led me, in moments free of memory and consciousness, to see the great brilliance of life again. Perhaps animals spend their whole lives in a world of terror and delight. They cannot escape, and have to bear reality until they have ceased to be. Even their death is without solace and hope, a real death. Like all human beings, I too was forever in hurried flight; forever trapped in daydreams. Because I hadn't seen the deaths of my children, I imagined them as being still alive. But I saw Lynx being killed, I saw the brain swell from Bull's split skull, and I saw Pearl dragging herself along like a boneless thing and bleeding, and again and again I felt the warm hearts of the deer cooling in my hands.

That was reality. Because I have seen and felt all that, it's difficult for me to dream in the daytime. I have a violent resistance to daydreams, and I feel that hope has died in me. It frightens me. I don't know whether I will be able to bear living with reality alone. Sometimes I try to treat myself like a robot: do this and go there and don't forget to do that. But it works only for a short time. I'm a bad robot; I'm still a human being who thinks and feels, and I shall not be able to shake either habit. That's why I'm sitting here writing down everything that's happened, and I'm not worried about whether the mice will eat my notebooks or not. Writing is all that matters, and as there are no other conversations left, I have to keep the endless conversation with myself alive. It will be the only report that I shall ever write, for when it is written there won't be a single little piece of paper left to write on in the house. Even now the moment when I shall have to go to bed makes me tremble. Then I shall lie with my eyes open until the cat comes home, and her warm proximity will give me the sleep I long for. Even then I'm not safe. If I'm defenseless dreams can assail me, black dreams of night.

It's hard for me to find my way back in my thoughts to that summer in the Alm, which seems very unreal and remote. Lynx, Tiger and Bull were still alive back then, and I had no inkling what was to come. Sometimes I dream I am looking for the pasture and can no longer find it. I walk through thickets and forest, on bumpy slopes, and when I awake I'm tired and depressed. It's strange, in the dream I'm looking for the pasture, and when I awake I'm happy not even to have to think about it. I would like never to see it again, never again.

In August there were two or three more storms, but

they were never very violent and lasted only a few hours. If something sometimes vaguely disturbed me, it was that everything had gone so well. We were all healthy, the days stayed warm and fragrant, and the nights were filled with stars. Finally, since nothing else happened, I got used to this state, and began to accept good things as easily as if I had never expected anything else. Past and future washed around a little warm island, the here and now. I knew it couldn't stay that way, but I didn't worry about it at all. In my memory, that summer is overshadowed by events that occurred much later. I can no longer feel how beautiful it was, now I only know it was. There is a terrible difference. That's why I can't draw the picture of the pasture. My senses have a worse memory than my mind, and one day they may stop remembering entirely. Before that happens I must have written everything down.

Summer was already drawing to a close. Bad weather set in in the last week of August. It grew cold and rainy, and I had to keep a fire going all day. At that time I was using up too many matches, for the sticks burned away immediately whenever I left the hut. Bella and Bull stayed in the meadow. They didn't seem to feel the cold, but looked less contented than they had in the summer. Tiger spent a miserable week in the hut, sitting on the windowsill and staring crossly into the rain. I completed my daily tasks, and quite slowly started yearning for the hunting lodge, for my dressing gown, the quilt and the crackling beech logs. At midday every day I took the loden coat, drew the cape over it and went into the forest with Lynx. I wandered aimlessly beneath the dripping trees, let Lynx rummage around a little to keep him in a good mood, and returned shivering to the hut. As I had nothing else to do I went to sleep early, and the more I slept the more sleepy I grew. I was annoyed by this, and began to grow melancholy. Tiger wandered, crying plaintively, from the kitchen to the bedroom and tried to tempt me to play, but soon grew weary himself and gave up. Only Lynx wasn't upset by the rain, and apart from our short expeditions he slept day and night in the stove door. Finally it even started snowing, in enormous wet flakes. Soon we were in the midst of the most awful snowstorm. I got dressed and led Bella and Bull to the stable. It snowed all night, and in the morning the snow lay four inches thick. The sky was overcast, and the wind blew cold. Toward afternoon it grew warmer, and a little rain fell. I now saw clearly that I couldn't put off our return home too much longer.

A week later I was woken by the sun on my face. It had actually turned fine again. The air was still cold, but the sky was clear and pale blue. The sun struck me as a little duller and smaller than before, but I'm sure I imagined that. The day was radiantly beautiful, but something had changed. The first snow shimmered from the rocks and made me shiver. Lynx and Tiger were already at the door, and I let them out. Then I led Bella and Bull to the meadow. The air smelt of snow, and it wasn't warm until midday. But now I wanted to wait a while before bringing the animals down from the pasture; in fact it stayed fine until the twentieth of September. In the evening I had to look at the stars through the window, it was already much too cold outside. They seemed to have retreated further into space, and their light was colder than it had been in the past summer nights.

I resumed my old life, went for walks with Lynx, played with Tiger and attended to my household tasks. But in a strange way I felt as if my illusions had been shattered. One night, when I was already starting to feel cold in bed, I realized that it was dangerous to wait any longer. In the early morning I packed the most necessary things in my rucksack, put Tiger in his detested box, fetched Bella and Bull from the stable and was ready to move. At seven o'clock we set off, and at eleven we arrived at the hunting lodge. First I let Tiger, crying pitifully, out of his prison and locked him in the house. After they had drunk at the spring I let Bella and Bull graze in the clearing. The weather was still fine, and it was warmer here than up in the Alm. When I went into the house Tiger was already lying in the wardrobe, where he seemed to feel safe. Lynx greeted the hunting lodge with joy. He understood that we had come home and accompanied me, yapping excitedly, wherever I went. I was busy in the house until late afternoon, and only after milking, and after I had brought Bella and Bull to their old byre, did I get something to eat. The fire was burning in the stove, a proper crackling fire of beech logs, and the house smelt of air and washed wood. Lynx crept into the stove door, and I too went to bed, tired. I stretched out, extinguished the candle and immediately went to sleep.

Something pressed damp and cold against my face, and woke me with little cries of joy. I put the light on, and then took the gray, dew-damp bundle into my arms and pressed it to me. The cat really had come home. With a lot of grrus, guarrs and meows she reported the experiences of her long, lonely summer. I got up and filled her bowl with warm milk, which she fell upon greedily. She had lost a lot of weight, and she was unkempt but seemed to be quite healthy. Lynx came over and the two of them greeted each other with something like affection. Perhaps I had always been unfair to the cat in thinking her cool and standoffish. On the other hand a warm oven, sweet milk and a safe place in bed are worth a bit of noise. In any case we were all happily united, and when I lay in bed again and felt the familiar little body against my legs I was very glad to be home again. It had been beautiful in the alpine pasture, more beautiful than it could be here, but I was at home in the hunting lodge. I thought back to the summer with something like unease, and was glad to have returned to my usual life.

Over the next few days I didn't have much time for the animals. Every morning I climbed up to the Alm with Lynx and brought back a big rucksack full of household equipment. It was less arduous than it had been in May, because this time it was downhill. Only the butter churn left a few blue marks on my back once again. When, before entering the forest, I turned around for the last time, I saw the meadow once more, rippling in the autumn wind beneath the high, pale blue sky. I was already out of place in the great breadth and stillness. I knew it would never again be as it had been that summer. There was no good reason why, but I knew it with great certainty. Today I think I knew it because I didn't want anything to repeat itself. Any intensification of that special situation would have placed me and my animals in great danger.

The way downhill led beneath dark spruces, along bumpy paths, and the little patch of blue above me had nothing in common with the sky over the alpine pasture. Every stone in the path, every little bush presented itself as familiar, beautiful, but a little ordinary compared with the gleaming snow on the rocks. But this familiar ordinariness was what I needed to live, if I wanted to stay a human being. In the pasture something of the cold and breadth of the sky had seeped into me and had imperceptibly distanced me from life. But that was already in the past. While I made my descent into the valley, the butter churn wasn't the only thing that weighed painfully against my shoulders; all the worries I had dismissed revived. I was no longer freed from the earth, but toiling and overburdened, as befits a human being. And it seemed a good thing to me, and I gladly assumed the heavy load.

After resting for two days I visited the potato field. The plants were dense and green and weren't starting to turn yellow. I had to spend a few weeks getting by with meat and flour, but I didn't have much flour left. I cooked nettle spinach, which wasn't as good as it had been in the spring but still filled the stomach. Then I went to look for my fruit trees. The damsons, which had blossomed and grown in abundance, must have dropped in the summer. On the other hand there were more apples than the previous year, and a large amount of crab apples. I had to wait for that harvest as well. I ate an apple, but it was still green and gave me stomachache.

My second autumn in the forest had arrived. Cyclamen blossomed in damp and shady places among the hazel bushes, and the gorge had a blue lining of gentians. The wind veered from east to south, bringing disagreeably warm air with it. Perhaps I had left the alpine pasture too early after all, but I knew already that very bad weather would follow the foehn. I felt tired and irritated, carted hay to the garage, and was happy that I'd chopped so much wood in the spring that I was spared that task at least.

Finally the rain came, but it stayed moderately warm. I had to light a fire in the evening, but you have to do that here. I stayed in the house and altered the old suit that Hugo had worn in the hut to fit me. I sewed very badly and ineptly, but then it didn't have to be a masterpiece. This task, which I disliked doing so much, occupied my hands alone. My thoughts set off for a stroll. It was pleasant to be in a warm room. Lynx slept in the stove door, the cat slept on my bed, and Tiger sent a ball of paper from one corner to the next. He was almost fully grown now, and already bigger than his mother. His fat tomcat's head was almost twice as wide as her delicate little one. After our return the old cat had greeted Tiger with hostility, until he, perhaps out of fear, had given her a good hiss. After that they tolerated, or rather ignored one another, and each behaved as if they were the only cat in the house.

Tiger hadn't recognized his mother. He had, after all, still been small when we'd moved to the Alm, and the old cat had stopped paying him any attention long ago. The wet weather meant that it grew dark early, and to be economical I went to bed early. I didn't sleep as well as I had done up at the pasture, where the very air made me tired. I woke two or three times in the night and tried not to think, so as not to drive sleep away entirely. I didn't get up until around seven o'clock, to go to the byre. Bella and Bull had settled down again completely, although Bella was giving less milk since switching to the inferior fodder in the clearing. But I hoped that would improve when she was fed on hay.

The weather very slowly turned cold and cheerless. I went to the forest with Lynx every day, and when the rain eased off I tried to catch a few trout. One afternoon I caught two, only one the next afternoon, and that one with my hand. I don't know whether fish sleep, but that one must have dozed off in its pond. Fishing had gone very quiet. The trout wouldn't bite anymore. Even though I couldn't respect the fishing seasons, I wasn't catching anything anyway. The arrival of the foehn had led to an early rutting season for the stags, and for that reason too my sleep was disturbed. It seemed to me that there were now more stags than there had been the previous year. My fears were confirmed; they were coming over to me from the other hunting grounds in which they could multiply unimpeded. Some day, failing an immoderately fierce winter, the forest would be overrun with deer. Even today I can't say how things will develop; but if I dig my way under the wall I will perform that last task very thoroughly and build a proper gateway of earth and stones. I couldn't deny my deer their last chance of survival.

The wind finally turned again, and now came from the east. It grew really fine once more. At midday the air was so warm that I could sit on the bench in the sun. The big wood ants became very industrious again, and marched past me in black and gray processions. They seemed to be extremely purposeful, and wouldn't be distracted from their work. They lugged spruce needles, little beetles and clumps of earth and toiled away. I always felt a little sorry for them. I could never bring myself to destroy an ants' nest. My attitude to the little robots vacillated between admiration, fear and pity. Only because I was looking at them with human eyes, of course. To a giant super-ant my own actions would probably have appeared extremely puzzling and peculiar.

Bella and Bull spent the whole day in the clearing, tugging, a little unenthusiastically now, at the hard, yellowish grass. They definitely preferred the fresh, fragrant hay that I gave them in the evening. Tiger played near me, but stayed away from the ants, and Lynx set off on little expeditions into the bushes, from which he came back every ten minutes, looked at me quizzically and, after a word of praise from me, disappeared again, reassured.

For almost the whole of October the weather stayed fine. I now made the most of the promising climate and doubled my wood supply. The entire house was now covered with stacks of wood as far as the veranda, and looked like a fortress with little windows peeping out like arrow slits. The woodpiles sweated yellow resin, and the whole clearing was filled with its odor. I worked on peacefully and evenly, without overtaxing myself. I hadn't managed that in the first year. I simply hadn't yet found the right rhythm. But then I had very slowly learned a little more, and adapted to the forest. In the city you can live in a nervous rush for years, and while it may ruin your nerves you can put up with it for a long time. But nobody can climb mountains, plant potatoes, chop wood and scythe in a nervous rush for more than a few months. The first year, when I still hadn't adapted myself, had been well beyond my powers, and I shall never quite recover from those excessive labors. On top of that, I had been absurdly proud of each new record I broke. Today I even walk from the house to the stable in a leisurely woodlander's stroll. My body stays relaxed, and my eyes have time to look around. A running person can't look around. In my previous life, my journey took me past a place where an old lady used to feed pigeons. I've always liked animals, and all my goodwill went out to those pigeons, now long petrified, and yet I can't describe a single one of them. I don't even know what color their eyes and their beaks were. I simply don't know, and I think that says enough about how I used to move through the city. It's only since I've slowed down that the forest around me has come to life. I wouldn't like to say that this is the only way to live, but it's certainly the right one for me. And so many things had to happen before I could find my way here. Before, I was always on my way somewhere, always in a great rush and furiously impatient; every time I got anywhere I would have to spend ages waiting. I might just as well have crept along. Sometimes I became quite clearly aware of my predicament, and of the demands of that world, but I wasn't capable of breaking out of the stupid way of life. The boredom that often afflicted me was the boredom of a respectable rose-grower at a motorcar manufacturers' congress. I spent almost my whole life at just such a congress, and I'm surprised I didn't drop dead with weariness one day. I was probably able to live only because I could always escape into family life. In the last few years, in any case, it often seemed to me as if the people closest to me had gone over to the enemy side, and life became really gray and gloomy.

Here, in the forest, I'm actually in the right place for me. I bear the motorcar manufacturers no grudge now;

they ceased to be of interest long ago. But how they all tormented me with things that repelled me. I only had this one little life, and they wouldn't let me live it in peace. Gas pipes, electrics and oil conduits; only now that people have ceased to be do these things show how truly pitiful they are. And back then they had been turned into idols rather than functional commodities. I too have one of those things standing in the middle of the forest, Hugo's black Mercedes. It was almost new when we came here in it. Today it's overgrown with vegetation, a nest for mice and birds. Particularly in June, when the wild grape blossoms, it looks very pretty, like an enormous wedding bouquet. It's beautiful in winter, too, glittering in the hoarfrost or wearing a white helmet. In spring and autumn, between its brown struts I can see the faded yellow of the upholstery, beech leaves, bits of foam rubber and horsehair torn out and pulled apart by tiny teeth.

Hugo's Mercedes has become a wonderful home, warm and sheltered from the wind. More cars should be put in the forests, they would make good nesting places. In the open countryside there are probably thousands of them, overgrown with ivy, nettles and bushes. But they are quite empty and uninhabited.

I see the plants flourishing, green, well-fed and silent. And I hear the wind and all the noises from the dead cities; windowpanes shattering on the pavement when their hinges have rusted through, the dripping of water from the burst pipes and the banging of thousands of doors in the wind. Sometimes, on stormy nights, a stone object that was once a human being tips from its chair at a desk and crashes with a boom to the parquet floor. For a while there must have been big fires as well. But they're probably over now, and the plants are hurrying to cover up the remains. If I look at the ground behind the wall, I don't see any ants, or beetles, not even the tiniest insect.

But it won't stay that way. With water from the streams life, tiny, simple life, will seep in and revivify the earth. I might have been quite indifferent to that, but strangely it fills me with secret satisfaction.

On the sixteenth of October, after my return from the Alm, I began to make regular entries in my diary again; on the sixteenth of October I took the potatoes out of the ground and collected the black dust-coated tubers in sacks. It had been a good harvest, and the mice had done little damage. I was able to be content, and to look forward to winter with some comfort. I wiped my black hands on a sack and sat down on a tree trunk. The time when my stomach would constantly be rumbling was over, and my mouth watered when I thought about my evening meal: fresh potatoes with butter. The last sunbeams were falling through the beech trees, and I relaxed, tired and content. My back ached from bending over, but it ached pleasantly, just enough for me to notice that I had a back at all. I was still faced with the task of lugging the sacks home on the branches. I always tied two of them on to the beech branches that served me as a cart in summer and a sled in winter, and pulled them along the beaten path to the hunting lodge. When I'd stored all the potatoes in the bedroom in the evening I was so tired that I went to bed without my supper and had to postpone the great feast.

On the twenty-first of October, while the weather was still fine, I fetched home the apples and crab apples. The apples tasted wonderful, although they were still a little hard. I stored them in the bedroom and made sure that they didn't touch one another. Those with bruises I put in the first row, for early consumption. They looked very pretty, grass-green, with flame-red, sharply contrasting cheeks, like the apple in the Snow White story.

Fairy stories were still very clear in my memory, but I'd forgotten a great deal else. As I hadn't known much in any case, only a little knowledge remained to me. Names lived on in my head, and I no longer knew when the people who had borne them had lived. I had only ever learned for exams, and later the dictionaries behind me had given me a sense of security. Now, without these aids, my memory was in a terrible muddle. Sometimes lines from poems occurred to me; I didn't know who had written them, and was seized by an obsessive desire to go to the nearest library and take out some books. It was some comfort to me that the books must still exist, and that I would one day get hold of them. I know today that by then it will be too late. Even in normal times I couldn't live long enough to fill in all the gaps. Neither do I know whether my mind could still retain these things. If I ever get out of here I shall lovingly and longingly caress every book I find, but I shall never read them now. As long as I live I shall need all my strength to keep myself and the animals alive. I will never be a truly educated woman. I must come to terms with that.

The sun was still shining, but from one day to the next it grew a little cooler, and in the morning there was sometimes a touch of frost. The bean harvest had been very good, and now it was time to fetch the cranberries from the Alm. I very much disliked going to the pasture, but I felt I couldn't do without the berries. The meadow at the pasture lay still and enchanted beneath the pale October sky. I visited the vantage point and looked out over the countryside. Visibility was better than it had been in the summer, and I discovered a tiny red church tower that I had never seen before. The meadows were yellow now, with the brownish haze above them, the sea of ripe seeds. And in between lay the rectangular and square surfaces that had once been cornfields. That year they had already been eaten away by big greenish patches, the flourishing weeds. A paradise for sparrows. Except that there wasn't a single sparrow there anymore. They lay in the grass like toy birds, already half sunk into the earth. I had gone with no expectations and yet, when I saw all that, not a cloud of smoke, not the slightest trace of life, I was once more overwhelmed by deep despondency. Lynx grew alert, and urged me to walk on. It was also much too cool to stay sitting down for long. I spent three hours picking berries. It was tedious work. My hands had quite forgotten how to deal with such little things, and were very clumsy. In the end I had filled my bucket, and sat down on the bench in front of the hut and drank hot tea. There were big patches in the meadow where it had been grazed and then had grown again. The grass was already yellowish and a little dry. There were low, lilac-colored gentian bushes here and there. They looked as though their blossoms were cut from frail old silk. Sickly, autumnal plants. I also saw the buzzard wheeling again, and plunging suddenly into the forest. I was overcome by the feeling that it would be better to keep away from the Alm forever.

I don't like being invaded by outside forces, and immediately got on the defensive. There was no sensible reason for me to stay away from the Alm.

I put my feeling of aversion down to fear of the troublesome move there. My suffering should be ignored; everything had been decided long ago and found to be good. And yet I shivered at the sight of the yellow meadow, the gleaming rocks and the unhealthy gentians. A sudden feeling of a great loneliness, emptiness and brightness made me get up and leave the Alm, almost as though I were escaping. Even on the familiar forest track everything struck me as very unreal. It grew cold quickly and Lynx pressed homeward to the warm hut.

The next day I made jam from the berries and put it in jars that I had to tie shut with newspaper. I used the last few days to cut straw for Bella and Bull with the sickle, and while I was about it I also scythed a piece of the forest meadow for the deer. I stored the straw over the byre and in one of the upper rooms, and I put the hay, once it was dry, under a protective roof, where the hay for the deer had been stored in the past. I left the potato field as it was, and had no intention of digging it and fertilizing it before the spring. Then I was tired and a little surprised that I had actually managed to make my preparations for the winter. But after all there had been good years in the past, so why should I not be granted a good year as well?

On All Saints' Day it suddenly grew warm, and I knew that this could only herald winter. All day, while I was doing my work, I couldn't help thinking about cemeteries. There was no immediate reason, but I couldn't help it, because for so many years we had been used to thinking about them at this time of year. I imagined how the grass would long ago have smothered the flowers on the graves, how the stones and crosses were slowly sinking into the earth and the nettles were growing over everything. I saw the vines on the crosses, the broken lanterns and the remains of the wax stumps. And at night the cemeteries lay quite abandoned. No lights burned, and nothing moved but the rustling of the wind in the dry grass. I remembered the processions of people with carrier bags full of enormous chrysanthemums and the industrious, surreptitious digging and watering at the graves. I have never liked All Saints'. The old women's whispering about sickness and decay, and behind it a malevolent fear of the dead and much too little love. For all the attempts to give a beautiful meaning to the feast, the primeval fear in which the living held the dead was ineradicable. The living had to adorn the graves of the dead in order to forget them. Even as a child it always offended me that the dead were so ill treated. Anyone could foresee that, in death, their own mouth would soon be stuffed with paper flowers, candles and fearful prayers.

Now the dead can rest in peace at last, untormented by the digging hands of those who had been indebted to them, overgrown with nettles and grass, slaked by moisture, beneath the eternally rustling wind. And if there should ever be life again, it would grow out of their decomposed bodies and not out of the stone things that were condemned forever to lifelessness. I pitied them, the dead and the stone people. Pity was the only form of love for human beings that remained to me.

The hot gusts of wind from the mountains agitated me and shrouded me in a sad gloom that I tried in vain to resist. The animals too were affected by the foehn. Lynx lay wearily under a bush, and Tiger cried and complained all day and pursued his mother with urgent affection. But she wouldn't have anything to do with him, and then Tiger ran to the meadow, and butted his head repeatedly against a tree, crying loudly. When I stroked him, horrified, he burrowed his hot nose into my hand, crying plaintively. All of a sudden Tiger was no longer my little playmate, but an almost fully grown tomcat, tormented by love. As the old cat wouldn't have anything to do with him, as she had recently become very sulky, Tiger would run into the forest and desperately search for a female, but there was no female there for him. I cursed the warm wind and went to bed overcome with foreboding. The cats both went out into the night, and soon I heard Tiger's song from the forest. He had a glorious voice, a legacy from Mr. Ka-au Ka-au, but more youthful and supple. Poor Tiger, he would sing in vain.

I spent the whole night in a half-waking state, in which I imagined my bed was a boat on the high seas. It was almost like an attack of fever, and made me weary and dizzy. I kept imagining I was falling into an abyss, and saw terrible images. Everything was happening on a dancing patch of water, and soon I no longer had the power to convince myself it wasn't real. It was very real; reason and order no longer counted for anything. Toward morning the cat jumped onto my bed and freed me from that terrible state. All at once my whole confusion dissolved into nothing and I finally went to sleep.

In the morning the sky was blackly overcast; the hissing wind had died down, but under the layer of clouds it was still stiflingly hot. The day crept on, and the air was thick and damp and lay heavy on my lungs. Tiger hadn't come home. Lynx crept sadly around. The foehn didn't affect him as much as my bad mood, which distanced me from him and made me unapproachable. I did my work in the byre, and had to rouse Bella from her slumbers before I could milk her. Bull too was peculiarly restless and unmanageable. After work I lay down on my bed. I had, after all, barely slept that night. The window and the door were open, and Lynx sat down in the doorway to watch over my sleep. I actually did get to sleep, and found myself in a lifelike dream.

I was in a very bright room like a hall, all decorated in white and gold. Magnificent baroque furniture was ranged along the walls, and the floor was laid with expensive parquets. When I looked out of the window I could see a little pavilion in a French park. Somebody somewhere was playing *Eine kleine Nachtmusik*. I suddenly knew that none of this existed anymore. The feeling of having suffered a terrible loss descended violently upon me. I pressed my hands to my mouth so as not to cry. Then the bright light went out, the gold sank into darkness and the music turned into a monotonous drumming. I woke up. The rain was beating against the windowpanes. I lay quite still on the bed and listened. *Eine kleine Nachtmusik* was silenced by the rain, and I couldn't hear it anymore. It was almost miraculous that my sleeping brain had roused a past world to new life. I still couldn't grasp it.

That evening it was as if we had all been released from a nightmare. Tiger crept in through the cat door, disheveled, his coat covered with earth and needles, but released from his frenzy. He cried out his fear and, after he had drunk some milk, he crept exhaustedly into the cupboard. The old cat kindly allowed me to stroke her, and Lynx crept to his bed after checking that I had turned back into his familiar human being. I laid out my old card game, and by the light of the lamp I listened to the rain beating against the shutters. Then I put a bucket under the gutter to catch water to wash my hair with, went into the byre to feed and milk the animals, and then lay down and slept deeply until the cool, wet morning. For the next few days, as it went on raining quietly and insistently, I stayed in the house. I had washed my hair, and it now floated, light and bushy, around my head. The rainwater had made it soft and smooth. Looking in the mirror I cut it short so that it just covered my ears, and I contemplated my tanned face under its sun-bleached cap of hair. It looked very strange, thin, with slight hollows in the cheeks. Its lips had grown narrower, and I felt this strange face was marked by a se-cret need. As there were no human beings left alive to love this face it struck me as quite superfluous. It was naked and pathetic, and I was ashamed of it and wanted nothing to do with it. My animals were fond of my familiar smell, my voice and my movements. I could easily cast off my face; it was needed no longer. At this thought a feeling of emptiness rose up in me, which I had to get rid of at any price. I looked for some kind of work to do, and told myself that in my situation it was childish to mourn a face, but the tormenting sense that I had lost something important would not be driven away.

On the fourth day the rain started to become tiresome, and I thought myself ungrateful when I thought of the release that it had brought us after the foehn. But it was simply undeniable that I had had it up to my ears, and my animals quite agreed with me. In this we were very similar to one another. We wished we could have gentle, cheerful weather, with a rainy day once a week for sleeping. But no one was concerned with our impatience, and we had to listen to the gentle rustling and splashing for four more days. When I went to the forest with Lynx the branches beat wetly against my legs, and the damp entered my bones. Sometimes the rainy days merge in my memory into a single day that lasted for months, during which I stared miserably into the gray light. But I know very well that in two and a half years it never rained for more than ten days at a stretch.

Meanwhile something had started happening in the byre that frightened me. Bella was calling for a mate, and roared all day. That was nothing new, it happened every few weeks, and I had become accustomed to ignoring it because I couldn't help her. But today I can hardly understand why I had never thought about it more. Something within me must have repressed the thought that Bull might one day be fully grown. At the same time I had been waiting for this moment since his birth. In any case, one day I surprised him approaching his mother in a very unambiguous manner. My first reaction was annoyance and fear. He had pulled loose from the rope, and stood before me, trembling, his eyes red-veined. He looked terrible, in fact. But he allowed me to tie him up, and nothing further happened.

First I went into the house and sat at the table to think. I had no idea what to do. Could I leave the two animals together at all without putting Bella, who was weaker than Bull, in danger? In the period that followed Bull became more and more insistent, and Bella seemed afraid of him. I had to keep them apart. However desirable Bull's masculinity was, it caused me nothing but annoyance at first. I came to realize that I needed to build him his own permanent partition in the byre, from which he could not break free. Boards were not strong enough for him, it had to be tree trunks. I did cut down two young trees, but then I saw that I wasn't up to building the partition. I was too weak and unhandy for real carpentry work. I wept with rage and disappointment, and then I started to look for another solution. Bull had to move into the garage. This decision caused me a lot of hard work. I had to store the hay in one of the upper bedrooms. It was arduous for me to carry the hay from there to two byres every day, and for Bull the transfer meant banishment into cold and darkness. But I had no choice.

I dug a runnel in the garage to allow the waste to flow away, and covered the floor with boards and straw, then I fetched the two bedsteads from the byre, which had always served as Bull's feeding racks, and as I couldn't stand the darkness I sawed a window out of the timber wall and, with strips of wood, nailed a windowpane from one of the bedrooms over the opening. Now at least there was a little light in the garage. Then I smeared the cracks in the walls with earth and moss, stuffed hay into the hay rack and put in a water tub. And then I fetched Bull. He wasn't happy about the move, and neither was I. He stood, with his great head sadly bowed, staring dumbly in front of him, and put up with it all. He hadn't broken anything; he was just being punished for being fully grown. I went into the forest with Lynx so as not to have to hear the roaring of mother and son anymore. I was left with two lots of work in the byres, and the sense of having committed some atrocity. The poor animals had nothing but each other and the endless, secret dialogue of their warm bodies. I hoped that Bella had conceived a calf and would soon be lonely no longer. I saw no hope at all for Bull.

Three weeks later it proved that Bull wasn't yet mature enough after all, or else that Bella, after such a long wait, was no longer able to conceive. I still don't really know for certain. When Bella started to roar again, I led Bull to her, and he trailed along delightedly behind me. The whole time I was beside myself with fear that Bull might injure or even kill his frail little mother. He was behaving like a wild thing. But Bella seemed to have other ideas, and that calmed me down a little. Three weeks later she was roaring once more, and the terrible business happened all over again. When things proved unsuccessful this time too I had no idea what I was supposed to do. Perhaps Bull shouldn't even have been acting that way. I decided to wait another few weeks. Before, I'd found Bella's roaring more bearable, whereas now, when I could have satisfied it, I couldn't bear to hear it. Every time it happened I had to go as far as possible into the forest with Lynx. On top of that, Bull was in a terrible state of excitement as well, and I barely dared go near him. At times he would turn back into a big, well-behaved calf and would be playful and affectionate toward me. Often enough over the next few months I cursed the cycle of procreation and conception that had turned my peaceful mother-and-child byre into a hell of loneliness and fitful madness.

Bella's roaring stopped long ago. Either she's actually expecting a calf, or else she's stopped being fertile, and all she has left is the tepid warmth of the byre, eating, chewing the cud and the occasional vague memory slowly fading. After all we've been through together, Bella has become more than my cow, a poor, patient sister who bears her lot with more dignity than I do. I really wish her a calf. It would extend the term of my imprisonment and burden me with new worries, but Bella ought to be allowed to have her calf and be happy, and I won't question whether it fits in with my plans.

November and the beginning of December were entirely

taken up with work on the new byre and concern about Bull and Bella. There could be no question of a peaceful winter. I have always been fond of animals, in the slight and superficial way in which city people feel drawn to them. When they were suddenly all I had, everything changed. There are said to have been prisoners who have tamed rats, spiders and flies and begun to love them. I think they acted in accordance with their situation. The barriers between animal and human come down very easily. We belong to a single great family, and if we are lonely and unhappy we gladly accept the friendship of our distant relations. They suffer as we do if pain is inflicted on them, and like myself they need food, warmth and a little tenderness.

Incidentally, my affection has very little to do with understanding. In my dreams I bring children into the world, and they aren't only human children; there are cats among them, dogs, calves, bears and quite peculiar furry creatures. But they emerge from me, and there is nothing about them that could frighten or repel me. It only looks off-putting when I write it down, in human writing and human words. Perhaps I should draw these dreams with pebbles on green moss, or scratch them in the snow with a stick. But I can't yet do that. I probably won't live long enough to be so transformed. Perhaps a genius could do it, but I'm only a simple person who has lost her world and is on the way to finding a new one. That way is a painful one, and still far from over.

On the sixth of December the first snow fell, welcomed with joy by Lynx and with disapproval by the cat, and marveled at by Tiger, with childlike curiosity. He clearly saw it as a version of the paper-ball game, and approached it trustingly. Pearl had behaved the same way, but more cautiously and with less spirit. She hadn't had time to learn. Back then I still had no inkling of how little time

Tiger had left. I set about my work as before, fetched hay from the barn and went in search of fresh meat. The roe deer seemed to sense the approach of winter, for they now came to the clearing often and grazed in the light of dawn or as dusk fell. I avoided shooting them there, and sought out their more distant trails. I didn't want to drive them from the forest meadow, where it was easiest for them to scratch out their fodder. I also enjoyed looking at them. Lynx had long ago understood that roe deer in the clearing were not fair game, but a kind of distant fellow lodger, who were under my protection and consequently under his as well, rather like the crows, who visited us again every day from the end of October.

Back then my legs suddenly began to give, and ached painfully, particularly in bed. My excessive efforts were making themselves felt, and in future they were to become a constant source of pain.

On the tenth of December I find a strange entry: "Time is passing so quickly." I can't remember writing it. I don't know what happened on that tenth of December that led me to write, beneath "Bella with Bull," "New-fallen snow," and "Fetched hay": "Time is passing so quickly." Was time passing particularly quickly back then? I can't remember, and can't give any account of it at all. And it isn't true. Time only seemed to be passing quickly. I think time stands quite still and I move around in it, sometimes slowly and sometimes at a furious rate.

Since Lynx died I feel that clearly. I sit at the table and time stands still. I can't see it, smell it or hear it, but it surrounds me on all sides. Its silence and motionlessness is terrible. I jump up, run out of the house and try to escape it. I do something, things race ahead and I forget time. And then, quite suddenly, it surrounds me again. I may be standing in front of the house looking across at the crows, and there it is again, incorporeal and silent, and it holds on to us, the meadow, the crows and myself. I shall have to get used to it, its indifference and omnipresence. It extends into infinity like an enormous spider's web. Billions of tiny cocoons hang woven into its threads, a lizard lying in the sun, a burning house, a dying soldier, everything dead and everything living. Time is big, yet it has room for new cocoons. A gray and relentless net, in which every second of my life is captured. Perhaps that's why it seems so terrible to me, because it stores everything up and never really allows anything to end.

But if time exists only in my head, and I'm the last human being, it will end with my death. The thought cheers me. I may be in a position to murder time. The big net will tear and fall, with its sad contents, into oblivion. I'm owed some gratitude, but no one after my death will know I murdered time. Really these thoughts are quite meaningless. Things happen, and, like millions of people before me, I look for a meaning in them, because my vanity will not allow me to admit that the whole meaning of an event lies in the event itself. If I casually stand on a beetle, it will not see this event, tragic for the beetle, as a mysterious concatenation of universal significance. The beetle was beneath my foot at the moment when my foot fell; a sense of well-being in the daylight, a short, shrill pain and then nothing. But we're condemned to chase after a meaning that cannot exist. I don't know whether I will ever come to terms with that knowledge. It's difficult to shake off an ancient, deep-rooted megalomania. I pity animals, and I pity people, because they're thrown into this life without being consulted. Maybe people are more deserving of pity, because they have just enough intelligence to resist the natural course of things. It has made them wicked and desperate, and not very lovable. All the same, life could have been lived differently. There is no impulse more rational than love. It makes life more bearable for the lover and the loved one. We should have recognized in time that this was our only chance, our only hope for a better life. For an endless army of the dead, mankind's only chance has vanished forever. I keep thinking about that. I can't understand why we had to take the wrong path. I only know it's too late.

After the tenth of December it snowed quietly and evenly for a week. The weather was just as I liked it, windless and calming. Nothing makes me feel more peaceful than the silent falling of the flakes or a summer rain after a storm. Sometimes a patch of the grayish-white sky would turn pink, and the forest sank behind delicate, luminous veils of snow. The sun, one sensed, hung somewhere behind our snowy world, but it didn't reach us. The crows sat motionlessly for hours in the spruce trees, waiting. There was something about their dark, fat-beaked outlines against the grayish-pink sky that touched me. Strange life, yet so familiar, red blood beneath black plumage, they symbolized stoic patience to me. A patience that has little to hope for and simply waits, ready to take the rough with the smooth. I knew so little about the crows; if I had died in the clearing they would have hacked and torn me to bits, in accordance with their task of keeping the forest free of carrion.

It was so lovely to go walking through the forest with Lynx on those days. The little flakes fell gently on my face, the snow crunched under my feet, I could barely hear Lynx behind me. I often considered our tracks in the snow, my heavy heels and the dog's dainty pads. Human being and dog reduced to the simplest formula. The air was clean but not cold, and it was a pleasure to walk and breathe. Had my legs been stronger, I could have walked for days like that through the snowy forest. But they were not strong. In the evening they ached and burned, and I often had to wrap them in damp towels so that I could go to sleep. In the course of the winter the pains eased a little, and didn't set in again until the summer. It irks me to be dependent on my legs. I paid them no attention for as long as that was possible. Up to a certain point one can get very used to pain; as I couldn't make my legs better, I got used to the pain.

Christmas was drawing ever closer, and everything presaged a glittering Christmas forest. I didn't like that much. I still didn't feel secure enough to think about Christmas without fear. I was susceptible to memories, and had to be careful. It snowed until the twentieth of December. The snow was now almost three feet deep, a fine-grained, blue-white layer under a gray sky. The sun no longer tried to break through the clouds, and the light stayed cold and white. I still didn't have to fear for the deer. The snow hadn't frozen, and the animals were able to scratch out the grass in the clearing. If there was a frost, a layer of frozen snow would form and the snow would become a dangerous trap. On the afternoon of the twentieth it grew a little warmer. The clouds turned slate-gray, and the snow fell in watery flakes. I didn't like thaws, but it was a boon to the deer. I slept badly at night, and heard the whistling of the wind blowing down from the mountains and rattling the tiles. I lay awake for a long time, and my legs were more painful than ever before. In the morning the snow had already fallen away in places. The stream was high, and in the gorge, too, the meltwater streamed into the road. I was happy for the deer. Wrongly, perhaps, because if a freeze followed the thaw it would be impossible to scratch up the hard ground. Nature sometimes struck me as one great trap for its creatures.

For the time being the weather was fine; the forest meadow lay almost free of snow in the sun, which suddenly broke from a purple sky between black clouds. The Christmas atmosphere had vanished, and I was now ready to deal with the foehn. I had pains in my heart, and the animals grew restless and irritable. Tiger had a new attack of the torments of love. His topaz-colored eyes grew dull, his nose was hot and dry, and he rolled plaintively around at my feet. Later he ran into the forest.

From all I've seen, being in love can't be a pleasant state for an animal. They can't know, after all, that it's a temporary thing; as far as they're concerned every moment is an eternity. Bella's gloomy calls, the laments of the old cat and Tiger's despair, nowhere a trace of happiness. And afterward exhaustion, dull coats and cadaverous sleep.

So poor Tiger had run crying into the forest. His mother crouched suddenly on the floor. She had hissed at him again when he tried to be affectionate. I took a good look at her and found that she had quietly grown plump under her winter coat. And her moody state on top of that. I could add two and two. Mr. Ka-au Ka-au had preempted his son long ago. The cat allowed me to examine her and gently feel her belly, and suddenly she caught my hand and carefully bit my knuckles. She looked as if she was laughing at my blindness.

Right then I was worrying less about Tiger. He had come back once before, after all, and he was fully grown and strong. But Tiger didn't come back, not that night, not ever. On the twenty-fourth of December I sent Lynx out to look for him. I took him on the leash, and he eagerly followed Tiger's trail. There were, of course, a lot of other trails in the forest, and Lynx sometimes became uncertain. For an hour he dragged me hither and thither, and suddenly he got very excited and almost pulled the leash from my hand. Then we were suddenly standing by the stream, far above the hunting lodge. Lynx looked up at me and barked softly. Tiger's trail ended here. We crossed the stream, but Lynx couldn't seem to find the trail again, and kept going back to the spot on the opposite bank. If

Tiger had fallen in the stream, something I was at pains to explain, the meltwater would have carried him off long before. I shall never know what happened to Tiger, and it still torments me today.

In the evening I sat by the lamp reading one of the diaries, but with my eyes alone; my thoughts were outside in the black forest. I kept looking to the cat door, but Tiger didn't come back. The foehn died down the next day, and it started snowing again. It snowed for days. I knew I would simply have to bear the new loss, and didn't even try to repress my anxiety about Tiger. The wall of snow by the hunting lodge grew larger, and I had to shovel the paths to the byres free of snow every day. I did my work and walked rather numbly around in the snowy desert. In the end I stopped waiting for Tiger every evening. But I didn't forget him. Even today his gray shade flits across my path in my dreams. Lynx and Bull have joined him; Pearl had gone on ahead. They have all left me, they have gone reluctantly, they would so much have liked to live out their short and guiltless lives. But I couldn't protect them.

The old cat is lying by me on the table, staring through me. Back then, a week after Tiger's disappearance, she withdrew into the cupboard and, whimpering terribly, gave birth to four dead kittens. I took them from her and buried them in the meadow beneath earth and snow. They were two tiny, beautifully marked little tigers, and two strawberry blondes. Everything about them was perfect, from their ears to the tips of their tails, and yet they hadn't been able to live. The cat was so ill that I was afraid of losing her, too. She had a fever, refused to eat, and kept uttering little cries of pain. But I still don't know what she needed, and can't imagine what it could have been. For days she could only lick milk from my fingers. Her coat was dead and unkempt, and her eyes were gummed up. And every night she dragged herself into the open and crept back wailing a few minutes later. She wouldn't befoul her bed or the hunting lodge at any price. I did what I could for her, made her drink chamomile tea with a tiny little piece of aspirin, which she swallowed only because she was too weak to spit it out. It was only then that I realized the cat had become a part of my life. Since her illness she seems to have grown more fond of me than before. A week later she started eating, and after four days more she resumed her old life. But something in her seemed to be broken. For hours she would crouch on the spot, and if I stroked her she would cry quietly and push her nose into the palm of my hand. She wasn't even up to hissing at Lynx when he sniffed at her inquisitively. She only lowered her head submissively and closed her eyes. During her illness she had had quite a strange smell, strong and rather bitter. It was three weeks before she lost that sick smell entirely. But then she quickly recovered, and her coat grew gleaming and thick once more.

Scarcely had the cat returned halfway to health than I fell ill. I had been pulling hay up the gorge for two days, and had come home exhausted and drenched in sweat. It wasn't until I came in from the byre and was on the point of changing my clothes that I noticed I was cold and trembling. The fire had gone out, and I had to light it again. I drank some hot milk, but it didn't make me feel any better. My teeth were chattering, and I could barely hold on to the bowl. I immediately realized that I was seriously ill, yet that struck me as extremely funny and made me laugh aloud. Lynx came by and prodded me reproachfully with his nose. And I couldn't stop laughing, unnaturally loud and long. But deep within me lay a very cold and clear awareness, observing what was happening. And I obediently did everything that this wakeful awareness commanded. I fed Lynx and the cat, laid fresh wood in the stove and went to bed. But first I took some more antifever tablets and drank a glass of Hugo's brandy. I had a high temperature, and tossed restlessly back and forth. I heard voices and saw faces, and someone pulled at my blanket. Sometimes the noise ebbed away, and I saw the darkness and felt Lynx moving by my bed. He hadn't gone into the stove door but now lay, as I had once hoped he would, on Luise's sheepskin. I was terribly worried about the animals, and wept inconsolably.

Toward morning the moments of daylight increased, and when the dawn of the snowy day entered the room I got up, put my clothes on, shivering, and went to the byre. I could think quite clearly, and hoped I would be able to milk Bella at least once a day. I climbed the slope and fetched hay for Bella and Bull, enough hay for two days. Then I filled their tub of water. Everything seemed to be happening very slowly, and I had violent pains in my side. Then I went back into the house, put out meat and milk for Lynx and the cat and laid fresh wood on the embers. I had left the door of the hunting lodge half open so that Lynx could get out. If I were to die he would need his freedom. Bella and Bull would easily be able to knock down their doors, the bolts were weak and the ropes were tied around their necks in such a way that they couldn't pull tight and strangle them if they tried to break them. And they weren't strong ropes. Even so, none of that would be any use to them because only cold and hunger awaited them outside the byre doors. I swallowed some more pills and brandy, and then sank dizzily into bed. But I had to struggle to my feet again. I went to the table and wrote in the diary: "Fell ill on the twenty-fourth of January." Then I carried a jug of milk to the bed and finally put out the candle and collapsed.

The fever beat hard in my veins, and I swam away on a hot, red cloud. The hunting lodge started filling up with people, but then it was no longer the hunting lodge but a dark, high-ceilinged hall. There was a constant coming and going. I had never known there were so many people. They were all unfamiliar to me, and behaved very weirdly. Their voices sounded like cackling; it made me laugh, and immediately I swam off again in my hot, red cloud and woke up in the cold. The big hall had turned into a cave, and was full of animals, enormous, furry shadows tapping along the walls, crouching in every corner and staring at me with red eyes. In between there were moments in which I lay in my bed and Lynx licked my hand, whining quietly. I wanted to comfort him, but all I could do was whisper. I knew too well that I was ill, and that I alone could save myself and the animals. I decided to keep that resolution in mind and not to forget it. I quickly swallowed pills and drank milk, and set off on my fiery journey once again. And they came, people and animals, enormous and very strange. They cackled and tore at my blanket, and their fingers and claws stuck into my side. I was abandoned to them, salt on my lips, sweat and tears. And then I woke up.

It was dark and cold, and my head ached. I lit the candle. It was four o'clock. The door was wide open, and the wind had blown snow into the middle of the hut. I put on my dressing gown, closed the door and lit the stove. It took a long time, but finally a quiet fire was burning and Lynx practically bowled me over and barked with joy. At any moment the fever might strike me again. I put on warm clothes and tapped my way to the byre. Bella greeted me plaintively. I suddenly suspected that I had been lying in fever for two days. I milked the poor beast and fetched hay and water. I think it took me an hour, I was so weak. I still had to attend to Bull, and it was dusk by the time I dragged myself back to the house. At least it had warmed up in the meantime. I put milk and meat on the floor for Lynx and the cat, and I drank a little milk, which tasted terrible. Then I fastened the door to the bench with a piece of string so that Lynx could only open it a crack. It was the best I could think of. I already felt the fever coming back. I put on some more wood, swallowed tablets and brandy, and new terrors engulfed me. Something lay heavy upon me, and suddenly they were clutching at me from all sides and trying to drag me down, and I knew I mustn't let them. I thrashed around and cried out, or thought I was crying out, and suddenly they were all gone and the bed stood still with a jolt. A figure bent over me, and I saw my husband's face. I could see it very clearly and stopped being frightened. I knew he was dead, and I was happy to see that face again, a good and familiar human face that I had touched so often. I reached out my hand and it dissolved. It was untouchable. A new wave of heat overwhelmed me. When I came to, the light of dawn was at the window. My temperature felt normal, and I felt weary and hollow. Lynx was lying on the little sheepskin rug, and the cat was lying asleep between me and the wall. She woke up although I hadn't moved, stretched out her paw and laid it slowly, toes spread, on my hand. I don't know whether she knew I was ill, but every time I awoke from the fever later on she lay beside me and looked at me. Lynx whined with joy the minute I spoke to him.

I wasn't alone, and I couldn't leave them. They were waiting for me so patiently. I drank milk with brandy and took more tablets, and when my temperature felt normal I got up and crept to the byre to attend to Bella and Bull. I don't know how often I did this, because every time I drifted into a restless half sleep I dreamed I was going to the byre to milk Bella, and immediately afterward I was lying in bed again, aware that I hadn't been to the byre. Everything grew inextricably muddled. But I must have managed to get up and do my work, or else the animals would not have got through my illness so well. I have no idea how long I spent in that twilight state. My heart danced great leaps in my breast, and Lynx kept trying to wake me up. At last he managed to get me to sit up and look around.

It was broad daylight and cold, and I knew I was no longer ill. My head was clear again, and the stitches in my side had stopped. I knew I had to get up, but it took me a long, long time to get out of bed. My watch and my alarm clock had stopped, and I knew neither what day nor what time it was. Stumbling weakly, I lit the fire, went to the byre and relieved the bellowing Bella of her burden of milk. I had to drag the water tub behind me in the snow because I couldn't pick it up, and when I was fetching the hay from the bedroom I sat down on the stairs three times. I did my work and somehow got back to the house after what seemed like an infinite length of time, Lynx constantly at my heels, licking my hands, pushing me, concern and joy in his reddish-brown eyes. Then I fed him and the cat, who were both very hungry, forced myself to drink warm milk and fell onto my bed. But Lynx wouldn't let me sleep. With indescribable difficulty I had undressed and crept under the blanket. I heard the fire crackling in the stove, and for a muddled heartbeat I became a sick child, waiting for my mother to bring me an eggnog in bed. Immediately afterward I went to sleep.

I must have slept for a very long time, since I was awoken by Lynx's whining, and felt quite well but very weak. I got up and, still stumbling a little, set about my usual tasks. The crows fell shrieking into the clearing and I set my watch at nine o'clock. From that moment it showed crows' time. I didn't know how long I had been ill, and after lengthy consideration I struck off a week from the diary. Since then the diary hasn't been right either.

The next week was very wearing and difficult. I didn't

do a stroke more than I needed to, but I was still very tired. Fortunately I had frozen half a deer and had no need to go far from the house. I ate apples, meat and potatoes and did everything I could to regain my strength. I had been seized by a terrible craving for oranges, and the thought that I would never have oranges again brought tears to my eyes. My lips were sore and blistered, and wouldn't heal properly in the cold. Lynx still treated me like a helpless child, yet when I slept he was sometimes gripped by fear and woke me up. The cat continued to lie in my bed and was very affectionate toward me. I don't know whether it was affection or a need for comfort. After all, she had lost her young and had been at death's door.

Very slowly we all returned to our usual life. Only Tiger's little shade cast a pall over my pleasure in recovering. I think that if he hadn't run away and the cat hadn't been ill, my illness wouldn't have affected me. I had often come home drenched to the skin in the past. But this time I hadn't had any resistance. Worry had made me weak and a prey to disease. My stay in the alpine pasture had transformed me a little, and the illness continued the transformation. I gradually started to break free of my past and find a new way of organizing things.

By mid-February I had recuperated to the point where I was able to go into the forest with Lynx and fetch hay. I was very careful and made sure not to exert myself too much. The weather stayed moderately cold, and the deer seemed to have survived the winter. I hadn't found any frozen or starved animals yet. It was delightful to be well again, to breathe the pure snowy air and feel that I was still alive. I drank a lot of milk and was more thirsty than ever. I tried to compensate Bella and Bull with especially loving care for the fear and distress my illness had put them through. But they both seemed to have forgotten everything long since. I currycombed their coats and promised them a fine, long summer in the Alm, and carelessly broke off pieces from my salt licks which I gave them as recompense. And they rubbed their noses against me and licked my hands with wet, rough tongues.

If I think back on that time today, Tiger's disappearance still casts a pall over it; I was almost glad that the kittens were stillborn, and that I was spared new love and worries.

At the end of February Bella called ardently for Bull, and I gave in again and risked another try. My hope later proved to have been in vain. I decided I would definitely wait until May. I felt a great uneasiness about the whole matter which developed into a constant source of irritation. Bull was still growing, and didn't seem to suffer from the cold. His coat grew thick and a little unkempt, and his big body always emanated a faint, tepid fragrance. Perhaps Bull would have been able to spend the whole winter in the open. I was still, of course, judging the animals' bodies on the basis of my own defenseless one. But the animals behaved in quite different ways, too. Lynx could bear heat and cold equally well; the cat, who had a much longer coat, hated the cold, and Mr. Ka-au Ka-au, although he was a cat as well, lived in the ice and snow of the forest in winter. I tended to feel the cold easily but neither could I have spent days lying in the warm stove door. And every time I saw a trout hovering in the pool shivers ran down my spine and I would feel sorry for it. I still feel sorry for the trout, because I simply can't imagine that it can be comfortable for them down there among the mossy stones. My imagination is very limited, and doesn't penetrate the smooth, white flesh of cold-blooded creatures.

And how strange insects are to me. I watch them and am amazed by them, but I'm glad they're so tiny. An ant the size of a man would be a nightmare to me. I think I exclude bumblebees only because with their downy fur they look like tiny mammals.

Sometimes I wish that strangeness would turn to familiarity, but I'm still a long way from that. Strangeness and badness are still one and the same thing for me. And I see that not even animals are free of this idea. This autumn a white crow appeared. It always flies a little way behind the others, and settles alone on a tree avoided by its companions. I can't understand why the other crows don't like it. I think it's a particularly beautiful bird, but the other members of its species find it repugnant. I see it sitting alone in its spruce tree staring over the meadow, a miserable absurdity that shouldn't exist, a white crow. It sits there until the great flock has flown away, and then I bring it a little food. It's so tame that I can get close to it. Sometimes it hops about on the ground when it sees me coming. It can't know why it's been ostracized; that's the only life it knows. It will always be an outcast and so alone that it's less afraid of people than its black brethren. Perhaps they find it so repugnant that they can't even peck it to death. Every day I wait for the white crow and call to it, and it looks at me attentively with its reddish eyes. I can do very little for it. Perhaps my scraps are prolonging a life that shouldn't be prolonged. But I want the white crow to live, and sometimes I dream that there's another one in the forest and that they will find each other. I don't believe it will happen, I only wish it very dearly.

Because of my illness, February seemed very short. At the beginning of March it suddenly turned warm, and the snow melted from the slopes. I was afraid the cat would set off on her adventures, but she showed no sign of being in love. The illness had taken its toll on her. Often she would play like a young kitten, and then fall back, weak and drowsy. She was friendly and patient, and Lynx enjoyed being near her. They even ended up sleeping side by side in the stove door. This transformation unsettled me slightly, it seemed to be a sign that the cat still hadn't quite recovered. I was still rather weak too, and that was dangerous. I absolutely had to regain my strength in time to do my work in the spring. I still had a little pain in my left side. I couldn't breathe deeply, and whenever I fetched hay or chopped wood this shortness of breath was an obstacle. The pain wasn't terrible, just troublesome, a constant reminder. I still feel it before a change in the weather, but since the summer I can breathe deeply again. I'm afraid the illness weakened my heart a little. But I can't pay much attention to that.

There was something tiring and dangerous about the whole of that March. I had to take care, yet I couldn't go all that easy on myself. The sun tempted me to sit on the bench, but it made me too drowsy and I had to stop. It's boring to have to think about one's own health all the time, and I usually forgot about it entirely. The earth was still cold, and as soon as the sun had set the air grew wintry, raw and cool. The grass had survived so well under the snow that in places it had stayed green. The deer found enough to eat in the forest meadow.

I spent the whole of March chopping wood. I worked slowly, since I was short of breath, but the woodcutting was of vital importance and had to be done. Everything I did was a little dreamlike, as if I was walking on cotton wool rather than the solid forest floor. I didn't worry much, and oscillated between hectic gaiety and superficial concern. I realized I was behaving like the cat, who, because of her illness, had regressed to a childlike way of life. Before I fell asleep I often felt as though I was lying in my walnut bed beside my parents' bedroom, listening to the monotonous murmur that penetrated through the wall to me and sent me to sleep. I kept telling myself I finally had to be strong and adult again, but I actually wanted to go back to the warmth and silence of the nursery, or even further back into the warmth and silence from which I had been torn into the light. I was vaguely aware of the danger, but the temptation to allow myself to fall after so many years was too strong for me to resist. It made Lynx unhappy. He urged me to go with him into the forest, to do this and that and shake off my drowsiness. My little childish self got very angry with Lynx and wasn't wanting any of it. So I walked out in the moist gleam of the March days that had prematurely tempted the flowers from the earth. Liverworts, cowslips, larkspur and buttercups. They were all very lovely, and created for my delight.

Who knows how long I would have gone on living like that if Lynx hadn't intervened. He had got used to going on little expeditions off his own bat, and one afternoon he came back whining and showed me his bloody, squashed front paw. I suddenly became an adult woman again. It looked as if Lynx had got caught under a heavy stone. I washed the paw, and as I couldn't establish if it was broken I made a splint with little bits of wood and wrapped a medicated bandage around it. Lynx gladly put up with all this, overjoyed by the interest I was showing in him. He spent the next two days lying in the stove door dozing. I reproached myself with the fact that it was my fault that the dog was in this state. I simply hadn't paid him any attention; I had abandoned him. I examined the paw again and saw that it wasn't broken. Lynx started to lick off the medication and I didn't replace the bandage. Lynx himself knew very well what was good for him, and he wanted to be able to lick his wound. After a week he was running again, with a limp at first, but soon as well as he had done before. The paw was left a little broader and more shapeless than it had been.

Suddenly the past few weeks struck me as entirely unreal. I thought about my work again and made plans to move to the Alm. Then winter started in once more. The snow buried the trees in the meadow by the stream and my dreams of the sheltered sleep of childhood. There was no certainty in my world, only dangers on all sides and hard work. And that suited me fine; the thought of what I had recently become repelled me.

The woodpile near the hut had all been burnt, and I set about dragging logs through the snow from a pile a little further away. The snow was smooth and hard, and I began to enjoy the work. My hands were soon chapped again, and full of pitch and little splinters. The saw had blunted a little, and I didn't dare sharpen it because I was afraid I would break the last blade in my clumsiness. So wood-cutting became hard work, and I went to bed completely exhausted every night. But in the end I worked up a hunger, and could even eat meat with relish. I soon noticed that I was getting stronger and more skillful again. Lynx ran all over the place with me, and didn't seem to notice his paw anymore. We were now three invalids, active invalids, since the cat had finally cheered up and cast aside her unnatural gentleness. Bull was growing even bigger and more magnificent, and the garage looked like a doll's house to me, he filled it so thoroughly. I looked forward to the day when he would feel the meadows of the pasture beneath his hooves once more.

Only the idea of the cat tormented me every evening when I thought of the move. There was no point in taking her. She would only run home again, and if I left her behind I could at least spare her the dangers of the long journey back. I watched her reverting to her prickly old self more and more, and could only hope she could cope with summer in the forest. If she had still been ill I should certainly have taken her with me. Her misfortune had made me so fond of her that the coming farewell quite spoiled any anticipation I might have derived from the Alm. I would much rather have stayed in the hunting lodge. My incomprehensible antipathy toward the Alm, incomprehensible after so fine a summer, had not quite disappeared as yet. Perhaps this was only due to my laziness, which made me shy away from exertion. Perhaps I should have obeyed my instincts, but I thought I owed Bella and Bull another summer in the pasture.

It stayed cold and damp all April, and in the last third of that month the weather was so stormy that I had to stay in the hunting lodge. I didn't enjoy this compulsory rest. I was filled with the desire to work, and now had to set about mending my clothes for the summer. My hands were so chapped that the thread kept getting caught on them, the needle slipped through my fingers and I had to look for it again and rethread it. For a while yet I didn't have to worry about clothes. The shoe situation was much worse. I had a pair of stout climbing boots with heavy, indestructible rubber soles, and also Luise's climbing boots which were a little too big for me, but which I would also be able to wear if I had to. But the shoes I'd been wearing when I arrived were in a terrible state. The lining was torn and the tips and heels worn down, and they could hardly last another summer. In the meantime I've sewn myself some moccasins from a dried-out deer hide. They aren't much to look at, but very pleasant to wear. Unfortunately they won't keep long. Back then I hadn't yet hit on that alternative. The sock situation was poor as well. My darning wool had been used up long before, and I had to make do with brightly colored woolen threads that I pulled out of a blanket.

I'd stopped wearing proper clothes a long time ago. I'd found the clothes that were practical for me ages before: Hugo's shirts, whose sleeves I had shortened; my old corduroy trousers; a loden Tyrolean jacket; a woolen vest and in the winter Hugo's long lederhosen, which flapped about me. In the summer I wore shorts tailored from an elegant pair of brocade trousers that Luise had worn in the evening in the hunting lodge. My dressing gown was still in quite good condition, since I wore it only in the house. All in all a less than flattering, but an appropriate wardrobe. I barely gave my appearance a thought. My animals didn't care about my outer shell, they certainly didn't love me for my appearance. They probably had no sense of beauty whatsoever; I can't imagine that a human being would have seemed beautiful to them.

So I spent a few days on this tiresome needlework. It was so cold and windy that not even Lynx showed any desire for expeditions. He sat in the stove door soaking in the warmth. The cat lay on my clothes on the table. She very much liked lying on clothes; Pearl and Tiger had always done the same. Whenever I said anything she started purring, sometimes a look from me was enough to set her off. The wind blew around the hunting lodge, and we were warm and comfortable. If the silence grew too great and oppressive I talked a little, and the cat answered with little cooing noises. Sometimes I sang as well, and the cat didn't mind. I could have been content if I'd managed to eliminate thoughts of the past entirely, but I managed to do that only very seldom.

On the twenty-sixth of April my alarm clock stopped. I was sitting taking in a shirt when it stopped ticking. I didn't notice at all, or rather I noticed only that something had changed. Only when the cat pricked up her ears and turned her head toward the bed did I consciously hear the new silence. The alarm clock had died. It was the alarm clock that I had found in the hunting lodge further up the hill on my expedition into the next valley. I picked it up, shook it, and it uttered a last ticktock and was then finished for good. I unscrewed the back with the scissors. It looked quite healthy as far as I could see, but refused to tick anymore. I knew straightaway that I would never manage to make it go again. So I left it in peace and screwed the back on again. It was three o'clock in the afternoon, crows' time, and that's what it has said ever since. I don't know why I kept it. It still stands by my bed, showing three o'clock. Now all I had was the watch, which had always been kept in the drawer of the table since I would only have broken it while working.

Today I don't own a single clock. I lost the watch on the way back from the Alm. Bella's hooves may well have stamped it into the earth. Back then I felt it wasn't important anymore, and I didn't go back looking for it. But I probably wouldn't have found it in any case. It was such a tiny watch, a gold toy that my husband had given me years before. He had always liked to see me wearing dainty and pretty things. I would much rather have had a big, practical watch, but today I'm glad I feigned delight over the present back then. So, the little watch was gone too. The time it showed had long ceased to be even accurate crows' time. Those little watches never go properly. At first I missed the alarm clock. For a few nights I couldn't get to sleep in the new, oppressive silence. I woke up in the night with the familiar ticking in my ear, but it was only my heartbeat waking me up. The cat was the first to understand the death of the alarm clock, Lynx hadn't noticed it at all. The stopping of a clock wasn't a sign of danger, of danger or deer, so he didn't notice it at all. He was quite insensitive to familiar noises, even if they were violent and loud. But if, when he was stalking, a twig snapped quietly, he would stop and stand sniffing the air. Now nobody can differentiate between harmless and threatening noises for me. I have to be very careful. The cat listens day and night, but not for me.

It was May by the time the weather really improved. Two years had passed in the forest, and it struck me that I now hardly ever gave a thought to the idea that someone might at last find me. I spent the first May digging the potato field and carting dung to it. The second May passed the same way. Overnight it was summer, and along with the frozen brown spring flowers everything was now bursting into the light, all at once. I returned to my wood-cutting work and stacked a new supply under the veranda. Winter was not to catch me by surprise. On the tenth of May, which had stayed summery and warm, I planted the potatoes, and noted with satisfaction that I had more left over this time. I'd also been able to enlarge the field some-what. I planted the beans as well, and that was the most important springtime work done. I decided to set off soon for the alpine pasture. There wasn't much hay left, and I let Bella and Bull into the meadow. Bull had eaten and eaten all through the winter, and had sometimes drunk the fine skimmed milk. I fetched hay from the barn again so as to have a little supply to hand in the autumn, when I came back. The fruit trees were in full bloom, and the grass had shot up in a week, and on the other side of the wall the nettles were already burgeoning around the cot-tage. The trees blossomed very late that year, but at least there was a hope that the frost wouldn't catch them.

Over the days that followed it grew cold and rainy again, but the saints' days in the middle of May turned out to be very mild, and on the seventeenth of May it was so fine again that I started the move. It seemed a lot more strenuous than the previous year, because I still couldn't breathe properly, and coughed as I carried my heavy loads. The grass in the pasture was already thick and green, and there was only a little snow left in the shady spots under the trees.

The cat observed my preparations morosely. If I tried to stroke her she stared coldly into my eyes and refused to purr. She had already grasped what was going on, and I could understand her indignation. I felt very guilty beneath her gaze. For the last few nights she stopped sleeping in my bed, and went instead to the hard wooden bench. On the morning of our departure she hadn't come home at all. The day was spoiled for me from the start. I could persuade myself today that the cat was trying to warn me. But that would be a lie. She just didn't want to be left alone, and there was nothing mysterious about that. No one wants to be abandoned, not even an old cat.

It was a glorious early-summer day, but I had a heavy heart. I've always found farewells extremely difficult, even if they're only for a short time. I like to stay in one place, and traveling has always made me unhappy. My thoughts were still in the old hunting lodge, which now lay in the morning sun, its doors locked and its shutters closed. An abandoned house is a very sad thing. As we climbed the hill I was in some intermediate place; I was at home nowhere. This time I hadn't left a note on the table, it hadn't occurred to me. Toward noon we reached the alpine pasture, and I was torn from my brooding. Lynx flew over the meadow toward the hut, barking jubilantly. He remembered the previous summer, and was immediately quite at home. I left Bella and Bull in the meadow. I still couldn't stop feeling uneasy, but I pulled myself together and went to work after a short rest. I fetched fallen wood from the byre and washed a year's dust from the floor. I kept thinking about Tiger, and when I opened the cupboard I expected for a confused moment to find the little cat rolled up asleep. I went weak at the knees and had to keep a grip on myself until my faint spell had passed.

Later I sat down on the bench by the house staring numbly before me. Everything was still there, the rain barrel, the chopping block and the woodpile, as if they were waiting for our old morning routine. I knew I couldn't go on like this, but I'd never been capable of simply nipping an anxiety in the bud. I always had to wait until it was ripe and mature and fell from me. But I was able to work. I went in search of kindling, and spent the whole afternoon carting one bundle after the other to the hut. I laid them out there to dry in the sun. I'd already laid the blankets and the pallet in the meadow in the afternoon. They weren't exactly damp, but they smelled a little musty. In the winter the snow must have covered the hut to the roof up here. This time I'd brought more potatoes with me, and stored them in the bedroom. There was no chance of finding flour anywhere. If there was any in one of the huts, it would have gone rotten long ago or been eaten up by the mice. On the third day I shot a young stag, and packed the salted meat into clay pots which I bound shut and buried in a shady hollow in the snow. I still felt dejected, but Bella and Bull were content. They sometimes interrupted their grazing, trotted to the hut and stuck their big heads through the door. They didn't come only out of affection, but because I'd become accustomed to letting them lick a little salt from my hand.

It wasn't until the fifth day that I went to the vantage point with Lynx. The landscape was now a single blooming, blossoming wilderness. I could hardly tell field and meadows apart by their color. The weeds had emerged victorious everywhere. Even in the first summer the smaller roads had been overgrown, and now the wide asphalt road was visible only in little dark islands. The seeds had taken root in the cracks left by the frost. Soon there would no longer be a road. The sight of the distant church towers barely moved me this time. I waited for the familiar onslaught of anxiety and despair, but it didn't come. I felt as though I'd spent fifty years in the forest, and the towers were now nothing to me but constructions of stone and tiles. They didn't affect me at all anymore. I even found myself thinking that Bella wasn't giving much milk now, and that it was a good thing that I'd left the butter churn in the valley. Then I stood up and went deeper into the forest with Lynx. My coldness alarmed me. Something had changed; I had to come to terms with the new reality. The thought made me uneasy, but I could escape that unease only by passing straight through it and leaving it behind me. I couldn't try to keep the old mourning alive artificially. The circumstances of my former life had often forced me to lie; but now every occasion and every excuse for lies had disappeared. I wasn't living among human beings anymore, after all.

By the beginning of June I'd managed to get used to the Alm, but it wasn't as it had been the previous year. That first summer there was gone irrevocably, and I didn't want a feeble repetition of it and therefore kept myself from succumbing once more to the old magic. But the pasture didn't make it hard for me, it had closed itself off to me and showed me an unfamiliar face.

There was less to do than there had been the previous year, because butter and fat production had declined. Bella wasn't giving much milk, and Bull finally had to start drinking nothing but water. Bella gave just enough milk for my daily needs, and I'd gone back to beating my little bit of butter with the whisk. Poor Bella, unless a miracle happened soon she wouldn't have another calf.

I often sat, as I had done a year before, on the bench by the house looking out over the meadow. It hadn't changed from before, and it smelt just as sweet, but I didn't go into the old raptures ever again. I industriously sawed my fallen wood, and I had a lot of time left over to go to the forest with Lynx. But I'd stopped making longer expeditions, for I'd drawn up my boundaries the previous summer. I no longer cared where the wall went, I had no desire to find ten more rotting woodmen's huts smelling of mice. The nettles would already have penetrated through the cracked doors into the huts, and would be flourishing in every cranny. I preferred just walking through the forest with Lynx for the sheer joy of it. It was better for me than sitting idly on the bench looking out over the meadow. A steady walk on the old paths, which were already starting to grow over, always calmed me down again, and it was a daily delight for Lynx in particular. Every expedition was a big adventure for him. Back then I talked to him a lot, and he understood the sense of almost everything I said. Who knows, perhaps he understood more than I thought. That summer I quite forgot that Lynx was a dog and I was a human being. I knew it, but it had lost any distinctive meaning. Lynx too had changed. Since I'd been spending so much time with him he had grown calmer, and didn't seem constantly afraid that I might vanish into thin air as soon as he went off for five minutes. Thinking about it today, I believe that was the only big fear in his dog's life, being abandoned on his own. I too had learned a lot more, and understood almost all his movements and noises. Now, at last, there was a silent understanding between us.

On the twenty-eighth of June, when I came back from the forest with Lynx toward evening, I saw Bull mounting Bella. I'd stopped paying attention to her bellowing in the night. When I saw the two great creatures merging together against the pink evening sky I felt certain there would be a calf this time. It had to happen that way, in a big meadow, against the evening sky, without human intervention. But even now I'm not sure whether I was right. In any case, from then on Bella stopped calling for Bull, and Bull occupied himself solely with stuffing as much sweet grass as possible into his big, strong body, dozing in the sun or flying across the meadows at a gallop. He was an extraordinarily beautiful and powerful animal, and very good-natured. Sometimes he would lay his head heavily on my shoulder and snuffle with contentment when I scratched his forehead. Perhaps he would later have grown wild and sulky. Back then he was just a huge calf, trusting, playful and always ready for a good feed. I don't think he was as clever as his mother, but then it wasn't his task in life to be clever. It was funny how he even obeyed Lynx, who looked like a mere yapping dwarf in comparison with him.

Today I think that Bella will have a calf. She's giving more milk than she did in the autumn, and she's grown significantly fatter. If that's the case, according to my farmer's diary the calf would be born at the end of March. Bella isn't conspicuously fat, but there's more fat on her than I can attribute solely to the fine hay. Even four weeks ago I didn't dare hope, and I still have my doubts today; perhaps I'm only convincing myself of things I wish very dearly. I shall have to wait and be patient.

Back then, in the alpine pasture, I was much more tormented by uncertainty. It was so important for me that Bella should have a calf. Otherwise I would very soon have had to work hard for two completely useless animals that I wouldn't have been capable of killing. Only Bella didn't seem in the least concerned about our future. It was a delight to watch her. She had kept her role as leader. If Bull got too uppity she would rebuke him by butting him with her head, and he would behave himself; he never strayed far from his dainty wife and mother. That was a great comfort to me, for I knew that Bella was sensible and that I could rely on her. Good sense filled her entire body and always ensured that she did the right thing. Lynx still didn't enjoy playing cowherd's dog, and did it only if I gave him express commands. I wanted to recover a little in the run-up to the hay harvest. I could still quite clearly feel the aftereffects of the illness. I was eating enough, getting a lot of fresh air and sleeping soundly.

On the first of July, it says in my diary, I could breathe deeply again for the first time. The last obstacle was removed, and only now did I realize how great a torment my shortness of breath had been, even if I hadn't noticed it. For an hour I felt as if I was reborn, and then I couldn't imagine that things had ever been otherwise. In a few weeks I had to start bringing in the hay harvest, and it was important for me to be able to breathe properly in the steep mountain meadow.

On the second of July I went into the valley to hoe the potatoes. It had rained, and the weeds had proliferated much more strongly than they had the previous dry summer. I worked in the field all morning. In the hunting lodge I'd found the familiar hollow on the bed, but I didn't know how old it was. I stroked the cover smooth, filled the rucksack with potatoes and climbed back up the hill. In the middle of July I made a second expedition and inspected the meadow by the stream. The grass was high, and much lusher than it had been the previous year. The summer was changeable; rainy and warm days followed one another in close succession. It was wonderful weather for anything that was supposed to grow and blossom. Since I still had time, I caught three trout and fried them in the hunting lodge. I would have liked to leave one for the cat, but I knew she wouldn't touch anything in my absence, sly and suspicious as she was. I wanted to wait for the waxing moon, which would perhaps bring rather more constant weather. I also decided to make the work rather easier for myself this year. Since Bella didn't have much milk she needed milking only once a day, and I was able to spend the night in the hunting lodge and start scything, well rested, in the first light.

So that's how things were at the end of July. I milked Bella and shut her and Bull in the byre. They weren't happy, but I couldn't do anything about it. I gave them a good supply of grass and water and went into the valley with Lynx. At eight o'clock in the evening I arrived at the

hunting lodge, ate a cold supper and went to bed immediately so as to be fresh in the morning. Since I no longer
had the alarm clock, I had to rely on the clock in my head.
I would imagine the number four, very large and clear, and
could be sure to wake up at four o'clock. I'd already had a
lot of practice doing that, back then.

But I woke up at three, because the cat jumped on my
bed and greeted me joyfully. She alternated between reproachful accusations and affection. I was wide awake,
but lay in bed another while longer, and the cat snuggled
up purring against my legs. I think we were both happy
with life for half an hour. I got up at half past three and
prepared my breakfast by the light of the lamp, which I
missed every evening in the Alm. The cat crept under the
cover and went back to sleep. I left her a little fried meat
and then, after I'd had my own breakfast and fed Lynx, I
set off for the gorge. It was still quite dark and cold. The
water ran down from the rocks in rapid rivulets and seeped
into the road. I had to walk slowly so as not to stumble
over the stones washed out by the last cloudburst. The
road seemed to be in a pitiful state. The water from the
thaw had already dug big channels in the spring, and by
the side of the stream the soil had crumbled in places
and fallen into the water. In the autumn I would have to
repair the road before winter destroyed it entirely. I should
have done it long before, but I hadn't been able to face it.
There was no excuse for that, and it served me right when
I almost broke my legs in the dim morning light. When
I'd arrived at the meadow I fetched the scythe from the
barn and started swinging it. The ice-cold water of the
stream drove the last sleep from me. By the time I started
cutting it was almost light. The scythe hissed through the
grass, and the moist swathes fell. I clearly noticed how
much better I scythed when I was well rested. I went on
for about three hours, and I was very tired by the end of

it. Lynx crept out of the barn where he'd been sleeping, and went back to the hut with me. I went to bed with the cat, who snuggled against me, purring furiously, and went back to sleep immediately. The hut door was open, and the sun cast a bright yellow glow on the doorstep. Lynx had lain down on the bench by the house, and lay dozing in the first warmth. I slept until noon, then had a bite to eat and went back to the meadow to turn the grass. When I came back the cat had gone away after eating the meat. That suited me fine, because I didn't want to see her disappointment when I had to leave her again.

At about seven o'clock we arrived at the Alm, and I immediately went to the byre to free Bella and Bull. I tethered Bella and left her outside for the night. Then I washed at the spring, drank some hot milk and went to bed.

The following day I milked Bella again in the afternoon and shut her and Bull in the byre. I slept in the hunting lodge, and the cat came and snuggled against my feet. I'd brought a flask of milk with me, and she thanked me by arching her back and pushing her head against me over and over. In the morning I scythed another large area, though I didn't go back to bed but turned the grass I'd cut the previous day a second time. It was half-dry and smelled sweet and mild. By the afternoon I was able to take some of it to the barn and turn the grass I'd cut in the morning.

With this new plan I was able to make quick progress. While the moon was waxing the weather stayed hot and fine. This time I wanted to harvest part of an adjacent meadow as well, because I didn't want to end up short of grass again. But the weather turned when I'd finished the big meadow, and it rained for a week with daily interruptions. It was pleasant weather that allowed the alpine meadow to grow with new vigor, but it wasn't haymaking weather. So I waited, since most of the harvest had already been brought in, and I had nothing to worry about. My legs were in a bad state again anyway. I bound wet towels around them and went to bed in the daytime when I could. Lynx was unhappy about my immobility at first, but I showed him my sore legs and explained everything to him, and in the end he even seemed to understand. He prowled about the meadow on his own, but always stayed within hailing distance. At that time he was devoting himself to the pleasure of digging up mice. The weather had turned at the right time. I couldn't let my legs heal entirely, but they did recover enough for me to return to my haymaking work after this break. It took me a week to harvest the smaller meadow. This time the cat's welcome was calmer, and I hoped I'd cheered her up a little. She probably didn't need cheering up, but thinking about her put my mind at rest.

Summer had gone curiously quickly, not only in my memory. I know it struck me as very short at the time. This year the raspberry patch was even more overgrown, and I found only one bucket of berries, unusually large but not very sweet fruits. But of course they were still sweet as far as I was concerned. I let them dissolve on my tongue and thought about all the sweet things of the past. I have to laugh when I think about the hero in adventure stories plundering the hives of the wild bees. There aren't any wild bees in my forest, and if there were I would never dare plunder their hives but would keep well away from them. I'm not a hero, not a resourceful person. I shall never learn to rub two sticks together to make a spark, or find a flint, because I'd never recognize one. I can't even fix Hugo's lighter, although I have flints and petrol. I can't even build a decent door for the byre. And that's constantly nagging at me.

I stayed in the Alm for the rest of August, always a little hampered by my aching legs. But I'd resumed the walks with Lynx, because if I lay idly on the bed I thought too much. I was already looking forward to the move, and summer had seemed a mere interlude.

I went into the valley again on the tenth of September to hoe the potatoes. They were particularly fine. The beans had multiplied a great deal as well. There had been few storms and no high winds or floods. This time I left Bull and Bella in the meadow. The fine weather tempted me not to rob them of this sunny day.

I got to the pasture at around five o'clock. Suddenly, before I had a clear view of the hut, Lynx gave a start and then ran across the meadow, barking furiously. I'd never heard him barking like that, ferocious and hate-filled. I knew straightaway that he'd seen something terrible. When the hut had stopped blocking my view, I saw it. A human being, a strange man was standing in the meadow, and before him lay Bull. I could see that he was dead, an enormous, gray-brown hill. Lynx jumped at the man and snapped at his throat. I called him off with a piercing whistle; he obeyed, and stood growling and bristling in front of the stranger. I dashed into the hut and tore the rifle from the wall. It took a few seconds, but those few seconds cost Lynx his life. Why couldn't I run faster? While I was still running I saw the glint of the ax and heard the dull crack as it fell on Lynx's skull.

I aimed and fired, but Lynx was already dead.

The man dropped the hatchet and collapsed with a strange spinning motion. I didn't pay him any attention as I knelt beside Lynx. I couldn't see any injury, but a little blood was dripping from his nose. Bull's execution had been terrible; his skull, hewed open by repeated ax strokes, lay in a big pool of blood. I carried Lynx to the hut and laid him on the bench. He'd suddenly grown small and light. And then, as if from a great distance, I heard Bella roaring. She was standing pressed against the byre wall, beside herself with fear. I led her into the byre and tried to calm her down. Only then did I give another thought to the man. I knew he must be dead, he had been such a big target that I couldn't have missed. I was glad he was dead; it would have been hard for me to kill an injured person. And yet I couldn't have left him alive. Or maybe I could, I don't know. I turned him onto his back. He was very heavy. I didn't want a clearer view of him. His face was very ugly. His clothes, dirty and dilapidated, were made of expensive material and had been stitched by a good tailor. Perhaps he had been a game-tenant like Hugo or one of the lawyers, directors and industrialists that Hugo had invited so often. Whatever he might have been, now he was just dead.

I didn't want to leave him in the meadow; not beside the dead Bull, in the virgin grass. So I picked him up by the legs and dragged him to the vantage point. There, where the rocks fall steeply to the scree slope and alpine roses bloom in June, I let him roll down the hill. I left Bull lying where he was. He was too big and heavy. In the summer his skeleton will bleach in the meadow, flowers and grasses will grow through him and he will sink very slowly into the rain-damp earth.

I dug a grave for Lynx in the evening. Under that shrub with the sweet-smelling leaves. I dug the hole deep, laid Lynx into it, covered it with earth and stamped the grass down over it. And then I was very tired, more tired than ever before. I washed at the spring, then I went to Bella in the byre. She didn't give a drop of milk, and was still trembling. I gave her a tubful of water, but she wouldn't drink. Then I sat down on the bench and waited for the long night. It was a bright, starlit night, and the wind drifted coldly down from the cliffs. But I was colder than the wind and didn't feel the chill.

Bella started roaring again. In the end I fetched my

pallet and carried it into the byre. I lay down on it fully dressed. It was only then that Bella fell silent, and I think she fell asleep.

At first light I got up, packed my rucksack and tied another bundle on top of it, took the rifle and left the Alm with Bella. The moon hung flat and pale in the sky, and the first pink light of dawn colored the rocks. Bella walked quietly, her head lowered. Sometimes she stopped and glanced back, bellowing gloomily.

Anything I didn't absolutely need is still at the Alm today, and I'm not going to fetch it. Or perhaps this will pass, too, and I will be able to set foot there again.

I took Bella to her old byre, fed her and moved back into the hunting lodge. During the night the cat came and lay down beside me, and I slept soundly, exhausted.

The next day I resumed my usual work. Bella went on roaring for two days, and then she was quiet. While the weather lasted I let her graze in the clearing. The very next day I set about mending the road. That took ten days. October came, and I harvested potatoes, beans and fruit. Then I dug the field and spread dung on it. I'd sawed up so much wood in the spring that I couldn't store any more under the veranda. The straw needed cutting, but that took only a week, and finally, physically beaten and broken, I abandoned my senseless flight and confronted my thoughts, to no purpose. I don't understand what happened. Even today I wonder why the strange man killed Bull and Lynx. I'd called Lynx off, and he had to stand there defenseless, waiting for his skull to be caved in. I'd like to know why the strange man killed my animals. I'll never find out, and it may even be better that way.

When winter came in November, I decided to write this report. It was my last resort. I couldn't spend the whole winter sitting at the table with that one question in my head, a question that no human being, nobody at all in the world, can answer. I've spent almost four months writing this report.

Now I'm quite calm. I can see a little further ahead. I can see that this isn't the end. Everything goes on. Since this morning I've been absolutely sure that Bella will have a calf. And, who knows, perhaps there will be kittens again. Bull, Pearl, Tiger and Lynx will never exist again, but something new is coming and I can't escape that. If there should come a time when I am without fire, without ammunition, I shall deal with it and find a way. But now I have other things to do. As soon as the weather turns warmer I shall set about converting the bedroom into Bella's new byre, and I'll also manage to break open the door. I still don't know how, but I'll definitely find a way. I shall be very close to Bella and the new calf, and shall watch over them day and night. Memories, mourning and fear will remain, and hard work, as long as I live.

Today, the twenty-fifth of February, I shall end my report. There isn't a single sheet of paper left. It's now around five o'clock in the evening, and already so light that I can write without the lamp. The crows have risen, and circle screeching over the forest. When they are out of sight I shall go to the clearing and feed the white crow. It will already be waiting for me.

Afterword

Recently, just after Christmas, I had a fairly pleasant conversation on the phone with someone I used to be in a relationship with. I told him about the daughters of two friends of mine, one of the girls is three, the other just turned four. After I'd finished recounting a couple of stories about them and the funny things they say, my ex said, "It's strange, isn't it, the way you're not really interested in all that." "Strange for who?" I said back, and he laughed, that slow luxuriant laugh that I occasionally still find attractive and irritating. I live alone and have done for many years and it doesn't feel strange to me at all. As a child, whenever I dared imagine myself as an adult, I always envisaged living on my own. I was deeply impressed by the cheerful dens I came across in folk tales and adventure stories, and invariably pictured myself in just such an abode. I liked the way the wily creatures who lived in these elemental dwelling places made ingenious use of the things around them: acorn cupules for bowls, pine cones to grate nutmeg, harebells as caps in the rain. A living space, in all senses of the word. Those early images of home never expired, and about ten years ago they manifested in reality—there, through the hedgerow, as if by magic, stood a four-hundred-year-old thatched cottage, my not-so-new home for a little while. It really was a dream come true. But how was I to live in it? This might appear to be a stupid question—who needs to think about how to occupy their home? Probably not many people since most homes are inhabited by a family, and are therefore designed to optimize security, comfort, and convenience; the kind of pact you have with those sorts of habitations is fairly straightforward. What are you supposed to do, however, if you are the sole tenant of an old stone and dank reed pile that is already bristling with mice and wasps and birds and spiders and perpetual drizzle? Shifting away from the popular perspective, which casts living alone as a grim state of affairs, I wanted to embrace it as a fruitful situation, which would entail, I anticipated, conceiving of the home as something other than a domestic space. In what other ways could it function? What does it mean to dwell? What does it mean to belong? I sought out a few books that explored various modes of inhabiting that did not revolve around family life and interior design, books such as *The Poetics of Space* by Gaston Bachelard, *In Praise of Shadows* by Junichiro Tanizaki, and *A Book of Silence* by Sara Maitland. Distinct in approach, each of these texts taps into the cosmic potential that the intimate relationship we have to our immediate surroundings engenders, and the capacity for reverie it can encourage. Beautiful, imaginative, and stimulating; yet occasionally a little far-flung—I had a yen for something more rugged and quotidian. I was aware of *Walden* of course, but didn't foresee that it would be much use to me, written as it is by a man. Men can live alone in the woods for years on end without anyone thinking too much about it. If you are a woman living alone, on the other hand, there must be something wrong with you; you are unappealing, or barren, or disturbed, or conniving, or frigid, or selfish, or degenerate, or bereft, or spent, or difficult, or abandoned, or deviant, or bonkers—someone to be wary of in any case, because it's quite unnatural, it's *strange* isn't it, to live on your own if you're a woman. What on earth do you do all day? Nothing good, that's for sure, since you're not involved with taking care of anyone. What kind of woman spends her days not looking after someone else? If you are a woman and you want to avoid causing offence there needs to be a legibility to your actions. You cannot be an unquantifiable presence on the periphery. The only way a woman can experience solitude, without judgment and recrimination scuffing up against her peace, is if the rest of the world has come to a complete standstill and there is no one around to see her. That's how it must have seemed to Marlen Haushofer, who, in writing *The Wall*, devised the most extraordinary scenario in order to imagine herself into a place where she could live alone and be free.

Born Maria Helene Frauendorfer on April 11, 1920, Haushofer grew up in Frauenstein, Molln, a mountainous and densely forested part of Austria. Her mother, a former maid, was strict, somewhat distant, and deeply religious. Her father was a forester in Effertsbach. When she was just twenty-one years old she married a dentist named Manfred Haushofer, they had two sons together and lived mostly in Steyr, where Manfred's dental practice was. The pair divorced in 1950, but reunited in 1957. Haushofer looked after the children, took care of the house, and helped out at the dental practice. She wrote at the kitchen table whenever the house was quiet and empty. Day-to-day life in a provincial Austrian town in the 1950s must have been tremendously suffocating. Haushofer, who was something of a tomboy growing up, responded to its conservatism and monotonousness by keeping herself to herself—when she died from bone cancer at the age of forty-nine her neighbors hadn't the faintest idea she was a writer. In her autobiographical novel *Nowhere Ending*

Sky, Haushofer gives free rein to her memories of growing up in rural Austria, depicting her boisterous antics, visceral relationship with nature, and the freedom from social constraint she enjoyed as a child with exuberance and humor. Of her own books it was her favorite, and it's reasonable to interpret her fondness for it as an indication of the enduring attachment she had to those formative years, a time when she had a direct, undistorted engagement with the world immediately around her. Haushofer felt that as we get older and accumulate experiences the capacity to see "the true picture" is significantly compromised. Our heads become crammed with memories and associations, making the eyes unreceptive, unable to see anything new. The irrevocable conditioning our perception undergoes is ruefully alluded to throughout *The Wall*, where the narrator concedes that, "Since my childhood I had forgotten how to see things with my own eyes, and I had forgotten that the world had once been young, untouched and very beautiful and terrible." She acknowledges that she can't be a child again and experience things in the way a child does. However, solitude, she discovers, brings on an emptying of the mind and a renewal of the senses; "loneliness led me, in moments free of memory and consciousness, to see the great brilliance of life again." It is this aspect of Haushofer's credo that resonated with me very strongly when I first read *The Wall*, some twelve or so years ago, while I was wondering how to go about living alone within my pile of stones without feeling that someone or something was missing from my situation. I was already beginning to experience for myself the dismantling effect that spending a lot of time on my own, quietly, can bring about. Like the stranded narrator in this novel I had serendipitously come by, I intermittently had the sensation that something which usually inserted itself between me and everything else had dissolved, allowing me to see things as themselves. There is a scene that expresses this revelatory occurrence beautifully. I read it over and over again. Every evening during the months she is at the Alm the lone woman sits on the bench outside the mountain hut with her dog at her feet and looks up at the night sky. She looks at it for a very long time, without thinking, without reminiscing, without any feelings of fear, and, divested of these intrusions, that normally "raced ahead of my eyes and distorted the true picture," she is able to see that the night isn't dark at all, it's very beautiful, and she starts to love it. When finally it grows cold she goes back into the hut, feeling calm. "It had something to do with the stars," she explains, "and the fact that I suddenly knew they were real."

It's amazing and unnerving how soon the frameworks that ordinarily define us and shape our encounters (while simultaneously getting in the way of them) quickly fall aside when we are alone. And when we force ourselves to recall the schemas that routinely orientate us throughout the days and nights of our lives, they seem abstract and insubstantial. Even our own name, if not heard for some time, can seem arbitrary and inessential. Indeed, while the stars have become real, the voice of the last woman left alive, almost as soon as she happens upon the wall, becomes "strange and unreal." She instinctively lets it drop to a whisper, until it becomes indistinguishable from the sound of water splish-splashing in the spring. Weeks later her name elapses; "No one calls me by that name, so it no longer exists," she says simply, and in this no-nonsense way dispenses with it once and for all. Perhaps there is something emancipatory about shedding these particulars with such efficiency, especially since the life she once lived was, in any case, "unsatisfactory in all respects. I had achieved little that I had wanted and everything I had achieved I had ceased to want." Her reflections on being a wife and a mother are brief and infrequent, yet it is clear she derived scant fulfillment from these roles which are typically presumed to give a woman's life meaning, purpose, and satisfaction. "Quite slowly they turn into strangers," she says of her two daughters, and describes the adults they have become as "unpleasant, loveless and argumentative." They too have entered the ranks of the unreal, and she candidly admits she doesn't mourn for them. "That probably sounds very cruel," she says, "but I can't think who I should lie to today...all the people for whom I have lied throughout my life are dead." In both senses of the word, she is not obliged anymore to keep up appearances. As far as her physical form is concerned it has become thin, angular, hardened, to the extent that she has lost the awareness of being a woman. No longer burdened by femininity, she feels herself to be more like a tree than a human. The woman she once was, "with the little double chin, who tried very hard to look younger than her age," seems alien to this being who now thinks of herself as a tough brown branch. Everything has been stripped away, and up there in the Alm, beneath a sky full of stars, she realizes in an instant that she had spent her whole life on the other side of the wall copying the thoughts and actions of other people.

The epiphanies that this unlikely survivor undergoes are profound and devastating—in essence her previous existence amounted to nothing at all—yet she relays all this calmly, with no hint of self-pity, or bitterness, or regret. The reason for this merciful equanimity is that Haushofer, who was familiar with Simone de Beauvoir's seminal text, *The Second Sex*, was cognizant of the limitations that are systematically placed upon a woman's life, narrowing her possibilities and severing her from her own impulses, so that the world she lives in is a very small, unvarying, and impersonal one, constructed entirely by the daunting yet indifferent demands and alienating mechanisms of capitalism. "But I shouldn't like to judge her too harshly," the arboreal woman says of the woman with the little double chin who was condemned to chase after a meaning that didn't exist and was quite unable to describe a common pigeon. "After all," she explains, "she never had the chance of consciously shaping her life. When she was young she unwittingly assumed a heavy burden by starting a family, and from then on she was always hemmed in by an intimidating amount of duties and worries. Only a giantess would have been able to free herself, and in no respect was she a giantess, never anything other than a tormented, overtaxed woman of medium intelligence, in a world, on top of everything else, that was hostile to women and which women found strange and unsettling." This censorious yet pragmatic evaluation of the domestic circumstances which enclose the lives of so many women is garnered no doubt from the author's own stifling experiences of womanhood. A reticent midcentury Austrian housewife, who preferred to remain on the edges socially, Marlen Haushofer may not have been a giantess, yet she was able to impart probity and strength while identifying the precise factors complicit in her subjugation, a feat which to my mind makes her absolutely colossal.

I have written this in a woodshed in Tipperary, my home for the time being. Most of my belongings are in a storage unit in the west of Ireland, where I lived at fourteen different addresses over twenty years until the interminable housing crisis finally made it completely unviable for me to reside there, however precariously, any longer. It's hard for anyone to find somewhere to live these days; it's impossible if you are a woman on your own. It's tough for a man too of course, but wage inequality persists, so it's likely they have a bit more money to spend on securing accommodation; prospective male tenants are still regarded with slightly less suspicion than female ones I suspect, and generally men don't need to concern themselves with personal safety to the same degree as women, which can be an obstacle because affordable homes tend to be in less salubrious areas. Society is structured in such a way that women are still being corralled into shacking up with men and reproducing—new homes are being constructed, but most of these, I notice, are family homes, which I've opted not to squander my inconstant income on since that's hardly sustainable and these houses are far too big for me anyway. When will planning, legislation, and attitudes change? When will it stop being anyone else's business if a woman chooses to live on her own and do god-knows-what all day? When will it finally be acknowledged that, as Haushofer observed, it is the world that is strange and unsettling, not the women it is so hostile to? We'd better hope it's soon, not least because by now we've really only got a few matches left.

CLAIRE-LOUISE BENNETT
NEWPORT, TIPPERARY
JANUARY 2022

About the Author

Marlen Haushofer was born on April 11, 1920, in Frau-enstein, a region in Upper Austria. She attended Catholic boarding school in Linz, and studied German literature in Vienna and Graz. Her adult life was spent in Steyr, an old industrial city with a strong working class culture and a history of militancy. She died in 1970.

Haushofer published the novella *The Fifth Year* in 1952 and earned her first literary award in 1953. Her first novel, *A Handful of Life*, was published in 1955. *The Wall*, published in 1963, is considered her greatest literary achievement. Variously interpreted as an ironic Robinson Crusoe story, a philosophical parable of human isolation, and dystopian fiction, *The Wall* is currently recognized for its important place in traditions of feminist fiction. Haushofer's last novel, *The Loft*, was published in 1969. Her short-story collection *Terrible Faithfulness* brought her the Grand Austrian State Prize for literature. She has been translated into several European languages.